Sinful King

A KINGS OF VEGAS NOVEL

NATALIE KANE

&
AMPERSAND
PUBLISHING, INC.

Content Warning

Please know that your mental health is always the most important thing. If you don't have triggers, you can skip ahead to avoid spoilers.

This book contains content that some viewers might consider troubling, including but not limited to: explicit sex, BDSM, public sex, the talk of child abuse, graphic torture, talk of loss of a parent, kidnapping and murder on the page.

Always protect yourself first.

-Natalie

For all of my dark romance girlies who love it when the hero finds his obsession.

Prologue

ROMAN

According to legend, along with songs, movies, and pop culture, the mob runs Vegas.

That's fucking bullshit.

Because my three brothers and I are the kings of Sin City.

Each of us has our specialty. Our niche, if you will.

Call us the Mafia, organized crime, or whatever label helps you sleep at night. It doesn't fucking matter.

We run this town. Nothing happens that we don't know about. Politicians? In our pocket. Police? Under our thumbs.

We own this city.

And we always will.

Nothing will ever derail our power.

One

LULU

"**I**'m going to be late for class," I announce as I walk into the kitchen, where I've been summoned to have breakfast with my father.

I have no interest in sitting anywhere near that man. *Ever.* I can't stand him.

He doesn't particularly like me, either, and he doesn't pull any punches with that. Literally. I still have bruises on my back from the last time I *got in his way.*

I'd like to avoid him as much as possible.

So why does he want to enjoy a meal with me now?

"Sit," he says, pointing at the seat across from him, where eggs, potatoes, bacon, and toast are already piled up just the way I like them, thanks to Iris, our house-keeper and cook. She's bustling about the kitchen, pretending not to listen. "You're not going to class today."

I don't trust this man, and I never cross him.

So I sit.

Dad's dressed in his black suit, the way he is every day. I've never seen him out of a suit in my life. Not once.

And the handgun on the table to his right is completely normal too. He doesn't know it, but I learned to shoot a gun just like it. Just in case. Because in this world I'm from, you never know when you'll need to protect yourself.

Or from whom.

"It's a nice morning," I say, trying to fill the quiet until he decides to tell me what's happening.

I do *not* want to miss class today. Dad thinks that I'm in college to get a business degree.

I'm not.

For the first year, I was enrolled in a culinary program. The second year, I learned massage therapy. My third year, I studied goldsmithing. I have a thing for sparklies.

And this year? I decided to submerge myself in all things alcohol.

Because why not?

I'm at the top of my mixology class, and it's freaking fascinating. A lot of chemistry is involved with alcohol. Making it, mixing it. You name it.

It's more than just shaking up some margarita mix with tequila and pouring it into a salt-rimmed glass over ice.

Not that my father will ever know about any of that. He had strict guidelines about where and what I should study. Thankfully, his accountant pays the college directly, so the asshole in front of me is none the wiser.

He might just pick up that handgun and press it to my temple if he got even a whiff of what I've been studying.

And given I'm only allowed to leave the house without a guard for class, I plan to keep it that way. *Not that he gives a shit about me anyway.*

"Excellent morning," he agrees, watching me with hard, dark eyes. I don't remember a time in my life when my father looked at me with kindness. "You'll need to change into something more appropriate. Slacks at the very least. A dress is better."

I do my best to keep my face neutral. My father *hates* emotions. "Are we going somewhere?"

My mom died when I was young. When I turned sixteen, it became my job to be my dad's *plus-one* to every social event you can think of. And because my father ranks so high in the Italian Mafia, there are a lot of events to attend. I hate them. I'm not friends with anyone, I don't have anything in common with any other women there, and I absolutely despise small talk. I'd rather be the one behind the bar, mixing drinks.

But since I've been in college, my father hasn't expected me to be on his arm quite as often, and I've welcomed the reprieve. It's why he'll think that I'm getting an MBA for the next two years.

I hate being a socialite.

"*You* are going somewhere," he replies calmly and cuts a piece of bacon with his knife and fork—who eats like that?—and puts it in his mouth. "I've agreed to an arrangement."

My potato-loaded fork stops halfway to my mouth.

No.

With my blood running cold, I shake my head, but he keeps talking.

"This partnership will benefit the family. Adam Damien will be a decent husband, and you'll give him babies so we both have an heir. It's mutually beneficial."

I would rather die.

I have no idea who Adam Damien is.

And I don't want to.

I'm still shaking my head.

"You knew this was inevitable, Eloise." He leans back, obviously bored with me, convinced he'll get his way. "This is our world. You're twenty-three. Most girls have been married off by the time they're your age."

"But I just—my education."

"I don't think they'll miss you in your bartending school."

My eyes fly up to his, and he smirks.

"Did you think I didn't know about all of that nonsense? That I don't have you followed to make sure you're safe? Come on, you know better than that, *cara mia.*"

My shoulders roll forward as fear wraps its talons around my neck. *Christ, he knew?*

"I let you have your *balordo* classes, but it's time for that to end and for you to do your duty to this family. Damien and his men will be here in less than an hour, and you'll go with them. Move in with him so you can get to know each other better before the wedding next month."

Bile rises in the back of my throat. "Can't I just get to know him by going on regular dates?"

Dad shakes his head. "He wants you under his roof to keep an eye on you. I don't have a problem with that."

I blink at him. "So you sold me."

I never speak out against my father like this, but holy shit, he sold me!

He lets out an aggravated breath, and I know I'm pushing him too far. "You've always been so damn dramatic. I arranged a good marriage for you. You should be grateful. Damien is a powerful man, Eloise. You'll be well taken care of."

I shake my head again, on the verge of tears. "No. You can't do this. I'm not marrying him, Dad."

If I thought his eyes were cold before, that's nothing compared to the glare he's aimed at me now.

"Yes. You are."

"I won't—"

Slap.

He backhands me across the face, making me see stars, and my jaw immediately aches. There's a coppery taste in my mouth from my tooth cutting the inside of my cheek.

God, he's strong.

"You'll shut the fuck up and do as you're told for once in your fucking life, Eloise. There will be no discussion. Playtime is over."

"Dad—"

He raises his arm again, and I flinch back. And for once, he doesn't follow through.

You concerned about the number of bruises this time, Papa?

"Go change your clothes," he says, dismissing me. "Do something with your hair. If you could lose thirty pounds in the next hour, that would help."

He's such a fucking prick.

Standing, I rush from the room and up to my bedroom with an aching jaw as my mind whirls. The men in my father's world are cruel. Violent. And they treat women like we're disposable pets. If he thinks that I'll marry some rich Mafia dude that he's chosen for me, he's a fool. I don't trust my father regarding anything in this life, particularly in his matchmaking skills. I bet this Adam Damien would beat me more than Dad does, and it would probably be way worse. He'd probably—

I don't want to think about it.

I have to run away, and I've been preparing for this moment for the past two years.

I may not know everything about my father's business, but I know enough. I had a fake ID made, and I've been squirreling away cash. I only have a few thousand, but it'll be enough to get me to a different city.

Do people still ride buses?

I'll find a bus.

"Not with this." I set my old cell phone on the nightstand and instead turn on the burner phone I bought. I actually have three of them, just in case.

I didn't know what *just in case* was. I figured I'd know it when I saw it.

And I'm looking at it right now.

I toss the phones, wallet with my new ID and cash, and some essentials like one set of clothes, underwear and deodorant, a toothbrush and my comb into my backpack. I take the back staircase down to the kitchen, planning to go out the back door, but Iris is kneading dough.

"Eloise," she says, narrowing her eyes as they fall to the bag on my shoulder.

She heard my conversation with my father, and she's not a stupid woman. She might be the only person in this world who's ever truly loved me. Who's ever shown me affection of any kind. *Will he hurt her when I'm gone?*

"I have to go," I tell her and rush over to embrace her. "I love you, but I have to go. You don't have to do anything. Just say you never saw me if anyone asks."

Her eyes fill with tears. "Oh, baby doll. You call me when you get where you're going."

I nod, but we both know I won't.

If I did, my father's men might find me.

I hug her again, then wink at her and press my finger to my lips before rushing out the back door.

There's a path I've taken often during my life that leads right into town. I always took this path when I needed to sneak away for a quiet afternoon. I got in trouble for it, too, but that didn't stop me from doing it.

Later, after I find the bus station and am headed out of Reno, I take a long, deep breath.

What the hell do I do now?

Two

ROME

"**M**r. Alexander?"

I turn and lift an eyebrow at Beth, one of my new employees whose job is to keep the clients happy in my club's playroom. She's beautiful, playful, bisexual, and has quickly become a member favorite. "Yes, Beth?"

"Um." She twists her hands at her waist and fidgets back and forth on her dainty feet. Beth is a tiny woman with fake tits that are on full display and long, riotous red hair.

"You can speak freely," I add, ghosting my fingers over her bare shoulder.

She looks around nervously as if she doesn't want our conversation to be overheard.

"You mentioned that I should let you know if I noticed anything ... *wrong*. This is just my gut talking, and I know I've only been here for three months—"

"I trust your gut," I reply and turn to lead her down the hallway to my office.

Owning one of the most prestigious sex clubs in the world comes with heavy responsibilities. My number one priority is safety for every person who walks through my doors seeking ... well, whatever it is they're looking for.

And when safety is compromised, we take out the garbage.

"Here," I say once I've closed the door and stepped several feet away, putting plenty of space between us so she doesn't feel any more intimidated than she already is.

Beth is small.

I'm a big man. A big, powerful man.

"What's your gut telling you, Beth?" I ask, keeping my voice calm.

She nibbles on that bottom lip again, then props her hands on her nonexistent hips.

"There was a client last night." She shakes her head as she looks at the floor. "I hadn't seen him before, but that's not unusual. Like I said, I haven't been here that long, and people come and go, you know?"

I nod once, wishing she'd get to the point. I have members from all over the world who come to Las Vegas just for the experience they get at Rapture. Of course, Beth hasn't seen all of them. She likely never will.

But something in her eyes shifts, and that has my attention.

"What did you see, Beth?"

"I'm no prude. Obviously, I'm a sex worker—"

"*Beth.*" My hard tone has her gaze whipping up to mine. "Tell me what you saw."

"Experienced. This guy. He didn't tell me his name. He … I didn't like his smile, but whatever. He wanted to play with the spanking bench."

I narrow my eyes. "Did you consent to that?"

"Yes, sir. I rather like to be spanked." It's endearing when she blushes. "So I agreed and told him my safe word. But I asked Libby to watch because I didn't like his smile, and I suspected something wasn't … right. I told her to make it out like she's a voyeur, but really, I wanted someone else there."

"Good girl," I say, pleased with the way she handled it so far.

Beth huffs out a breath. "I had to say my safe word *three times* before Libby finally stepped in and made him stop."

Oh fuck no.

"Say that again."

"I wasn't quiet or coy, and I definitely wasn't playing. I was firm, and I yelled it out because he got too rough. I thought he was going to break the skin, and I'm not into that."

"What time was this?" I ask her. "And did my men get involved?"

"No," she admits. "He stopped and apologized, said he was in the *zone* and didn't hear me, but that's not how it works."

"No. That's not how it works. Time?"

"Around one in the morning, I think."

"I'll check the security footage and find him. He won't be back, and I apologize that that happened to you in my club."

"It's not your fault—"

"We screen our members thoroughly. That's not acceptable. You'll be compensated. Do you want tonight off?"

She blinks in surprise. "No, I'm fine, sir. You don't have to pay me—"

"I will anyway. Are you sure you don't need time off?"

She frowns as if she's confused. "No, I'm happy to be here. I *love* this job. I was worried I'd be in trouble for telling you because I know it's expensive to be a member here—"

"You're not in trouble," I assure her. "We have rules. End of. I'll take care of this."

She nods and heads for the door, which I open for her, and when she's gone, I call Luke, my head of security and second-in-command, into my office.

"Hey, boss," he says when he walks into the room. "It's fucking busy tonight. It's Wednesday. Why is it so packed in here on a Wednesday?"

"It's Vegas, Luke. Every day is a holiday in Vegas. Beth, the new playroom girl, was just in here."

"Yeah?" He grins. "Did you finally hit that? She's fucking *hot*. A little small, but she really does it for the guys who have a daddy kink."

I stare at him. Most men would wither under my glare, but Luke smirks, the asshole. "I don't fuck any of the employees. You know that."

He blows out a breath. "You should. Or the members, at the very least. You'd probably be less of a grouch."

He's one of the few people in this world who can get away with speaking to me the way he does.

And only because he's my cousin.

"We have a problem."

That makes the smile disappear from his face, and now he's all business. "Tell me."

It takes thirty seconds to clue him in, and by the time I've finished, he's good and pissed off.

"Why didn't my boys take care of this piece of shit?"

"That's my question," I reply.

Luke paces my office. "I'll pull up the footage of the playroom last night and find him. And I'll have a talk with the boys, along with Libby and Beth."

"I'd also like to look through the footage," I reply. "Because when we find him, we'll take him to the cell."

He nods.

We have a zero-tolerance policy for anyone who puts anyone else in danger, regardless of the hundreds of thousands of dollars they've paid to be here.

Ignoring a safe word is not fucking tolerated.

I might be a shit human being, but I take care of what's mine. These people trust us and pay me a fuck ton of money to keep things safe.

So that's what they'll get.

"I'm surprised you weren't watching in real time," Luke says as he crosses to the door. "You usually monitor everything from the control room."

"I was busy."

Just because I don't fuck the women who work for me or the members doesn't mean I don't fuck at all.

Luke simply nods and walks out of my office, and I head down to the control room.

My cousin is right. I usually spend a good deal of time in here, keeping an eye on the entire club. I have twelve monitors that show live video feeds of every area. The playroom is our largest area, so there are three monitors and twelve cameras. I can see everyone who comes and goes through the main entrances, from both streets. I also keep an eye on the bar in the main lounge, where members can sit and enjoy a drink before they go into the playroom. The lounge requires full clothing, no sex, and we have a two-drink max.

I'm short a bartender tonight, but it appears that Max and Rita are keeping up okay for now. Our patrons come in wearing ensembles curated specifically to be noticed—suits, sparkly dresses, lots of jewelry, and expensive watches.

It's a place to flirt and be seen before walking through the doors to the carnal delights beyond.

I see Mr. and Mrs. Foley are on the hunt for a third tonight. They're chatting with a man at the bar.

Mrs. Foley likes to fuck men who aren't her husband. And Mr. Foley likes to watch.

I learned long ago not to judge anyone based on their

sexual preferences. There are plenty of kinks that I indulge in, including the occasional threesome. If you want to judge people for their lifestyle, this isn't the place for you.

My playroom manager, Madam Loveland, is in her office. Before long, she'll move into the playroom to keep an eye on things there. I wonder where she was last night when Beth was strapped to the spanking bench.

That's a question to ask her later.

It's early enough in the evening that most of the privacy rooms are empty, but those will fill up before the night is out.

My phone pings with a text from Luke.

> L: There's a man asking for you at the loading dock.

The loading dock is where I conduct the ... less legal side of my business. Just as I'm about to tell Luke I'll be right there, someone on a monitor catches my attention.

I lean forward and hit the key that brings the reception area up on full screen, then turn on the audio.

"Who are you?" I murmur, watching intently.

Luke texts again, and I type out a quick response.

> Me: Take care of it. I'm unavailable.

She looks nervously around as she pushes her long dark hair over one shoulder and pauses before approaching the front desk.

She's not a member.

She's not an employee.

My hand balls into a fist on the desktop as a smile spreads over her perfect face, and even though I've never seen her before in my life, it's as though every cell in my body recognizes her.

She's mine.

Three

LULU

I didn't die today.

To be fair, it's only eight in the evening, so there's plenty of time for my status to change before midnight. I'm sure my father and his men are on the hunt for me. There's no way they're not. It's been two days since I ran, and it's not like I went very far.

Reno to Vegas is almost laughable.

But I decided to make it simple. Sure, I could have drained all my funds and spent a week on a godforsaken smelly bus to Florida or New York, but then I figured they'd probably expect me to go as far away as possible. They wouldn't expect me to stay so close to home.

So I came to Vegas and checked into a motel using my new fake ID. The motel is just on this side of sleazy, meaning there aren't any bedbugs. But the room hasn't been updated since the 1980s, the carpet and drapes smell like cigarettes and pesticides—hence, no bedbugs— and I refuse to drink the water out of the tap. I won't even brush my teeth with it. I did see a housekeeper and witnessed them changing the sheets, so at least it's relatively clean.

However, it's on a shitty side of town. I got mugged this morning, and they took all the cash I had left, along with my burner phones. I was stupid and put up a fight because it was *everything* I had left, so the two bastards kicked my ass. Literally. They also managed to kick my ribs, and I'm so sore it hurts to breathe.

At least they didn't hit my face. I already have a bruise on my jaw from my father's *farewell gift*.

On the upside, before the mugging, I managed to buy a few items of clothing yesterday, and a few more staples like shampoo, a hair dryer, and makeup to cover my facial bruises.

The motel I could afford didn't offer those amenities.

My room is only paid through the week, which means I have to figure out my financial situation within the next two days.

My father sold me.

My own flesh and blood fucking sold me, and even with my ribs singing and my money gone, that's all I can think about. Although I don't respect or trust my father, I never believed he would have sold me as if I were an old car. I know that arranged marriages are common in the Mafia, but he's *never* uttered a word about it to me. I didn't even know that it was a possibility or a consideration.

I'm royally fucked. Stranded in Las Vegas, with no

money and nowhere to go, I feel like I lost a fight with an MMA champion.

If I'm going to survive, I need a job. Now. Without money, I'm a sitting duck. I'm taking this one minute at a time. I can't reach out to any friends to help me financially because I don't have any friends. And even if I did, I wouldn't trust them not to call my father.

With the hundreds of establishments on the Strip and in this city, someone will hire me on the spot. I'm dressed in a pair of brown slacks with a cream blouse that I found at a discount department store. I knew I needed something semi-nice for job interviews, and the jeans I ran away in wouldn't cut it. My dark hair was styled earlier, and if I tease it with my fingers, it'll be okay.

Although I admit, I'm a mess. I'm shaky because I'm exhausted and hungry. I don't even want to know what my makeup looks like since I've been walking around the Strip aimlessly, trying to decide where to apply for a job. I could start crying at the drop of a hat, but I don't have time for that now. If I keep my wits about me, I'll survive the rest of this godforsaken day.

And hopefully end it gainfully employed.

Blowing out a breath, I look up and see a discreet sign.

RAPTURE.

I haven't heard of this club before, but I like that it's not over the top. There aren't a ton of flashing lights around the name. It's not ... obvious.

Maybe they need a bartender. I can't show my license

thanks to having to use a fake ID, but I can make just about any drink under the sun. I'm good at it.

When I step inside the building, my jaw drops. This is *fancy.* I know without a doubt that I'm way underdressed for this place, but I already like the vibe. I push my hair over my shoulder and glance around. The two men by the front door watch me, but they don't kick me out on my ass, so I take that as a good sign.

I'm relieved when I find a restroom off the opulent lobby, because I need to freshen up before I speak to anyone. The floors are gleaming gray marble, the walls black, and the club's color scheme continues in the restroom, with gold light fixtures and finishes. A quick look in the mirror has me cringing. The makeup situation isn't great, but after wetting a towel, I wipe the mascara from under my eyes and tidy my face up. My hair is okay after I drag my fingers through the dark curls, but my outfit is rumpled after walking around most of the day.

At least I don't have sweat stains in the armpits.

"Well, shit." I smooth my hands down and then resign myself to having less-than-stellar clothes on. I've learned how to hide my bigger body with fashion. My father always hated that I'm curvier, with zero resemblance to the lean, statuesque women he wished he'd had on his arm in public, but after years of diets and exercise and hating myself, I realized that this is simply who I am.

I also learned to keep my makeup simple, so I didn't draw the attention of my father's soldiers. I hated it when they leered at me.

And what does it matter what he thinks of me? He no longer has a say in anything I do. And at twenty-three years old, it's about damn time.

Squaring my shoulders, I push out of the restroom and approach a receptionist. I've never been in a club with a receptionist before.

"May I help you?" She's tall and blond, with bright red lipstick and a perfect smoky eye, and she's not wearing much of anything at all. Black leather straps crisscross over her body, strategically covering any of the bits that could get her arrested.

It's actually pretty badass, and I wish I had the balls to wear that outfit.

"Hi, I was wondering if I could speak with a bar manager? I'm interested in a bartending position."

Her eyebrows climb in surprise, and her pretty blue eyes travel up and down my torso, but she raises a walkie-talkie from her desk.

"Sure. What's your name, honey?"

I start to open my mouth and then remind myself that I can't give her my real name. Everyone will be looking for Eloise Rizzo.

"Lulu," I reply. "Lulu Monroe."

At least, that's the name on my ID. I kept my nick-name as the first name because I'll need to respond when someone talks to me, and changed the last name alto-gether. Thank God my muggers left me the wallet. They just took the cash and then kicked me again because I didn't have any credit cards.

Fuckers.

She raises the device and speaks into it. "Madam Loveland, I have a woman here to speak with you. She's interested in the bartending position."

The bartending position. Does that mean one's available?

Maybe my luck is about to change after all.

A voice comes through the device. "I'll be right down. Thank you, Scarlett."

I smile at Scarlett, who smiles back at me.

"Can I offer you some advice?" she asks me, leaning just a little closer as if she's going to tell me a secret.

"Sure."

"Unbutton those top buttons, untuck the shirt, and tie it under your bra line. Show a little midriff."

I lift an eyebrow in surprise. "Really?"

"Yes. Trust me on this."

"I'm not too ... curvy for that?"

"No way, you have a banging body," she replies, and I can't help but snort.

No one, not once in my life, has called my body *banging.*

But she works here, and she's the expert.

Just as I've finished doing what she says, a door opens, and the most beautiful woman I've ever seen in my life walks through it.

Scratch that. She doesn't walk.

She ... *glides.*

She has to be over six feet tall in those black stiletto boots. She's in a tight white dress that shows off her hourglass figure and does little to hide her massive breasts.

Her glossy black hair is perfectly straight and falls over her shoulders, framing an angular face with sharp cheekbones, nose, and chin.

Dark chocolate eyes scan me from head to toe before she offers me her red-tipped hand.

"I'm Madam Loveland," she says.

"Lulu," I reply and shake the offered hand. "I'm hoping you have a bartender position open."

"I see." She nods once and turns away. "Come to my office, please."

I glance back at the receptionist, who offers me a thumbs-up and an encouraging smile—I like her—and then follow Madam Loveland through the door, where I have to blink for my eyes to adjust to the dim lighting. Sconces on the wall light the way, but they're not bright, and the wallpaper is gray and black.

It's ... *rich.* The whole building feels lavish. Hell, it even smells extravagant. Like leather and whiskey, with a hint of citrus.

She leads me through yet another door, then closes it behind her and gestures for me to sit while she takes a seat behind the desk.

"Where did you hear about the position?"

"Oh." I blink rapidly. "Honestly, I didn't hear about an opening. I came in hoping there would be one available."

Her eyes narrow, and I feel like I've done something

wrong. Like she doesn't believe me. "You *randomly* chose this establishment to walk into?"

"Yes." I don't drop my gaze. She might be the most impressive and intimidating woman I've ever met, but I learned a long time ago to keep my chin up in every situation.

Never let them see you sweat.

Her eyes drift down my body again, and she almost sneers.

"Where is your résumé?"

"I don't have one on me." I lean forward slightly. "I have experience. Show me a bar, request a drink, and I'll make you the best fucking drink you've ever had. I can talk about just about anything. I'm not shy, I'm not a wallflower, and I'm also not a pushover."

Her pink tongue pokes out to run along her bottom lip.

"But you don't have a résumé with any references, and you walked in here looking like *that.*"

I lift an eyebrow and resist the urge to look down at myself. "Like what, exactly?"

"Listen, Lisa—"

"Lulu."

"We cater to a very specific clientele. Elite. Wealthy. Important. They expect to be served by someone who looks ... well, not like you."

"Not like me in what way? They don't like brunettes? Short girls? Green eyes?"

Yeah, bitch, I'm going to make you say it.

"Fat girls," she finally replies, and although I was expecting it, it doesn't sting any less.

But I keep my face bland.

"I see." I nod and stand from the chair. "You could have told me that in the lobby, Madam Loveland."

"I think that would have been rude," she replies, making me laugh.

"Yes. *That* would have been rude."

I shake my head and walk out, back down the dark hallway and make it to the lobby where Scarlett's still operating the reception desk.

"How did it go?" she asks.

"She's not interested in fat girls," I inform her and watch her face transform into shock. "I know, right?"

I walk out the front door, keeping my integrity around me like a shield. Once I get to the sidewalk, I take a deep breath.

Well, fuck.

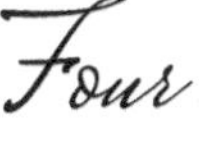

Four

ROME

"Fat girls."

Rage. Rage unlike anything I've ever felt before bubbles through my veins as I watch my manager insult the most gorgeous woman I've ever fucking seen.

I barely hear the confident response that comes out of her lips as I push back my chair and stomp out of the control room.

I watched my girl follow Loveland to her office and listened to her explain, with confidence, that she can do the job.

And then she was insulted so deplorably, I'd like to put a bullet through Loveland's brain.

Too bad I don't kill women.

I could call Carson. He doesn't mind pulling the trigger if the mark has a pussy.

By the time I get to Loveland's office, my little firefly is gone, and Loveland is already back to work.

"Get her," I say, startling her, "and give her the fucking job. She starts tonight. And if you *ever* talk to someone like that again, I'll fucking kill you myself."

Her jaw drops as she stands from her desk.

"Rome—"

"My name is *sir*. Or Mr. Alexander."

She blinks in confusion.

"Go get her and give her the job. *Now*."

"Yes, sir," she says, her voice full of confusion as she rushes out of the office. *Never seen her rush before.* "But she's probably gone by now."

"Then you'd better find her."

Five

LULU

Fuck that bitch. We're living in a world of body positivity, and she has the goddamn nerve to tell me that I'm too fat to pour drinks?

She doesn't know me or anything about me. I could probably run circles around her. Okay, maybe not *run*, because I only run if something's chasing me, but it's not like I can't stand on my feet for an eight-hour shift and pour drinks.

"People suck," I mutter to myself as I continue walking down the sidewalk, dodging people. I can't get away from there fast enough.

"Lisa!"

You have got to be fucking kidding me.

"Lisa, wait."

Yep, that's her voice. But that's not my name.

So I ignore her and keep walking.

"*Lisa!*" I hear her heels working in triple time, and

then she tugs on my arm, spinning me around. "Please, come back to the club."

I lift an eyebrow and pin the hand on my arm in my gaze.

She drops it.

"I'm asking you to come back."

"I'll pass."

"Wait." She reaches out again but then thinks better of it and steps back. "Look, it doesn't matter what I think because the boss wants you, so you're in. I was instructed to come get you, so please, it could be life and death if you don't come back with me."

"Dramatic much?"

"I'm not kidding."

I narrow my eyes on her. "That doesn't sound like it's my problem."

Okay, I don't buy for a minute that her life depends on me bartending at that club, but even I don't want someone to die for me.

I need the job. It's not like I have any other offers banging down the door of my crappy motel room.

"Please," she says, huffing out a breath as she pushes her hair over one shoulder. She actually looks a little frazzled.

I'm enjoying it too much.

"Fine, I'll come back."

She nods once and turns to walk back to the club, her head high, her hips swaying back and forth in that tight dress. She's getting plenty of looks. One guy whistles.

She doesn't even bat an eye.

Madam Loveland pushes through the door to Rapture, and Scarlett's head comes up. She offers me a beaming smile.

"You're back!"

"Hey," I reply with a little wave. "I guess fat girls aren't so bad after all."

"I told you, you're not fat. You're *hot*," Scarlett says with a wink.

Is she hitting on me?

Unlikely.

But I smile at her before following Loveland through the door I went through earlier. Rather than stopping at her office, she leads me to another room resembling a swanky locker room. It's nothing like what you'd find at a gym. The lavish color theme follows inside, and there's even a water feature, like something in a spa.

"Am I getting a massage?" I ask with a smirk. "This is ... different."

"You can stow your things in this locker," Loveland says, opening a top locker for me. There's a clean robe inside, I guess in case I want to take a shower later? That's nice. "What you're wearing isn't our standard requirement for our bartenders, but it'll do for tonight, I suppose."

"I can wear jeans and a T-shirt from now on," I assure her and watch as her face transforms into something horrific as if I just told her I'd play Christmas music in July.

"*No.* Absolutely not. Don't you know anything about this place?"

"Actually, no. Because I went from being told I'm too fat to work here to being escorted to a locker. I've never even seen the bar."

She sighs, closes her eyes, and pinches the bridge of her nose. "This is an elite sex club, Lisa."

"Lulu," I say, correcting her, and then feel the blood leave my face when her words sink in. "Wait. A *sex club?*"

I immediately have visions of a sea of bodies, gyrating and making noise, and bodily fluids, and I want none of it.

"Um, I don't think—"

"You'll be in the lounge," Scarlett says, and my head whips over to her. I didn't even hear her walk in. "Not in the playroom."

"Is that ... better?"

Loveland smirks. "Depends on who you ask."

"There's no sex in the lounge," Scarlett continues, side-eyeing Loveland. "Everyone's dressed. It's where our clients begin their evenings before they're ready to move on to the playroom and all of the fun inside."

Okay, that makes me feel moderately better. I don't have to watch people having sex.

"And I don't have to, you know?"

Loveland shakes her head. "No. You don't have to do anything you don't want to. One of the perks of the job is a complimentary membership to the club. That in and of itself is worth a quarter of a million dollars."

My tongue sticks to the roof of my mouth.

Jesus, I was just hoping for medical and dental. Maybe a 401k.

"But you don't have to use it," Scarlett adds. "I'll fill you in more later."

"We're short a bartender tonight," Loveland says, "so you can start right away."

"Wait. Will *you* be my manager?" I ask her. Because if so, I don't think I want this job.

"No, I don't run the bar. Rita does, and she's bartending right now. She'll be your direct supervisor."

Good.

"Can I help her with her outfit before you take her out there?" Scarlett asks, and Loveland nods.

"I'll let Rita know to expect you," Loveland says before walking out.

"She's lovely," I say, my voice dry as the Nevada desert, and Scarlett smirks.

"She's a Domme. She's not the warm and fuzzy type."

"Shocking."

Scarlett taps her finger to her red lips. "Can I please help you with this outfit? The better you look, the more tips you'll get."

"I can use all the tips," I reply, meaning every word.

"Okay, take off your shirt and your bra." When I hesitate, she adds, "Trust me."

As she hurries off, I do as she asks and sigh in relief when I take off the cheap bra I bought yesterday. Sometimes the girls need a break.

And my girls are big, and they require space.

But they're not free for long because suddenly, Scarlett is in front of me with a corset.

"Uh, that doesn't look comfortable for moving around the back of the bar."

"It's going to look hot." She moves toward me, and then her eyes widen in shock. "Oh God, what happened?"

I look down and wince. "I got mugged and beat up a bit."

"*A bit?*" She bites her lip and looks at the corset in her hand. "This won't feel good at all. Plan B it is, then."

She tosses the corset aside and passes me a pretty orange bralette that will go well with my brown slacks. I pull that over my head and get the girls situated, and then she hands me a flowy orange top. It's cropped, so when I reach up, you'll be able to see my midriff. It's a little see-through, but it's classy and pretty, and I actually like it.

"We have all kinds of costumes around here," she says with a wink as I pull on the top. "It's fun to play with them. This is a great color on you and matches your pants. Now, let me touch up your makeup."

"You're being really nice to me."

She pauses and glances back at me as she opens her locker and pulls out her makeup bag. "Why wouldn't I? I like you. You're new here, and I was new here once, too."

"How long have you been here?"

"About three years. I work reception some nights, and some nights, I'm in the playroom."

I swallow hard. "Do you …?"

"Have sex with the members? Of course, I do. And it's fun as hell. But it's not for everyone. Rita doesn't. I don't think she's ever set foot in the playroom, let alone

one of the private rooms. It's whatever you prefer. Mr. Alexander is firm on everyone being comfortable."

"Mr. Alexander?" I ask as she brushes some eye shadow on my eyes.

"He's the owner. He's hot, like, *so fucking hot*, but he doesn't fraternize with the employees or the members. He's professional. And he's really, really good to his staff. Generous. He looks intimidating because he hardly smiles, but he's fair."

I nod, trying to take it all in.

"I don't even know what my salary is."

"Well, I know they're eager to fill that spot at the bar, so they'll go over it all with you soon. They're generous. I don't think you'll do better on the Strip."

She smiles as she steps back and takes in her handiwork.

"Okay, you're ready. Have a look in that mirror and tell me what you think."

I step over and then stare. *Wow.* My makeup isn't over the top, but it's bolder. The outfit is really pretty. I raise my arms, and sure enough, I get a full view of my midsection, bruises and all, but I'll be careful.

"Come on," Scarlett says. "I have to get back to reception, and you have a new gig to get to."

I THOUGHT Rita was going to cry when Scarlett introduced me. Max grinned, raised his chin in hello, and kept pouring drinks.

They're both gorgeous. Everyone here is stunning. Rita's a tiny thing, with bleach-blond hair and piercings everywhere. She moves fast, and the customers love her.

Max is a Greek god. He's tall, wide, cut, and has the most perfect white smile I've ever seen. He looks like he should be on the cover of *Men's Health*.

And based on all the smiles, waves, and flirtatious kisses blown his way, he's clearly popular with the ladies. I mean, what's not to love?

"How are you with an old-fashioned?" Rita asks me.

"I'm great with it."

She nods. "The guy at the end of the bar wants one."

I glance over and feel my heart thump in my throat.

Holy fucking shit.

That man is ... I don't even know.

He's sitting, but I can tell he's a big man. His broad shoulders fill out his suit perfectly, his biceps bulging under the material. Tattoos peek up from the collar of his shirt and run down his hands to his knuckles. His dark hair is styled perfectly, while vivid blue eyes stare right back at me.

He wings up an eyebrow, and it shakes me loose from my stare.

He wants an old-fashioned, idiot.

I get to work making the drink, and when I set it in front of him, I manage a smile.

"Here you go."

He sips, then licks his lips, and my stomach tightens.

"That might be the best old-fashioned I've ever had." His voice. Jesus, it's deep and rich and makes my nipples pucker, and I have to swallow hard because this guy is dangerous for my libido, and he's a customer. I might be *allowed* to mess around with the members, but that doesn't seem like a good idea.

I've been working at this job for about two hours ... and I'd like to keep it.

So I wink at him and try to keep my hormones under control. "Of course, it is. Flag me down when you need another."

Six

ROME

I couldn't stand watching her through the screens anymore, so I came down to the lounge to see her in person. I needed to get closer to her, to be in her orbit. To see if the attraction was just as strong when she's mere feet away from me as it was through the video feed.

It's stronger.

When I sat down, I made it clear to Rita that I wanted to observe without the new woman being made aware that I'm her boss. Of course, Rita didn't bat an eye. She's been with me a long time and is used to my odd requests.

My firefly was gorgeous on screen, but she's absolute perfection in person. Her curves have drawn the eye of every man in this lounge. Any one of them would haul her into a privacy room to fuck her if given the chance.

I want to pull my gun from the small of my back and shoot every one of them.

Yet I can't blame them for it. As she bustles back and forth behind the bar, that orange top sways and lifts, giving me a small glimpse of her soft skin.

It's late enough in the evening now that most members have moved from the lounge into the playroom, so the bar is slowing down. My firefly laughs at something Max says, and he pats her on the back.

Touch her again, and you'll lose your hand, Max.

She returns my way and flashes me that bright smile. Her eyes are green with flecks of gold. Her lipstick is long gone, but her lips are plump and pink and beg to be wrapped around my cock. She's twisted her hair up into a messy bun that none of my employees would ever wear on the job, but it looks perfect on her.

"I'm Lulu," she says with a smile as she approaches. That smile brings light into my cold, dead heart. "Can I get you another?"

I nod. I never drink more than one when I'm here, but I want to watch her make my drink.

"You got it. What's your name?"

"Rome," I reply, and she nods as she takes my empty tumbler and sets it in the sink, then reaches for a clean one.

Before I can say anything else, she turns and reaches above her head for a bottle on a top shelf, granting another view of her gorgeous fucking—

Bruises. New and old, marking her entire rib cage. *What the fuck?* Is that a scar on her lower back?

Before I can question it, I'm off my stool and behind

the bar. Lulu startles, glancing around in alarm, those green eyes wide, while backing away from me.

"Stop." My voice is hard, and she stops moving, but her face is full of fear now, and that pisses me off almost as much as the bruises. I don't want her to fear me. "What happened to your ribs?"

She frowns, and suddenly, Rita's by her side, patting her on the arm as if to comfort her.

"Wh-what?" Lulu asks.

"The bruises," I say again.

"Oh." Lulu frowns and then cringes. "I'm sorry, I'm sure that's not something any of the customers want to see. Don't worry about me, I'm making you that drink now."

"I don't give a fuck about the drink," I reply and step closer. "I want you to answer me."

"This is Rom—" Rita says, and I shake my head, cutting her off. "It's okay, girl. You didn't do anything wrong."

Lulu's mouth opens, and she licks her lips.

I shake my head once, losing my patience. "How. Did you get. The bruises?"

"I was mugged this morning," she replies, her voice full of disdain. "Got a little roughed up, but I'm okay."

"Are you in pain?"

"No, I—"

"Don't lie to me."

She blinks at my hard tone but then offers me a small smile and reaches out to touch my arm. Rita's eyes widen because she knows I don't like to be touched, but Lulu's touch—*somehow*—calms my rage-fueled heart. "I mean, I'm sore, but I've had worse. Really, it's okay. Take a seat, and I'll make your drink."

When she pulls her hand away, it's like the sun going behind a cloud, leaving a chill behind, but rather than reach for her and pull her against me, I return to my seat, watching her with a more critical eye.

She's cheerful, smiling, and hasn't slowed down in the few hours she's been behind the bar, but I can see fatigue in her eyes. And I fucking hate that someone bruised her. That someone had the audacity to lay a hand on her.

My firefly resumes making the drink and slides it over to me with her confident smile back in place.

"Here you go," she says.

"How long have you been a bartender?" I ask her.

"If I'm being honest?"

"Always."

She chews that plump bottom lip, and my cock stirs. "Not long. But I took a mixology class for almost a year and loved every second of it. There's a lot of science that goes into a good drink."

"So you enjoy science, then?"

"Not really."

She blinks in surprise when my lips kick up in a grin.

"I mean, I never liked science in school, but I like unexpected things, and it surprised me that alcohol isn't just beer and frat parties, you know?"

I tip my head to the side, watching her. "Fascinating."

"Exactly." She twists to take an order, and she must move too fast because I catch the wince from the pain in her ribs. I don't like that.

I don't like it one fucking bit.

Seven

LULU

My ribs are *killing me*. I would give all of tonight's pay for some painkillers. I don't have any in my purse. Hell, I don't even have any at the motel, and unless they let me leave here with tips tonight, I won't be able to stop by the pharmacy on my way back either.

"Lulu," Rita says as she joins me, "why don't you go home for the night? It's slowing down, so Max and I have this covered."

"Oh, did I do something wrong?"

"Not at all. In fact, you're great, and I'm happy to have you on board. I'm hoping you can come back tomorrow night. Well, tonight now, since it's well past midnight."

I sag with relief. "Yes, I'd love that. Thank you. I'm assuming I have to fill out paperwork, and I don't even know what my salary is—"

"We'll get all of that tomorrow," she assures me.

"Your shift starts at nine, but come in at eight thirty, and we'll get you squared away."

"Will I be working until six in the morning?" I ask.

"Yes. Unless—"

"No, I can do that. I'm just clarifying. I appreciate the job."

She presses a wad of bills into my hand, and I do my best to keep my face neutral.

Thank God. Ibuprofen, here I come.

"These are your tips for tonight. You'll get paid out for tips at the end of every shift."

"Great. Thanks."

"You'll want to keep dressing sexy," she continues. "You'll get better tips. But not over-the-top sexy."

"Classy," I reply with a knowing nod. I've seen what everyone has been wearing tonight. "Got it."

"See? You're going to be great." Rita pats my shoulder. "I'll see you tomorrow."

"Okay. Thanks, Rita."

Leaving the bar, I toss a smile to Rome, who's still sitting at the bar but hasn't touched the drink I made him, and wave to Max. I walk down the long hallway and into the fancy locker room. I change out of the borrowed top and bralette into my own clothes, and with my purse slung across my body, I walk out the front door and onto the sidewalk.

Scarlett wasn't at the reception desk. In fact, *no one* was at the reception desk, but the two burly guards were by the door, so I assume they'll let someone know if a member walks in.

Not my job, I remind myself. But at least I *do* have a job.

Tonight was everything I knew I'd love when working as a bartender. It was fast-paced, interesting, and that's just the behind-the-bar work. The people-watching was truly fascinating. Rapture certainly caters to a higher class of people than I'm used to, yet I felt I held my ground well.

Practice from being on my father's arm came in handy.

I knew how to schmooze. And the tips? I shake my head, still amazed. I didn't dream I'd walk out of Rapture tonight with hundreds of dollars in my purse.

Even though my motel is at least a mile from here, in a city that never sleeps, plenty of people are around, and it's all well-lit. So I start walking. I duck into a pharmacy and buy painkillers, a bottle of water, and some snacks because I'm starving, then set off for the motel.

The hair on the back of my neck prickles. Is someone watching me? Following me?

Shit, is it my father's men?

I stop and glance around, feeling paranoid as my heart rate kicks up. But I don't see anyone paying any attention to me.

Even so, I walk faster, and when I get to my motel and unlock the door, I breathe a sigh of relief. I lock up behind me and go the extra mile by laying a towel in front of the door and covering the peephole with a tissue.

People yell on one side of me. On the other side are lewd sounds of sex. Someone is screaming out to God, and I roll my eyes. *Such an act. As if sex can make someone scream ridiculous things.*

I empty the bag of purchases. Immediately opening the ibuprofen, I wash three down with some water, then open a bag of barbecue potato chips and shove some in my mouth. *I'm so hungry.* When was the last time I ate an actual meal and not just snacks?

Before I ran from my father. No wonder I'm hungry.

I bought a super-cheap pair of flip-flops because I don't like walking on this floor barefoot, so I slip out of my shoes and into them, wiggling my toes.

I'm tired. At least I don't have to go back to pounding the pavement to find a job tomorrow. I do have to go shopping for clothes, though, so I'll go back to the department store and try to find things that look nice and not too cheap.

I don't know if that's possible, but I'll do my best.

Maybe I won't have to renew my stay at this motel. Perhaps I'll be able to afford something nicer. I made a few hundred bucks tonight and didn't even work a full shift.

Things are looking up.

Ready for a shower and some sleep, I walk into the tiny bathroom. I wonder who, exactly, Rome is? He's intense. He seemed so angry that I had bruises on my ribs that, at first, I thought he was pissed at *me.* But he wasn't. I don't know if anyone has ever been mad on my behalf before. Maybe Iris, but she'd never speak up to my father for treating me badly. No one in that house is that brave.

"How did you get the bruises?"

"I was mugged this morning. Got a little roughed up, but I'm okay."

"Are you in pain?"

"No, I—"

"Don't lie to me."

Every word, despite the fury in his tone, has my temperature spiking even now. Why was he so angry?

Should I have been scared of him? I've seen men like him before. Powerful. Formidable. Yet my injuries prompted his ire. Honestly, Rome's indignation gave me the warm and fuzzies.

Also, he's hot as fuck. Holy blue eyes, Batman. Combined with the olive skin and dark hair, and I might have been drooling.

Not to mention, the tattoos make my core pulse.

God, I'd like to see *all* of the tattoos. Obviously, they run down his arms. Does he have them on his chest? His back? I want to know.

"You probably shouldn't try to picture the customers naked," I say as I turn on the water in the shower and get my night clothes ready.

Yet as I step under the stream, still wearing the flip-flops because this tub doesn't look clean at all, I can't help but think of the handsome stranger and wonder ... *why did he care?*

Eight

ROME

Standing in the shadows, I watch the light in the first-floor room that Lulu disappeared into. It's a wonder my teeth don't break from clenching my jaw so fucking hard.

She walked here, more than a mile from my club.

This *motel*, if you can even call it that, is seedy as fuck and in the worst part of town.

It would have shocked me if she *hadn't gotten* mugged, now that I know where she's staying.

But she won't be staying there long.

I want to know everything there is to know about my little firefly.

I press my phone to my ear.

"Hey, boss," Luke says.

"I need you to bring me my car," I tell him and give him the name of the motel.

"What the fuck are you doing there?" he demands. "Are you by yourself? Jesus, Rome—"

"Just bring the car." I cut off the call and slip the phone back into my pocket.

If she's staying here, she won't be doing it unprotected. No one's ever going to touch her in anger again. The mere thought of the bruises on her precious skin makes my blood heat. I want someone to pay for them with their blood. And I want to march into that room and make her leave with me, take her back to my place, and keep her safe.

And I will. But not quite yet.

Less than ten minutes later, Luke pulls into the parking lot, and I meet him as he shoves out of the vehicle.

"What the fuck?" he asks me, and I simply stare at him. "Seriously. I'm your head of security. You never leave without me."

Going out alone is careless, and I'm not a careless man. But I had to follow her.

He looks between me and the motel.

"Are we taking care of someone in there?"

"Not in the way you mean. Her name is Lulu Monroe. She's the new bartender. And from this moment on, she's never alone. I'm going to stay here tonight to watch over her, but I want a man on her, from a distance, starting tomorrow morning."

Luke scowls. "Why?"

"Because I fucking said so. She's mine. No one touches her."

His eyebrows shoot up. "Whoa. I'm sorry, I was looking for *Roman Alexander*."

"You're a riot. And you're walking back."

"I'm not leaving you."

I huff out a breath and get in the driver's seat. Luke walks around to the passenger side and climbs in.

"If you're here all night, I am, too."

"I have an eight o'clock meeting."

He eyes the clock. "That's in four hours."

I don't reply.

"You're fucking grumpier than usual tonight."

"Handle the detail for her. Now."

"Yes, boss." He sighs and pulls out his phone, and the light in the window goes out. My hands tighten on the wheel.

She's lying in bed in a disgusting motel on the wrong side of Vegas. *Fuck that.* She should be in luxury—in *my* bed, naked and spread open for me.

And you will be soon, my little firefly.

You were made to be mine.

Nine

ROME

I've been through the hours of footage of Lulu from last night, with audio, and listened to her conversations with Scarlett, Rita, and Loveland. She mentioned several times that she didn't know her salary, and based on the motel she's in, she needs money.

I'll take care of that.

However, I need to have a conversation with Loveland, my general manager, because she did everything wrong last night.

I've had a long fucking day with no sleep. Luke and I stayed in the parking lot of that fucking place until Bruno, our replacement, arrived at seven, so I could come home and shower and get ready for my busy-as-fuck day.

"Where is she?" I ask as soon as I see Bruno's name on my phone's screen.

"Shopping, boss," he says. I scowl when he gives me the name of the cheap department store and pull my hand down my face. It makes sense that that's where she's shopping, but again, it'll be the last time.

Where did you come from, my firefly? And why are you here in Vegas with so little when you deserve the world?

And who the fuck hurt you because only those recent bruises were from a mugging.

Why am I so enamored with her? Why do I have this deep-seated desire to claim her?

I don't know, and it doesn't matter. I took one look and knew in my soul that she belonged to me. Then I heard her voice, smooth like whiskey, and it became an ache in my chest.

She touched me and cemented her fate.

"She keeps looking over her shoulder," Bruno continues.

"Are you staying out of sight?"

"Of course, but she's paranoid about something."

I tighten my jaw. I want to know everything there is to know about Lulu Monroe.

"Keep me informed," I tell him. "She's going to walk to the club tonight. Let her. Follow her."

"That's a hike, boss."

"I know."

I check the time. Lulu's shift starts in three hours. Just three more hours until I get to see her. I'd have my men put cameras in her shitty motel room, but she won't be living there after tonight, so it's a waste of time.

"Don't let her out of your sight. I'll see you when you get here."

I end the call just as Loveland walks into my office

and closes the door behind her. She strides to the chair across from me, sits, and crosses her long legs.

"You fucked up last night," I inform her.

She swallows hard, but her gaze stays on mine.

"You didn't even tell her how much she'd earn?"

"I'm not her manager."

"No, but Rita was swamped, and you knew it. I told you to hire her. That includes getting her paperwork, informing her of her benefits and salary, and all the other shit that goes with it. You've been here for almost ten years. What the fuck?"

"You're right, and in those ten years, you've never *once* threatened to kill me over the way I do my job."

My eyes narrow, but she doesn't shrink away. "I've never heard you speak to someone the way you did to her. Ever. We hire people of all shapes and sizes, and you know it."

"Not true." She shakes her head adamantly. "I've never hired someone who looks like her."

I go still, and now she won't look me in the eyes.

She's jealous.

I've known this woman for a long fucking time. Once, in the beginning, we thought we could be in a relationship, but it failed spectacularly. I caught her fucking a member and killed him on the spot.

I've never touched her since.

Or any other employee. I learned that lesson the hard way.

"I'm going to make myself clear, in case you weren't listening last night. You will *never* speak to anyone the way you did to Lulu in your office. I don't care if we wouldn't employ them if the world was falling apart, you will be respectful."

"I was simply honest."

"If you choose to defy me in this, you're done."

Her eyes jump to mine now.

"You can't fire me—"

"I can do whatever the fuck I want to you." I stand and circle the desk, dragging my hand over her perfect hair. "Fire you. Kill you."

I lean down until my mouth is next to her ear.

"Are you jealous, Sarah? Jealous that I might want to fuck that woman when I wouldn't touch you with a ten-foot pole?"

She stills and takes a sharp breath but doesn't look my way.

"She's beautiful. And she's mine. And if you so much as hurt her feelings, I'll destroy you without a second thought. She's everything, and you're nothing. Don't push me on this."

She clears her throat as I stand to walk away.

"I need to get to my office." Her voice is strained.

"Go."

She doesn't pause. She's on her feet and out the door before my ass is back in the chair.

My phone rings, and when I see that it's Julian, I answer.

"We have a situation," he says. "And it needs to be handled tonight."

"Have you called the others?"

"They're my next call."

I pull my hand down my face. "When?"

"My plane leaves at midnight."

"Where are we going?"

"LA."

"I'll be there."

I hang up and immediately stride out of my office and down to the control room, where I get to work setting up the camera feeds on my phone. I won't be here for most of my firefly's shift, but I'll be able to see her.

By the time I have my work squared away and have briefed Rita on what I want for Lulu, I see my girl walk through the front door and smile at Beth, who's working reception tonight.

"Hi, I'm Lulu," my girl says. "I'm the new bartender."

"Heya," Beth says. "So you're the cool new girl I heard all about. Welcome aboard. I love that dress."

Lulu glances down at the black dress that hugs her tits and ends just north of her knees. It's basically a nun's habit compared to what the other girls wear, but it's sexy and classy, and as long as she's comfortable, that's all that matters.

However, it would look better on the floor next to my bed.

"Thanks. I have to be comfortable behind that bar, you know?"

"Oh, totally," Beth agrees. "Go on in, hon. Rita said to send you straight to her office. Third door on the left."

"Thanks, Beth." Lulu grins, then pushes through to walk the hallway to the offices.

She's going to pass right by me.

I want to pull her in here, boost her up against the door, and fuck her until she can't remember anyone before me.

But not yet.

I listen as Rita outlines the salary and benefits for my girl, and judging by the quick intake of breath and the lift of her hand to her chest, Lulu's shocked.

That's nothing, firefly. You'll never want for anything ever again.

It doesn't take long for Rita to finish everything. Lulu moves on to the locker room, and I'm distracted by work.

Determined to look in her gorgeous green eyes before I have to go take care of business in LA, I leave my office.

Ten

LULU

"**Y**ou're doing great," Max says with a wink as he stands next to me to pour a beer. "How are you feeling?"

"Good." And it's the truth. Today is *so much better* than yesterday. I bought a few outfits to wear to work and had a real meal of spaghetti and meatballs. I'm planning to switch to a nicer motel now that I know how much money I'll make.

I've never had to worry about money in my life, but even I know that a six-figure salary is pretty damn good, and that doesn't even include tips.

"If you need anything, I'm right here. Rita's coming on in an hour, too."

"Are we the only three bartenders on staff?" I ask him.

"No, we have Brandy as well, but she only works two nights a week because she's a single mom. You'll meet her Sunday night."

I nod, then deliver the Guinness I just poured to a member before I make my way to the next customer.

"A filthy martini," the redhead says. She's in a slip dress that looks made of diamonds, and I have to say, it's freaking gorgeous. "With extra olives, please."

"You got it."

"The dirtier, the better," she adds.

"Is there any other way?" I ask, earning a grin.

"I like you," she decides, and with my confidence buoyed, I turn to make her drink.

I've been here for a couple of hours, and so far, there has been no sign of Rome. Maybe he's not coming in tonight. Or perhaps he arrives later in the evening. It hadn't even occurred to me that he never left the bar to go into the playroom last night.

But he's a member of this sex club, and that means he probably usually goes into the playroom and the private rooms to have sex. Right? For all I know, he could be married, but he comes here to get his rocks off.

And I'm not judging. Maybe the wife knows. Perhaps they have an open relationship, and this works for them.

After sliding over the martini, movement at the end of the bar catches my eye. It's not Rome, but it's a handsome man.

He also has a ton of tattoos and dark hair that's cut super short to the scalp. He's dressed in a white button-down with the top two buttons unfastened. No tie. No jacket. And the sleeves are rolled almost to the elbows.

He's a giant of a man, with muscles that flex under his inked-up skin. His hands look rough.

And when I look in his face, I almost stumble back because he's ... *scary.*

This man hurts people.

I've seen enough of them through my father's line of work to recognize them.

But his lips curl up into a half smile as I approach him.

"Hi there," I say, proud that my voice doesn't shake. "What can I get for you?"

"Just a shot of Macallan will do it," he replies. His voice is like gravel. And his dark eyes are pinned to me. "You're new."

"Yeah, I just started last night." I set the glass on the bar, then reach for the bottle and pour. "I'm Lulu. And you are?"

"Intrigued," he replies.

"That's smooth." I wink at him. "Does it work with all the girls?"

He barks out a laugh and shoots the whiskey back. "I'm Carson."

"Nice to meet you, Carson. Would you like another?"

"Better not. I'm working tonight."

I blink at him. "Oh, do you work here?"

That smile returns to his handsome face, but it looks foreign on him, like he's too mean to smile so much.

"Would it disappoint you if I said no?"

"Why would it disappoint me, Carson?"

He leans in. "Because then I wouldn't be here on the regular to rock your world in one of the private rooms. Or are you more of an exhibitionist? Would you rather I bent you over one of the couches in the playroom?"

I tip my head to the side, watching him, not backing down an inch. I'm not at all attracted to him sexually. Definitely not like I am Rome. And he makes me ... uneasy.

"I don't think I'd take you up on any of the above, if I'm being honest."

I hear a chuckle behind me and turn to find Rita tugging on her apron.

"Leave my girl alone, Carson," she says with a good-natured smirk. "She's not your type."

"Why not? She's fucking hot."

"Rome saw her first," she says, and Carson leans back in his chair as if he's putting space between us.

What the hell does that mean?

"Pity." He shakes his head. "Well, it's time to get to work. Have a good evening, pretty Lulu."

He raps his knuckles on the bar, and then he's gone. I turn to Rita with a frown.

"What do you mean *Rome saw me first?*"

"Just that." She winks at me but doesn't elaborate, which is not helpful. "Now, get back to work. Looks like Blondie over there needs her second martini."

"Why do we have a two-drink max?" I ask.

"Because the things that go on in the playroom would be dangerous if people were sloppy drunk. This way, they can lower their inhibitions without getting out of control."

I nod as it all makes sense. "I like that."

"Good. *Always* remember the number one rule."

"Never serve anyone more than their allotted two drinks."

Rita smiles like I'm her favorite student. "You've got this, girl."

Eleven

ROME

"I'm riding with you," Carson says as he walks into my office. I've just slipped two guns in their holsters under my jacket, and I'm putting throwing knives on my belt.

"Why?"

"Because I was in the neighborhood anyway, and I wanted a drink, so I stopped by the bar."

"You mean, you were at your casino next door and decided to come over here to bum free liquor off me when you have plenty of your own bars to drink at?"

Carson owns King of Spades, and our buildings are connected via a sky bridge, which is convenient for our businesses.

"I paid for my whiskey, thank you very much. Cheap asshole."

I grab my long-range rifle just in case I need it and turn to Carson. "Where are your weapons?"

He holds his hands up and smirks. "Got everything I need right here."

"Okay, badass, let's go."

Luke's waiting outside the office for me along with Spider, Carson's second-in-command, and they walk right behind us as we make our way through the back doors to the alleyway, where my SUV is waiting.

"So you have a sexy new bartender," Carson says as he climbs into the back seat with me. "She's … *feisty.*"

"I'll kill you," I say, and he bursts out laughing, but when I don't smile back, he sobers.

"You interested in her?"

I turn to look at him and don't reply.

"But you don't hook up with employees," he goes on, and I notice Luke flicks me a look in the rearview mirror. "What's so special about this one?"

"A man can't change his mind?"

"You *never* change your mind." Carson shakes his head. "You've got the hardest head out of all of us. So the pussy must be thermonuclear—"

"Want a bullet to the brain?" I look at him again.

Carson sobers and then nods. "It's like that."

"It's like that. Now what the fuck is happening in LA that requires our attention tonight?"

"I'm assuming Julian will let us in on that when we get on the plane."

We never ask questions. If one of the four of us needs help, we simply go. Between us, we run this city. On the street, we're called the Kings of Vegas. But among us, we're simply brothers.

Not by DNA.

But absolutely by blood.

We've shed enough blood for each other, that we've bonded in ways that we can never get out of. Not that we'd ever want to.

We each have our own businesses. I have the sex club, but I also deal with dirty money. Julian is the diamond guy. Mateo runs drugs and guns. And Carson owns casinos, which is a great front for more money laundering and pretty much everything else he can get his hands on.

His preferred job? Carson is an assassin.

He's a bad motherfucker. Then again, no one wants to cross any of us, so I'm interested to find out what's going on tonight.

Luke and Spider climb out of the car first, and when they give the all clear, we follow suit and board the plane. Julian and Mateo, along with their men, are already here.

"Jesus, it's a party," I say as I sit facing Julian. "What's going on?"

"The Italians have decided they want my shipments," he says coldly. "They killed ten of my men at the port and have settled in to take over my receiving."

"Fuck that," Carson says.

"Exactly," Mateo chimes in. "We're killing them all tonight and sending their heads back to Salvatore Rizzo."

"I hate that fucker," I mutter, shaking my head. "He tried to buy a membership to the club."

Julian's eyes narrow. "When?"

"Last year. What he didn't know is that every application is run by me first. He didn't try to hide his identity. Piece of shit."

"He's about to lose half of his men tonight," Mateo growls. "And it will be my pleasure."

WE'RE in four different black SUVs. We never ride with more than two of us in each car, just in case it gets taken out. That way, all four of us don't go out at once.

I've done it this way for a decade.

Before we reach the port, I check the video feed on my phone. It's after two in the morning, and my firefly is halfway through her shift. She's still smiling, bustling about behind the bar. She looks relaxed and like she's having fun.

She's safe.

That's the most important thing. We left Bruno behind to follow her back to her motel in case I'm not back in time to do it myself.

I pocket the device just as Luke pulls up behind Julian's car about a hundred yards from the port.

We'll walk in from here and catch them by surprise.

"There's a rooftop here," Julian says, pointing at a map of the area, "where I think Rome should snipe from."

"You don't want me on the ground?" I ask him.

"I want your eyes in the sky," he replies as he puts his

earpiece in. We all follow suit. "I think twenty of Rizzo's men are in and around the building."

"There are twelve of us," Mateo reminds him. "I fucking like those odds."

"And we're hitting them unaware," Carson says, cracking his knuckles. "It'll be quick."

Julian turns the page and shows us the building's blueprints. Thanking fuck I brought my rifle, I break off from the others to climb a series of fire escapes up the abandoned building.

Won't lie. I would have liked to get my hands on some of the Italian fuckers tonight, but taking out more as a sniper will also satisfy my need to take revenge for Julian's men.

Who the fuck do they think they are, trying to take Julian's run?

I slow my steps, sure to stay perfectly quiet as I walk up to the motherfucker already on top of the building. He must see my guys come into view because he raises his rifle, but I pull my knife, jerk his head back, and slice him open from ear to ear.

He gurgles as he falls, and I scowl at the blood that spurted onto my shirt.

I hate getting dirty.

With a shrug, I assume his last position and lift my rifle.

"In position," I murmur so the others can hear. "One down."

"We're a go," Julian says, and then all hell breaks loose below, sending adrenaline through my veins.

As the Italians scatter, I take aim.

"Two down," I say, squeezing the trigger of my Barrett MK22, picking off men one by one. "Three."

"Four," Carson says, hardly breathing hard after pulling a man's throat apart with his bare hands.

Scary motherfucker.

"Five," Mateo says.

"Six and seven," Luke announces.

One by one, we count them off. None of our men are hit.

"Twenty-two," Julian says. "That was the last one."

But I see more movement.

"No, there's two more," I say, taking aim. "Back of the building, hiding behind crates. I can't get a shot."

"On it," Mateo says. "Only cowards fucking hide."

He hits one, and the other runs right into my crosshairs, and I take the shot.

"Twenty-four," I say calmly. "I'm coming down."

By the time I walk into the warehouse, our foot soldiers are working on removing the heads from the bodies, so I stay out of the way of the blood.

It's not that I'm afraid to get messy, as I've been covered in my fair share of blood. But tonight, there's no need.

Spider swears as he slices his knife through a man's throat.

Decapitating grown men is hard work.

"Why didn't you just send their tongues?" Luke asks Julian with a grunt.

"Because receiving a crate full of twenty-four heads

sends a message," Julian replies smoothly as he takes photos.

"You're not wrong," Carson says as we walk back toward the cars. Julian's men will stay behind and finish up here, but it already took far longer than I expected it to. It's past six in the morning when we reach the plane.

I pull out my phone and see the texts from Bruno.

> B: She got back to the motel fine. I'll stay here until I have more instructions.

Without replying, I slip the phone back into my pocket and prepare to sleep on the flight back to Vegas.

Twelve

LULU

What a night. It was exhausting, exhilarating, and another steep learning curve. My mixology classes had given me excellent knowledge, but working somewhere like Rapture, where most people ordered classier drinks than white wine, beer, or a cosmo, I was being stretched every shift. I love it. The walk back? Not so much.

I still had that niggling feeling of being followed, so I took a roundabout route back this morning, hoping that on the off chance my father's people had thought to look for me in Vegas, that I was outsmarting them.

Could they have found me this quickly?

That thought kept going around and around in my mind, and I had to believe no, they couldn't.

So my plan is to sleep the whole day away; I can just feel it. I'm not stupid enough to completely let my guard down, but I feel it's okay to rest, take a breath, and then find a better hotel closer to the club. I made almost a *grand* in tips tonight.

I smile to myself and wiggle my butt, trying to get comfortable in this crappy bed.

If I'm honest, I had hoped I'd see Rome again last night. But what was I really expecting would come of seeing him anyway? He was a good-looking, sexy-as-sin man who possibly only came to Rapture once a week. But what had Rita meant by *Rome saw her first?* Of course, I didn't ask anyone about him because even I knew that was foolish. *Let it go, girl. You're not here to meet a man.*

You're here to start a new life.

End. Of.

Sleep. Find a new hotel. Eat. Work. That's what you need to focus on.

I'm just about to drop off to sleep when I hear something at the door. My eyes pop open, and I strain to listen. A rattle? Maybe just someone walking by. But then I hear something brush against the thin wood.

Oh shit.

Someone is definitely at my door.

Suddenly, the mechanics of the lock move, as if someone has opened it with a key card, and I bound out of the bed and run for the bathroom. I turn to close the door and see a huge man rush in. His sneering face is the last thing I see as I slam the door closed and lock it, shoving wet towels from my shower along the bottom, and try to breathe through my hammering heart. I feel like I just ran a marathon.

"Do you think this will keep me out, you stupid bitch?" He's jiggling the door handle while I desperately search for a weapon.

Shit!

I have hair spray. That would probably hurt his eyes.

I arm myself with the can, but then the asshole goes quiet, and there's a thud on the floor right outside the door.

It's a trap.

He wants me to open the door so he can attack.

"It's not going to fucking work, you piece of shit," I call out. "I'm calling the cops."

I'm absolutely not calling the cops, but he doesn't know that. I know he's one of my father's men. I recognized him as a foot soldier who I've seen around the house.

And if he found me, then my father knows where I am.

Fuck! How? How could he find me this easily? I've covered my tracks, used cash for everything I've bought. What am I going to do? How am I going to get out of here?

And where the hell will I go *if* I get out of here?

God, I'm so fucking tired.

"You can come out." There are two knocks on the door. "I won't hurt you."

"Right. I've heard that one before. Go fuck yourself."

Shit, he didn't pass out after all. Oh God, what am I going to do? There's no window in here. I can't escape. The only way out is through the room. Through *him.*

"No, you don't understand. I'm really not going to hurt you."

"I won't go back," I yell in return as the panic attack starts to set in. "You can tell my father to kiss my ass. You'll have to kill me first."

I gasp and push my hand against my mouth. *Oh God.* They'll kill me. Or, at the very least, beat the shit out of me, and my dad will still make me marry that guy. Whoever he is.

It's hard to breathe in here. There's not enough air. Am I using up all the air? Am I running out of oxygen? I'm going to die in this bathroom. *Fuck.* I am going to *die.*

"Boss?" a man says from the other side of the door. "We have a situation."

Thirteen

ROME

"What kind of situation?" I ask Bruno as I step off the airplane.

"Some goon broke into her room," he says, and I fill with anger. "She managed to run to the bathroom, but she's scared out of her mind and won't come out. She keeps saying she won't go back."

"Did you kill him?"

Won't go back where? What secrets are you keeping, firefly?

"No, he's just unconscious."

"Good. I'll be there in less than ten minutes."

"We're all going with you," Carson says after I hang up.

"I've got this."

"If it has to do with your little bartender, we're all going."

"What bartender?" Mateo demands.

"He's got a girl," Carson replies, but I let them talk their shit as I run for my car. Luke has it started, and we're on our way within seconds, with the others on our tail.

"Who the fuck would want to hurt her?" I ask no one specifically.

"Maybe she has a past, boss." Luke shrugs. "I mean, we all do."

I narrow my eyes, and as soon as he pulls up to the motel room, I jump out and rush inside.

"I won't come out!" she screams, and I can hear the panic, the terror, in her voice. "Please just leave."

After a moment, I hear her cry more softly, "I'd rather kill myself than let him marry me off."

What the fuck?

Bruno shrugs. "She's been like this since we hung up."

I look down at the man on the floor. "He's the one who broke in?"

"Yep."

"Get him into the cell. We'll deal with him later."

Bruno nods, and with Spider's help, they lift the man and get him out of the room.

Julian, Carson, and Mateo file in, looking around in disdain.

"You let your girl live like this?" Julian asks, and I roll my eyes.

"Lulu," I say calmly. "Open the door."

"No way."

"Listen to me. You're safe. This is Rome."

She's quiet for a second, then she unlocks and cracks the door. I don't push inside. She's fucking terrified.

"Are you one of my father's men, too?" She has tears rolling down her sweet cheeks. "Oh God. My man radar is so fucked up."

"No." I shake my head and step closer, but she moves to close the door, and now I press my hand against it, keeping it open. "Listen to me, firefly, I don't know who your father is. I'm not here because of him."

"You're lying."

I narrow my eyes. "I'm a lot of things, but I'm not a fucking liar."

Her eyes flick over my shoulder and fill with more fear. "Carson."

Before I can ask how the fuck she knows my brother, Carson replies, "At your service."

"Oh God. He hired all of you, didn't he? That's why you've been hanging out at the club."

She retreats into the bathroom, huddles against the wall, and I walk in after her.

"It was all a setup. I'm so fucking stupid. *So fucking stupid.*"

I raise my hand to brush her hair off her face, but she flinches as if I'm going to hit her, and I pause.

A woman only reacts like that when she's been hit before.

"I won't hurt you."

She's sobbing now, and she shakes her head.

"She's panicked," Julian says from behind me. "You

won't be able to calm her down like this. She doesn't know any of us. She's terrified."

"Lulu."

She sniffs and swallows, but she won't look at me.

"Just do it," she whispers. "If you're going to hurt me, just do it. You have blood on you. Obviously, you're going to hurt me."

Shit. Of course, the blood scares her.

"Baby, I'm not going to hurt you." Christ, she's breaking the dead black heart in my chest.

"Someone did," Mateo says behind me and passes me a water bottle. "Here. Get her to drink this."

"Have some water and take a breath." I glance back at the others to find them all crowding into the tiny bathroom. "Jesus, get out of here. No wonder she's terrified."

The three of them back out, and it's just the two of us now. I want to scoop her to me and kiss her head. I want to soothe her and reassure her that absolutely nothing can hurt her.

But there's no way she'll let me right now.

"Hey, this will feel good on your throat. Take a drink."

She's shaking, and her eyes are on mine as she takes a sip, then another, and wipes a drop off her mouth with the back of her hand before passing it back to me.

"That's my girl. I promise you, I won't let anything happen to you."

She frowns and presses her lips together. Christ, she's so full of life, so full of fire and flirtation at the club, and now she's been reduced to this?

When I find out who's responsible for this, they're going to lose their head—right after I'm finished removing their limbs and internal organs.

"I don't believe you," she whispers.

"That's okay. It doesn't make it less true."

After a few minutes, her eyes get heavy, and she scowls at me. "Did you drug me?"

I glance over my shoulder and see Matteo looking in on us. He just nods.

The fucker.

"Yeah, baby, we drugged you. I need to get you home."

She whimpers. "I don't want to go back. Please. Please don't take me back home. He'll hurt me. He sold me."

She's swaying, and I catch her in my arms as she finally passes out.

Who the fuck sold her? Her father?

"Who the hell are you, firefly?" I whisper, holding her close to me. She feels so right in my arms, which is only just keeping my fury at bay.

"You're going to pay for drugging my girl," I inform Matteo, who just smirks.

"It's easier than pulling her out of there kicking and screaming," he replies.

I carry her out of the bathroom and turn to Luke. "Pack up whatever she has here and meet me back at the penthouse."

"Sure thing, boss."

"What's next?" Julian asks.

"I'm going to get her settled in my bed, and then I have some questions for the asshole in the cell."

"Oh, good. I'm coming along." Carson grins. "I have some new toys to play with."

"You're a sadistic son of a bitch."

"I know."

Fourteen

ROME

Mateo holds the door of my penthouse open so I can walk through with Lulu in my arms.

"How long will she be out?" I ask as I pass by.

"Let me do some math." He winks one eye closed and looks at the ceiling. "She didn't drink much. I'd say a couple more hours, probably."

Hours? The fuck? What if she'd drunk more than a few sips? I turn and scowl again at Mateo.

He shrugs. "I had to think fast on my feet, man," he argues.

"Fuck you. I'm putting her in my bed, then we're going down to the cell."

"Let's hope Carson hasn't killed him already when we get there."

"He knows better," I say over my shoulder as I climb the stairs.

I've never enjoyed holding women. I'm not a snuggler. But having *this* woman in my arms, against me, feels like nothing I've ever experienced.

I want to feel her. I want to hold her. Yes, I want to fuck her until we're both unconscious, but it's more than that.

I want her.

And now, she's mine.

Gently, I lay her on top of my bed and cover her with a spare blanket. I felt their glances. Thankfully, they were wise enough not to say anything ... to my face. They all know I fuck women. Often. But I never bring women here. I've never let a woman come into my bedroom and certainly have never had one sleep or fuck here.

Hell no.

But it feels right to have my firefly here.

Yet they've said nothing. They've only had my back.

"We're all going with you."

That's family. Fuck, that's my family.

"Sleep it off," I murmur and kiss her sweet forehead. She smells like roses.

With one last look, I stride out of the room and down to where Mateo is waiting. Julian and Carson are already at the cell.

We take the elevator to the basement. Each of our main properties has a room just like this one for interrogation purposes. Hooks hang from the ceiling for strapping men up. A few wooden chairs sit off to the side of the room. There's a drain in the middle and a workbench placed next to the chair where the man who tried to hurt my firefly is tied up, already swollen and bloody.

"You started without us," I say casually as I approach the man. I shove my hands in my pockets as I stare down at him.

"Just warmed him up a bit," Carson says from where he leans casually against the wall.

Julian is at the workbench, pulling out tools, and Mateo walks behind him.

We have four men outside the door. We won't need them, but they're there, just in case.

"I'm going to start nicely," I inform him, looking into his hard brown eyes. I can already tell he has no intention of speaking.

That will pass when I start to skin him.

"Fuck you," he growls, and I nod, then pace away two strides before I take my jacket off and toss it aside. I'm still wearing all of my weapons from the op in LA. *I still have blood on my shirt.* That will have to go before my girl wakes up.

I tug off my tie and roll my sleeves before I turn back around, and when the man looks at me again, his eyes narrow.

"I know you," he says.

"Do you?" I lift an eyebrow. "I'm intrigued. Who am I?"

He tips his head to the side as if trying to place me. "You're Alexander." He looks around the room. "Why do the Kings of Vegas give a shit what I do with that little slut?"

I backhand him and watch with satisfaction when blood flies out of the corner of his mouth.

"I'm the one asking questions."

He spits blood onto my shoe, then grins up at me. His teeth are red. "I'm not in the mood to answer them."

"No?"

I nod and walk over to Julian, who hands me a cleaver off the tool bench.

In one smooth move, I sever three of his fingers from his left hand, and he wails in pain.

"Good one," Carson says with a satisfied nod. "You always have the best aim. You must spend a lot of time practicing."

"It's an art form," Mateo adds.

"That probably hurts," I agree, eyeing the hand bleeding down the chair and onto the concrete floor. "Who do you work for?"

He shakes his head.

"You're about to lose *all* of your fingers, and I don't like repeating myself," I inform him. "Who do you work for?"

More headshakes.

So I take the rest of the fingers on that hand.

"Fuck." Mateo smirks. "How's he supposed to jack off now?"

"He still has another hand," Julian says with a negligent shrug.

"For now," I add. "Who do you work for? And before you shake your ugly head, remember that I have no qualms about skinning you alive. Your death will be a slow one."

"I'm going to die here anyway." His face is a mask of pain.

"True." I shrug. "But I can make it fast, or it can last for days. So I'm going to ask you one more time. Who the fuck do you work for?"

"Look, I'm just a foot soldier," he says, but that's not what I asked.

"Listen. I'm going to call you Vinny, okay? Listen, Vinny, I didn't ask what you do."

"Christ, just remove his spleen," Carson growls as Vinny licks his lips.

"I was just supposed to kidnap her, not hurt her." He's talking fast now, as if this will keep him alive. "Okay, maybe rough her up a little, but that's nothing she's not used to. I had to deliver her alive."

I backhand him again, wishing I could kill the fucker right now. "...*but that's nothing she's not used to.*" Fuck.

Her bruises.

The scar on her back.

Someone hurt her ... often.

I fist his greasy hair in my hand and pull his face back. "Who. Do you. Work for?"

He folds his lips together, and I hold my hand out. "Pliers."

"Now it's getting fun." Carson's voice is full of glee as he rubs his hands together. "Start with the molars."

He's a sick son of a bitch.

"Last chance," I tell him. "Before you lose all of your teeth."

Now, he starts to cry.

But he doesn't talk.

When the last one is gone, I squat before him. He passed out from the pain twice. Maybe from a little blood loss.

We woke him right up again.

This could go on for days.

"You're going to tell me who you work for, Vinny, and why you were trying to touch something that belongs to me."

"Doesn't," he whispers, and I narrow my eyes.

"Who does she belong to?"

"The boss."

"This is fucking tedious," Mateo says as he drags his hand down his face. "And she'll wake up soon."

"Let's take his foot," I announce as I stand, and Vinny moans. "TELL ME WHO YOU FUCKING WORK FOR!"

I pick up an axe and swing it around.

"Tell me. Now."

"Rizzo."

The room stills.

My eyes find Julian's.

"Salvatore Rizzo?" I ask as I let the axe fall to the floor.

"Yeah." He's breathing hard. "Kill me."

"Why does he want the girl?" Julian asks.

"Do kno. Jush do wha tol."

I spin on my heel and leave the room. There's a scream and then silence behind me as Carson's the last to leave.

"Christ, Rome," Julian says.

"Not here," I reply as I press the call button for the elevator, then press my hand to the palm reader for the penthouse floor.

We're silent as we ride up, and when we walk inside, I peel off to go check on my firefly.

She's still out cold.

I trash the clothes I was wearing, take a shower to get any blood or body matter off my body, and change into fresh slacks and a shirt then walk downstairs.

"Who the fuck is she?" Julian demands. "Because if she has the Italian Mafia after her, she's not just an anonymous bartender, and she kept saying she's not going back to her father."

"Is she a setup?" Mateo asks with a scowl.

"No." I pace in front of the windows that give me a view of the Strip. The glass is bulletproof, and treated so I can see out, but no one can see in.

"Rome, listen," Julian says. He's always the most reasonable of us, and that's not saying much because the man can be unhinged. "It's a little too convenient that Rizzo tried to take over my port, and his men tried to steal your bartender at the same time."

"You really don't know her," Carson adds. "She's worked for you for two fucking days. She could be a scout for them. A spy."

I shake my head, but they keep going.

"Stop thinking with your dick," Mateo says with growing impatience, and I cross my arms over my chest.

"You didn't see her the night she came in here," I

reply evenly. "I *know* she had nothing to do with what happened in LA. I have questions, and we'll get the answers, but I'm telling you she's not a fucking spy."

"I don't trust her," Julian says.

"That's fine," I reply. "Because you *do* trust me."

He's already shaking his head when I hear a noise come from upstairs, and we all go perfectly still. Suddenly, feet slap on the hardwood floors, and we turn to the stairs as Lulu runs down them and toward the front door.

Fifteen

LULU

My head is killing me, and my mouth is dry. I turn on the bed and pry an eye open. Then I sit up straight, and my heart feels like it's going to pound out of my chest.

Where the fuck am I?

I'm not in my motel room.

And then I start to remember. I was going to sleep, but someone burst into my room. I hid in the bathroom. He was going to hurt me.

Then Rome came.

Rome works for my father.

Panic rises up my throat and threatens to choke me as I look around. This bed is too nice. The bedding feels too good for it not to be something my father is paying for.

He may beat the shit out of me every chance he gets, but he makes sure I'm always in the lap of luxury. *Fucking hypocrite.*

I need to get out of here.

I move to stand and feel woozy but take a deep breath.

Hold it together. Just get out of here. Run away and fall apart later.

I walk to the door and turn the knob, surprised when it isn't locked, and open it just a crack. I don't hear anyone, and no one guards me from the other side.

For a second, I stand and try to listen, but I don't hear anything through the rushing in my ears. It feels still.

I can see I'm on the second floor ... in a house? I must be in a house.

Maybe I can run to a neighbor for help.

Just run!

I swallow hard, then do what my gut tells me. I run. My bare feet slap against the floor, but I don't care. I see the stairs, and I manage to get down them without falling and breaking my neck. Just when I see the door, a huge body steps in front of me and takes me by the shoulders before I crash into his chest.

No.

"Going somewhere, firefly?"

"Let me go," I say and feel the tears come. "Just let me go."

"I can't do that," he replies. "Look at me."

He takes my chin in his fingers and makes me look way up into his bright blue eyes. I know I should be petrified.

Rome is a *big* man who far outweighs me and is so much stronger than I am.

But I'm not scared.

I also don't trust him because I'm not *that* stupid.

"I'm not letting you go," he says, staring into my eyes. "And I'm not going to hurt you."

I clamp my mouth shut. Christ, I'm going to be sick.

And he must see it because I'm suddenly airborne, cradled in his arms, and he's hurrying past the other men from the motel room.

"What happened to Rome?" one of them asks.

"Never seen anything like it," another says.

He gets me to the toilet in time, and I throw up until I can't breathe and I'm covered in a layer of sweat.

"God, I'm sorry," Rome murmurs, and I realize he's pressed a cold, wet cloth to the back of my neck. "I'm going to kick Mateo's ass for drugging you."

"Didn't my father tell you to?"

"No." His big hand rubs up and down my back, and I want to lean into his touch and purr. "I don't know who your father is, Lulu."

Is he telling me the truth?

I want him to be. From the moment I laid eyes on this man, I've been pulled to him. I can't explain it, but I don't think it's all because of my vagina.

"Better?" he asks.

I nod, and he leads me to the sink, where I swish water in my mouth. Then he leads me out of the bathroom.

Three huge men stare at me, and I stop dead in my tracks.

"We do *not* work for your father," Carson says. His voice is still hard and gravelly. "We don't work for anyone but ourselves."

"And we need to know who your father is," another of them says.

"Wh-who are you?"

"This is Julian and Mateo," Rome says, pointing at each of them. His arm is still wrapped around my shoulders, holding me to his side.

Julian is the one who asked about my father.

My gaze bounces between them, and I think they're telling me the truth.

I don't think they work for my dad. If they did, wouldn't they just take me to him rather than bring me ... wherever I am?

I take a shaky breath, and when my knees want to give out, Rome picks me up and carries me to a couch, where he sets me down and covers me with a blanket.

"I'm not cold," I tell him.

"I don't want them looking at you without more of you covered," he replies simply, calming me with an even, deep tone that seeps into my nervous system.

I'm in my sleep shirt and shorts. No bra.

Because that's what I was wearing when everything happened.

"Oh." I tug the blanket around me. "Okay. I'm not trying to cause trouble."

"Great," Julian says. "We don't want trouble. Who's your dad, Lulu?"

I can't escape. Rome won't let me out of this place, and the three men in front of me—who all have splatters of blood on them—quietly terrify me. Yet, unexplicably, I feel safe. Even though I was drugged.

Fuck.

"Salvatore Rizzo." It's a whisper, and all four seem to lean closer to me.

And they look mad.

"My real name is Eloise Rizzo, but my friends call me Lulu. I use the term *friends* loosely because I don't really have any, but my classmates and our housekeeper call me Lulu. I had to run away, so I came to Vegas. I found a job, and I like it, and I don't want to leave, but obviously my dad found me, and I won't go back to him, so I have to leave Vegas. I have some money, so I can just go and be out of your way. Wait. Why do you care who my dad is?"

I frown up at them.

"If you don't work for him, and you're not going to make me go back, what does it matter?"

They share a look.

"What don't I know?" I ask them. "Oh God, is my dad dead?"

I blink at the thought.

"Why don't you look upset by that idea?" Rome asks me.

"I'm only upset that I didn't get to watch," I mutter and look down at my hands. "I hope it was painful. The bastard sold me."

I shake my head. Out of all of the horrible, painful things he's done to me through the years, that's the one thing that I can't reconcile. He *sold* me.

"He didn't send you here?" Julian asks me.

I shake my head but then feel dizzy. "No. And you didn't answer me. Is he dead or not?"

"As far as we know," Mateo says, "he's alive."

"Shit." Tears fill my eyes. "I have to go. It's not safe for me here."

I go to stand, but Rome urges me back on the couch and turns to the others.

"Give us some time," he says.

"She needs to answer—" Carson begins, but Rome shakes his head.

"She'll answer, but she's sick, thanks to Mateo. Give us some time."

The three of them don't look happy about it, but they do file out of the—apartment? I still don't know where I am.

"I don't want you to be in danger," I whisper.

"I'm not," he says, lifting me off the couch, blanket and all.

I'm not a petite girl. The fact that he can just carry me around is ... alarming.

And a reminder of just how strong he is.

He stops in the kitchen and pours me some water, and as I sit on the counter, I drink some of it, watching him over the rim.

"How's your stomach? Do you want some food?"

I wrinkle my nose. "Definitely not."

"Hold on to your water."

I do as I'm told, and he lifts me again, this time carrying me up the stairs and back into the bedroom where I woke up.

"Is this your bedroom?" I ask him.

"Yes." He sets the glass on the bedside table, pulls the blankets on the bed back, and gestures for me to climb inside. "Lie down, firefly."

"Why do you call me that?"

I don't fight him. I scoot over in the bed and turn on my side so I can watch him. Rome unbuttons his shirt, removes it, and tosses it aside, and my eyes are plastered to his naked torso.

Holy fucking Jesus in a rowboat.

How? How is he so … muscly? And covered in ink, from his jawline to his fingers and everything in between. There are words and images. An angel. Flowers. It would take hours to look at them all, and my fingers itch to touch him.

"My eyes are up here, firefly."

My cheeks darken as I roll my lips together and lift my eyes to his.

He's *grinning.*

"You have a nice smile," I say, surprising us both.

Leaving his slacks on, Rome climbs onto the bed, but he doesn't touch me. He rolls onto his side, facing me, and pulls the covers up to our shoulders.

"What are we doing?" I ask him.

"Hopefully, we're going to nap," he says. "You need

to sleep more of that off, and I haven't slept in two days, so a few hours sounds good."

"Why don't you sleep?"

"Work," he says simply. "Why did you run from your dad?"

I tuck my hands under my chin and let out a breath. "I should have run away a long, long time ago, but I didn't have any resources, and despite what he did … well, I guess it was easier to stay. That makes me sound weak, and I hate that."

"I haven't known you long, but I know you aren't weak."

I feel warm with his words. I can't believe I'm telling him so much. That I feel safe to.

"I don't know how much you know about the Mafia." I cringe. "That sounds like something out of a movie, but my father is kind of a big deal in that world."

"I know who he is," Rome replies, surprising me.

"You do?"

He nods.

"He's not a good man. Not even to me." I shake my head. "Anyway, he came to me not quite a week ago and told me that he'd arranged a marriage for me, and I'd be expected to go with this guy within an hour of his little announcement."

Rome's eyes go cold.

"I know that arranged marriages happen all the time in organized crime. It just is what it is. But he'd *never* talked about it with me before. Not that he really talked to me much. I know very little about what he does, except that he makes a lot of money, and he gets off on hurting people."

Rome takes a breath. "How do you know that?"

I chew on my lip, looking at the angel on his chest. *I don't want to tell him how I know.*

"Anyway, when I told him that I wouldn't marry whoever this guy was—I'd never met him before, and I didn't know the name—he hit me."

Rome's jaw clenches.

"Wasn't the first time, but I knew that I couldn't stay. That I wouldn't just blindly go to whoever my father sold me to and hope that my home life there would be better than it had been before. I'd prepared to leave during the few years leading up to this, and I grabbed my go-bag and left. I knew he'd look for me, I'm not stupid, and he'd never just let me go. That's why I found the cheap motel because he'd never think to look for me there. Well, that, and I didn't have much money. I don't know how that guy found me."

"Why Vegas?" he asks as he reaches out to push my hair behind my ear, and it sends warmth down my whole body. I love this man's hands.

"It was convenient," I admit. "I'm from Reno, and it was a quick and cheap bus ride. I didn't lie to my boss, as I really do have a background in mixology, so I figured I'd find a job here pretty quickly." Am I digging myself a deeper hole right now?

I feel so stupid.

"I like the job, and I'll miss it. I like my coworkers. It sucks that I have to leave."

Rome reaches out and brushes his finger down my cheek, sending a shiver through me.

"You don't have to do anything right now. You're safe here. No one can get to you. So why don't you relax and sleep off the rest of that drug?"

My eyes *are* heavy. And this bed is so comfy, and I feel good when I'm with Rome.

So without fighting him, I let my eyes drift closed and fall asleep.

Sixteen

ROME

She fell asleep so easily and quickly, as though she could finally let her guard down. Her plump lips part as she breathes deeply in sleep, and she looks so *right* in my bed. I can't help but reach out for her and hug her to me, careful of her bruised ribs.

She said she was mugged, and I don't think she was lying. Some of the bruises look fresh. But I now know that the more advanced bruises, and possibly the scar on her back, were caused by a man I despise. It makes me see red, but she nuzzles her little nose against my chest, and some of the tension within me settles.

Even more strangely, despite the question marks that hover over Lulu's life story and my brothers' valid concerns, I have no desire to back away from her.

I plant my face in her hair and kiss her head, breathing her in.

You're not going anywhere, firefly. You're home.

And her father is going to die.

Seventeen

LULU

I don't know if I've ever felt so ... *cozy.*

I'm surrounded by warmth. My face rests against a hard, warm chest, and when I open my eyes, it's to see the rest of a tattooed torso in my line of vision.

Rome.

We weren't touching when we fell asleep, but here we are now.

Cuddling. Actually, that term's too simple for it. We're wrapped up in each other. His arms are holding me against him, and it feels so good. I don't know if I've ever been held like this before. I'm not a virgin, but the few sexual encounters I had with just one man weren't followed up with cuddling in bed.

There was no bed.

My arm is draped over his stomach, and my leg is hitched up high on his thighs. For fuck's sake, I'm clinging to the poor man like a monkey in a tree.

What if he doesn't like to be touched?

I guess he would have rolled away from me if that were the case.

He's relaxed beneath me, breathing in long, deep breaths, obviously still asleep. I want to drag my fingers over his eight-pack abs. Over the ink and the soft, warm skin.

Holding my breath, I ease my head back to see his face. It's relaxed in sleep, but he still looks grouchy, with that little line between his dark eyebrows, as if even in dreams something pisses him off. His full lips are closed. They look like they could do all kinds of naughty things to me, and just the thought of it has my core tightening.

Rome has a good nose. It might have been broken once because he has a bump on the bridge.

Full, dark eyelashes lay against his tanned cheek, and his dark hair is tousled from sleep.

Everything about this man is sexy. His voice. The way his blue eyes watch me as he listens to me. Hell, the *listening* is sexy. Even though we've only had a few conversations, and they haven't been long or of much substance, I feel like he sees me. Like he wants to know me.

With my eyes pinned to his face, I let my hand drift over his abdomen, and God, if I don't love the way his smooth skin feels under my touch. Each muscle is defined, and I enjoy exploring each hill and valley up to his chest.

I want to kiss his neck. Maybe bite him there and leave a mark.

Mine.

I mentally shake my head at my audacity. He's not mine; he's just being nice to me. And I don't even really know why. I don't know how he knows who my father is or why it's important.

I have a lot of my own questions.

"You're thinking way too hard."

I startle at the rough words, but I don't stop touching him until he takes my hand in his and kisses my palm before bringing them both to his stomach and resting them there.

"How long have you been awake?"

He opens one eye and peers down at me. "Since you started getting handsy."

I bite my lip. "Not sorry."

He huffs out a laugh. "I didn't think you were."

In the quiet of the next few seconds, it feels good to lie here like this, as if we do it all the time. As if we've done it for years and it's the most natural thing in the world.

"Thank you for everything," I whisper.

"Mm-hmm. Go back to sleep."

I grin. God, I like this guy. "I can't. I really do have to go."

"No." His hold on me tightens, and he rolls onto his side and hugs me against him. "You're staying. Go back to sleep, firefly."

I lean in and press my lips to his chest, and he stills. I couldn't resist it. It's *right there.* And his skin feels good against my lips.

"I have to figure out what I'm going to do, Rome. I don't know where I am. I guess I'll go to work tonight and tell them it'll be my last shift, but I have to walk there, and I don't know where we are right now or how far away it is."

I feel his gaze on me and look up to find him frowning.

"You don't know who I am," he says as if he's just now realizing this.

"You're Rome. A member of the club. Kind of a scary guy, but I'm not scared of you, surprisingly, and you snuggle well. I sincerely hope you're not married, but if you brought me to your house, I assume you're not. Or she's super understanding, which would make her a better woman than me because I would haul me out of here by the hair. Anyway. That's about it."

He blinks. "There's a lot to unpack there. No, I'm not married or attached to anyone in any way. Well, I *wasn't*. I'm Rome Alexander. Rapture is downstairs, so the commute is pretty short. I own this building. We're in my penthouse on the top floor."

My jaw drops.

Oh God.

This is Mr. Alexander.

This is my boss.

Well, technically, my boss's boss.

And what did he mean by he wasn't *attached to anyone?*

"I'm *so sorry*." I pull out of his arms, my cheeks flaming from being completely mortified, and roll away from him, then cover my face with my hands. "Oh Christ, I'm so sorry. I am *not* this unprofessional, Mr. Alexander. Give me ten minutes, and I'll be out of your way."

"You're cute."

I peek through my fingers and find Rome—I mean Mr. Alexander—lying on his back with his hands tucked behind his head, watching me with humor-filled eyes.

"What?"

"Adorable. Tonight isn't your last shift, by the way."

"I could have sworn you were here for the conversation before I fell asleep."

"I was. You're safe here, Eloise."

Eloise. Why does it sound so sexy rolling off those lips?

"I appreciate the offer, Mr. Alexander, but—"

"Rome."

"Huh?" He sits up and lets the blanket fall to his waist, and once again, my eyes feast on his tattoos.

"You call me Rome. When we're here, or in the club, or wherever, you use my name. Got it?"

"Uh, okay."

"Second, you live here now."

I shake my head, but he takes my face in his hands and leans in to kiss my forehead.

God, he has good lips.

"Are you telling me you'd rather live in that roach coach you called a motel?"

"I only found one roach," I inform him, but he doesn't laugh. "No, I hated it there."

"See?"

"No, I don't see."

"I'll lay it out for you. You'll live here, in my penthouse. With me. You'll continue working as a bartender downstairs."

"Am I being held prisoner?"

He scowls and honestly looks offended. "Of course not. But if you leave the building, you take guards with you. Until I speak with your father."

"And I'm out." I pull away and get out of bed. "If you're speaking with my father, I'm leaving. Absolutely not."

"Do you think after what he's put you through, I'll stand by and let him get away with it?"

"My father is a powerful man, and I will not put you or anyone else in danger, and if one of his goons found me, others are on the way. I have to go."

He stands and faces me, pushing his hand through his dark hair. "You're also looking at a powerful man, Eloise. Your father doesn't fucking scare me."

He should. He scares the shit out of me.

"I'm not kidding, Rome."

Suddenly, his face goes hard, and it makes it hard to swallow. *Shit, he's intimidating.* "Neither am I, firefly. Those three men you met earlier? The four of us make up the Kings of Vegas. We run this city. Your father sent his man into our territory. For that alone, we need to have a conversation."

He steps up to me and brings his hand up to my cheek, and it immediately calms me.

"Added to that, he hurt you and threatened you. He'll pay for that."

"I left one organized crime household and fell into another. That's what you're saying?"

He lets out a frustrated breath. "I will never hurt you. You're safe here, Eloise. I promise."

"Why do you call me firefly?"

He leans in, and I think he's going to kiss me. My thighs press together, and I lick my lips in anticipation.

But then he simply kisses my forehead again.

"Because I can." He walks away, leaving me feeling cold. "Shelly will be here at seven."

I scowl. "Who the hell is Shelly?"

"A personal shopper. You need more clothes."

And with that, he closes the bathroom door, and I can only stare after him.

I'm in an alternate universe.

Eighteen

LULU

I'm in the middle of eating an entire pizza by myself —I'm *so* hungry—when a woman waltzes into the penthouse, pulling two racks of clothes, and then another woman follows, also pulling two more racks of clothes.

I stop chewing and stare. Rome left after the pizza came and told me to make myself at home, so I'm sitting at the dining room table, still in my sleep clothes, legs crossed under me, and I'm no longer alone.

"You must be Lulu," woman number one says with a bright smile. "I'm Shelly. This is my sister, Sheila."

Now that I get a good look, I see that they're twins.

"Hi," I reply, setting my slice of pepperoni down. "You're early."

"I know," Shelly says, brushing a lock of her red hair out of her eyes, "but Mr. Alexander mentioned that you have to work at nine, and I wanted to give you plenty of time. Men don't understand that this can be time-consuming."

"Nice to meetcha," Sheila says with a wave.

Abandoning my plate, I cross to where the women are fussing with the clothes, but I don't know what I'm supposed to do. I'm not a stranger to shopping, I've done plenty of that in my lifetime, but the store has never come to me.

"I think we got your size right," Sheila says with a nod. "And if anything doesn't fit, but you love it, we can exchange it."

"I don't really have a big budget," I inform them.

"Oh, honey, don't worry about that. Mr. Alexander already paid for everything."

I shake my head and take a few steps back just as the door opens, and Rome walks in. He surveys the scene and nods at the women.

"Ladies," he says. "Does the living room work, or would you rather use the den?"

"I'll change in the bathroom," I say as I cross to him and grab his hand, linking my fingers with his. He glances down at our hands but doesn't pull away from me. "Can I please speak with you privately?"

"Of course," he says, leading me toward his office.

"We'll start with work wear," Shelly calls out to me. "And we'll meet you in the den."

"Thanks," I call back, then prop my hands on my hips when we get to the office. "You can't buy me all of those clothes."

He leans back against the desk and crosses his arms, then rubs his finger over his lips. "Why not?"

"Because that's ... ridiculous."

"Fine. You pay for them."

I narrow my eyes at him. "I'll buy a few things, but you just wasted their time, Rome."

He shakes his head and pushes away from the desk to cross to me. "Are you always this difficult?"

"I'm not being difficult."

"Yes, you are. You'll take whatever you like. It's all been paid for, so don't worry about that."

"But—"

He shuts me up by wrapping his arms around my shoulders and pressing his lips to the top of my head. It's the nicest way I've been shut up, that's for sure. This is the nicest a man has ever been to me in my life.

And I can't believe it, but I trust it.

"Are you buttering me up with cuddles?"

"Is it working?"

I sigh and wrap my arms around his waist. "Kind of."

He chuckles and tips my chin up so he can kiss the tip of my nose.

This man still hasn't kissed my lips yet. And man, do I want him to.

"They're just clothes, firefly."

"Those are expensive. I didn't look at the labels, but I know expensive clothes when I see them. I *wore* them once upon a time."

"And you'll wear them again, but they won't come

from your father." He drags his fingertip down my cheek to my neck.

Suddenly, all I can picture is his hand around my throat, forcing me to my knees, and holy shit, that's my new goal in life. I wonder if I can manifest that?

Except he hasn't made any moves on me at all.

I don't even know if he's attracted to me like that.

"What?" He skims his finger over my eyebrow.

I bite my lip. "I'm struggling to see how this makes sense, Rome. You were a stranger only hours ago, it feels, and now you're cuddling me, when I've never been cuddled by a man before. And ... are you even attracted to me?"

Fuck, I feel like a fool. Of course, he's not. Maybe he wants a pet. I've read romances where the alpha hero just wants a pet.

His eyes darken, and his hand slides into my hair at the back of my head. He makes a fist and tugs my head back more.

"You're in my home, slept in my bed, in my arms, and I just brought all of the ready-to-wear items in the city for you to choose from. Why would you think that I'm *not* attracted to you?"

"You haven't even kissed me." It's a whispered confession, and his eyes immediately drop to my lips.

"Not yet," he murmurs and leans in, but his lips land on my forehead. "You're the most beautiful woman I've ever seen in my life."

I can't stop the "psh" that pushes through my lips. "Right."

That hand loosens, letting go of my hair, but he holds the back of my neck.

"Since the moment I saw you, I wanted you. I want to get you naked and fuck you so hard and for so long, you'll only ever remember me. I want to kiss you for days. I want to listen to you laugh, and talk, and anything else you want to do until we fall asleep, and then do it all over again. I don't deserve one minute with you, but I'm going to take them all."

I swallow hard. I don't know what to say. All of the words have left my brain, and my blood has pooled between my legs.

"I'm going to kiss you," he murmurs, staring down at my lips again, "but it won't be a sweet peck, and it's not going to be when there are two women in my house, *when I never let women into my house*, who are waiting for you."

I lick my lips. *I never let women into my house.*

"A simple 'Yeah, I'm attracted to you' would have worked."

His lips quirk up into a half smile. "No. It wouldn't have. Now, go choose some clothes. I don't want you to be late for your shift."

He takes my hand and leads me out of the office and through the living room to the den, where a three-way mirror has been magically set up in the middle of the space.

"Don't fuck around," he says to Shelly and Sheila. "I don't want you here longer than you need to be."

He turns to me.

"I'll see you later, beautiful."

"Where are you going?" I ask him, then feel my eyes widen. "Don't answer that. It's none of my business. I'm sorry."

In front of the two women who are watching unabashedly, Rome steps over to me and grips my hand, and gives it a squeeze.

"I'm your business, firefly. There's nowhere in this building that's off-limits to you except for the basement. If you feel the need to venture down there, please talk to me first. Anywhere else, you're welcome. Even my offices. You don't even have to knock, but don't be offended if we pause the conversation upon your arrival. Now, I'll be downstairs. Have fun."

With one last kiss on my forehead, he turns and saunters out of the room, and I can't help that my eyes fall to his ass.

It's a supremely gorgeous ass. Especially in dress pants, with his white shirt tucked in. Even with the gun at the small of his back.

Let's be honest. Every inch of Rome should be illegal.

"Wow," Shelly says with a sigh.

"We've known him a long time," Sheila adds. "I've never seen him like that."

I turn to them with a frown. "How is he usually?"

"Grumpy," they say at the same time, making me smile.

"Yeah, he can be grumpy. Okay, I have to work in two hours. Let's do this."

Nineteen

ROME

When I walk into the lounge, Rita's already here, taking inventory of the bottles.

"You're here early," she says to me.

"I was thinking the same about you." I slip onto a stool to stay out of her way and watch her hustle back and forth, stopping only long enough to write notes on a sheet of paper. "I don't like that you're putting in twelve-hour nights."

"I'm fine."

I narrow my eyes at her. Rita's been with me since the beginning, and she's like a sister to me. To all four of us. We saved her from a sex trafficking ring, and she just never left us. Not that we'd let her leave now. She runs this lounge impeccably, and the employees and members love and trust her.

Given her history, Rita has no interest in the sex club. She's never set foot in the playroom or private rooms and doesn't attend the special shows we put on. Not to mention, she's the best at deflecting interest from members.

And I can respect that.

"You work too much," I reply.

"Hi, pot, I'm kettle." She laughs and pushes her hair —blue tonight—over her shoulder. Rita is a colorful woman, and not just her hair falls in that category. She's tattooed all over her chest and arms, and she has more metal in her face than anyone I've ever seen, but it doesn't look out of place on her. "Let me guess, you're here to talk about Lulu."

I lift an eyebrow. "Why do you think that?"

Rita laughs again. "Come on, Rome. You've never looked at someone the way you look at her. Not to mention, you let her touch you and didn't take her hand off."

"I rarely do that."

But it's not unheard of.

No, I don't like to be touched. That's why, when I do fuck, I like to tie the woman up so she can't reach me. Yet earlier today, I couldn't get enough of Eloise's hands all over my skin.

It was unsettling and addictive, all at the same time.

"So you're going to break your rule for her? The no-touching-the-employees rule?"

"Looks that way. Has she been given a tour of the facilities?"

I know she hasn't.

"No, we've been so busy when she comes on shift

that she's mostly just been behind the bar and in the locker room."

I nod. "I'm going to have Scarlett give her a tour tonight. Can you do without her for an hour?"

"Sure, especially if it's at the beginning of her shift."

"I want her to go after midnight."

"Are you trying to see if you can scare her off? She seems like a tough cookie to me."

"No, I don't want to scare her." But she should see what happens here. She needs to know all of it. I don't have that many kinks, but there are a few, and I will want to explore them with her. I want to see her reactions, so I'll be watching on the screens. It'll tell me what she's into.

It better not be threesomes because I won't share her. Man or woman, no one touches her ever again but me.

Looks like my threesome kink has officially ended.

The thought of being with anyone other than my firefly makes my gut clench.

"You can have Scarlett come get her anytime," Rita assures me. "We'll make do."

I nod, head up to my office, and find Luke waiting for me.

"Do you just hover in the hallway outside my office, waiting for me to appear?"

He smirks. "You wish. I just got here. We have a shipment coming in tonight."

I nod and sit behind my desk. "Two o'clock. Are we ready?"

"I have eight men lined up," he assures me.

"Good. I have a meeting in thirty with the boys."

The boys is code for Julian, Mateo, and Carson, and Luke knows this.

"How's Lulu?" he asks.

"She's safe," I reply. "If she needs to go anywhere, she's driven with a four-man detail."

He nods and pulls his phone out of his pocket to make notes. "For how long?"

"Forever."

His head whips up, and he stares at me. "Seriously?"

"Seriously. I need you to get her a phone and program my number into it. Add yours as well, and when you've finished assigning her detail, add those numbers, too. I want it tonight."

"Good thing this is Vegas, where you can get anything twenty-four seven."

"Isn't that convenient?" I check the weapon at the small of my back, then slide on my suit coat. "Let's go. We're meeting at Carson's."

Luke nods, leading me out of the building to my waiting SUV.

I want to get work wrapped up so I can get back to Rapture and escort my firefly to work.

Twenty

ROME

"Do you believe her?" Julian asks after I explain everything I learned from Eloise this afternoon to the three of them.

"He can't be impartial," Mateo pipes up, and I glare at him.

"I believe her," I reply. "I *don't* think she knows much about what her father does. I think he's an abusive fuck who either ignored her or hurt her. I don't know who he was trying to marry her off to."

"I still say it's a crazy coincidence," Carson says, shaking his head. "I'm not saying you're not right, but it's just so fucking unlikely, and I don't trust it."

"We need to get in contact with Rizzo," I say. "I'd like to invite him here, but I won't."

"Why the hell not?"

"Because if Lulu got wind of it, it would terrify her. She's been scared enough in her life, I won't add to it. He doesn't come here."

"We don't have to take him to the cell at Rapture," Julian reminds me. "There are a dozen or more other locations to meet with the asshole."

"We're not going to his turf," Julian growls. "Fuck that. He stole a couple of million dollars of my product, then sent his man to Vegas? Fuck him. He comes here."

The others nod, and I realize that I'm outvoted.

"Not to Rapture," I reiterate.

"Not a problem," Mateo says, watching me steadily with hard, dark eyes. Energy is sparking off him, and I know he's holding back.

"Just say what you have to say."

He shrugs. "You're *sure* about this girl?"

I shove my hands into my hair and lean back in my chair. "I can't fucking explain to you why, but yes. I'm sure. And you three are the only ones who can question me like this and live to tell about it."

"Quite a coincidence," Carson says again, shaking his head. "But your gut hasn't steered us wrong yet."

"Now, how do we get Rizzo to Vegas?" Julian glances at me. "We could use her as bait."

"Fuck no."

"Just her name," Julian clarifies. "Not *her*. She'll be safe in your building."

I don't like it. But it might be the only way to get that asshole here.

"Just get him here."

Twenty-One

LULU

"Did you save this one for last on purpose?" I ask as I step into the den wearing a black dress I'm officially obsessed with.

"Maybe," Shelly says with a pleased nod. "He was right."

"Who?" I frown at her in the mirror.

"Mr. Alexander picked that one out for you. And he was right because it hugs you in all the right places."

I turn to the side and check out my ass. "I'm not even wearing shapewear under this."

"You don't need it," Sheila points out.

"But also, I'm not wearing a bra," I add, biting my lip. The dress is hooked together in the front with silver safety pins down to just above my navel, so I can't wear a bra because it would show. "I'm too big-chested to let the girls go free."

"Says who?" Shelly demands. "Are you uncomfortable?"

"No," I admit.

"As long as it feels good," Sheila says, "you're good to go. Honestly, Lulu, you look amazing. I'd kill to wear something like that, but you have the perfect body for it. We also got you these super cute wedge heels that are so comfortable."

They *are* really adorable, and when I slip them on, I immediately know that they won't kill my feet.

"Sold." I smile at the two women who have been so nice to me. "I just have to brush my hair and put on some mascara."

Sheila scowls. "Please let me do your makeup."

I blink at her. "Oh, you don't have to do that."

"I honestly want to. With that dress, you need something more dramatic than mascara. Don't worry, I won't go overboard."

"I honestly don't have much makeup to work with," I admit. "I only have the basics."

I always dressed down before, so I didn't draw any attention. But I admit, I kind of like having my makeup done and looking nice. Especially since I don't have to worry about my father's men eyeing me as I walk through my own house.

Not that it ever really felt like my house.

"Let me help. I have a kit with me," Sheila says with a smile. "Just have a seat right here. It won't take long."

I don't argue, and less than thirty minutes later, I stand in front of the mirror and grin. She was right. The makeup elevated the whole outfit.

"I need to invest in some nice makeup and have you give me pointers."

"I'm always down for that," Sheila says with a wink.

I hear the front door open, so I walk out of the den. When Rome glances up at me, he does a double take and stops in his tracks.

Yep, the dress works.

"Fuck, you're gorgeous."

I laugh and cross to him. "Thanks. Done with work so soon?"

"No, but I'm escorting you to the lounge. I have to show you some things, and I wanted a few minutes with you before I have to share you with everyone else."

I slip my hand into his and enjoy the way his palm feels against mine.

"I guess I'm ready. I won't have to store my purse or anything in a locker if I'm coming back here in the morning."

Suddenly, Shelly and Sheila come out of the den, pulling mostly empty racks behind them.

"We're done here, Mr. Alexander," Shelly says. "You'll be refunded for the things that didn't work."

"Thanks for your help," he says.

"I had fun," I tell them both. "Thank you *so much.*"

"It was our pleasure," Sheila says with a wink. "Hit me up when you want that makeup lesson."

I smile at her, and once they're gone, Rome turns to me and brushes his finger along my jawbone.

"Did you really enjoy your time with them?"

"Actually, yes. They're nice girls."

He leans in and presses his lips next to my ear. "I can't wait to get you out of this stunning fucking dress in the morning."

I swallow hard and brace myself with my hands on his sides. "They said you picked it out. Does getting me out of it mean you don't like it?"

Rome ghosts his lips over the shell of my ear. "Not at all. It's fucking perfect. And it's going to look even better on the floor of my bedroom."

I swallow thickly and then chuckle when he presses his lips to my forehead.

"I have to go to work," I remind him.

"I'm aware. Before we go, I want to lay some ground rules."

Here we go. I should have known. I'm not under my father's control anymore, but I'm under Rome's roof now, and there are always fucking rules.

"Okay."

"Number one, you'll keep this on you."

He passes me a cell phone, and I frown up at him.

"It has my number in it, along with Luke, my second-in-command, and the men who will accompany you if you leave the building. That's rule number two. No leaving without my men to keep you safe."

I blink up at him. "Let's go back to rule number one. You got me a phone?"

"Yes. I need to be able to reach you and vice versa. It's yours."

I sigh. "You've already done so much. I don't need a phone. I don't have anyone to call."

"You have me," he says, hooking his finger under my chin, forcing me to look him in the eyes. "And *I* want to be able to call you. Especially if something comes up and I have to leave unexpectedly."

I lick my lips and slip the phone into my pocket.

This amazing dress has *pockets*.

"Thank you," I murmur. "What else?"

"I want you to make a grocery list at some point so we have all of your favorites here."

"No, you don't." I shake my head and start to laugh.

"I'm missing something."

"Rome, I went to culinary school. If you set me loose on your kitchen, which is so freaking beautiful I might want to marry it, I'll never come out of it. I'll be cooking enough for twenty people every day. It's my favorite hobby."

His smile is beautiful. "The kitchen is yours, Eloise. Make your lists or take your detail and go to the grocery store whenever you want."

"Holy shit," I whisper. These rules are nothing like the ones at my father's house.

"What other talents do you have?"

"I got a certificate in massage. Oh, and I took classes on goldsmithing."

He blinks at me. "Goldsmithing."

"Yes. You know, jewelry. Setting stones and designing things. It's really interesting, actually."

He smirks, and then he laughs. "Julian is going to love that. Anything else I should be aware of?"

"When I'm nervous or scared, I clean. Oh, when I'm mad, I also rage clean. Basically, I hope you have a mop."

"I don't want you cleaning this penthouse."

"I plug in a spicy audiobook and clean. It's not a big deal, Rome."

He looks uncomfortable. "You don't work here."

I let out a laugh. "Actually, I do. And I think I'm going to be late."

"Luckily, sassy woman, I'm the boss, so it doesn't matter. Okay, we can figure out the rest later."

"Those are the only rules?"

"The only ones off the top of my head. Not fucking other men is a given, but if you need me to lay it out for you, that's fine. Let's move it up to rule number one."

I shake my head as I walk with him to the door.

"I don't think I planned to do that." I glance up at him. "Does that mean that you won't—"

I clear my throat, and he corners me against the still-closed door. "No, firefly. The only woman I'm even remotely interested in is you. The rule applies to both of us."

I lick my lips. "Okay."

"Okay." He kisses my forehead, and then we're in the hall, where two men are standing.

"This is Luke, my second. You probably don't remember him from earlier."

I shake my head and don't reach out to shake hands.

"I'm glad you're feeling better," Luke says with a wink.

Rome turns to the other man. "And this is Sebastian. He's one of our men, and you'll see him from time to time. Tonight, his duty is outside of our door."

"Do you always have someone guarding the door?" I ask as he leads me to the elevator.

"Yes. When I'm in residence, there are two guards outside. There are also always men outside the elevators on each floor. You'll eventually learn their names."

I frown up at him as we walk into the elevator, and he presses a button, making it stay where it is.

"This is a palm print. You'll need to use it to get to this floor. Go ahead and lay your hand on the glass."

I do as I'm told, and a few seconds later, a green light blips.

"Now you have access to the penthouse. If you want to come up here on your break or for any reason, you have full access. Always. This is your home, Eloise. Understand?"

I nod, feeling overwhelmed. Jesus, he wasn't lying earlier.

Rome is an important man.

He truly wants me to stay here. I have no idea how long that will last, but if I can save money, I'll be ready for when he doesn't want me here anymore. I'm anything if not savvy. Sophisticated security and two men at the elevators when he's in residence also scream that Rome wasn't lying about being an important man.

It's daunting.

Exciting.

But can he really keep me safe from my father?

"The lounge is on the second floor, as you know," he says, pushing the correct button. "As are several of the offices, like for Loveland, Rita, and Luke."

Luke's in the elevator with us, not saying a word.

I glance back at him.

"My office is one floor above, on the third floor. You now have access to that as well."

"You're just allowing me to waltz all over your property?"

"Is there any reason I shouldn't trust you, firefly?"

"Of course not, I guess I'm just not used to ... it doesn't matter. I won't snoop around or anything."

He smirks, and the doors open to the second level. I step out, but Rome doesn't release my hand. He doesn't leave the elevator, so I turn back and raise an eyebrow.

"Have a good night, Eloise." He kisses the back of my hand.

"You too, Rome."

He releases me then, and the doors close on him. I walk over to the bar area where Rita and Max are already working.

The lounge seems to fill up quickly early at night, as people come in to socialize before moving on to other areas.

And when I check the time, I see I'm five minutes late.

"Sorry, Rita," I say with a wince. "It won't happen again."

"All good, Lulu. Rome mentioned you might be late." She shrugs. "No big deal."

I don't have time to talk to her, to ask questions, or tell her I'm living with him now. Which is still crazy to me.

I'm living with the hottest man I've ever seen in my life.

How did that happen?

"There are a couple of members on that end of the bar who I haven't gotten to yet," Rita says with a friendly smile. "Jump on in, honey. Also, you look *scorching* in that dress."

"Thanks," I say with a grin as I tie the apron around my waist, then walk down the bar to my first customer.

"Hey there, handsome," I say with a grin as I approach the member. "What can I get for you?"

His eyes skim over the black tank dress I'm wearing, pausing at my exposed cleavage. Sure, I'm showing off more of myself than I normally would, but this is a freaking sex club, and I'm completely covered.

"One hour in a privacy room." His response makes me grin but also feel on edge. There's something about this guy that I don't like.

"Sorry, I'm working," I reply, deciding to forgo any more flirtation with him. "Pick your poison."

"Whiskey, neat," he replies and leans on the bar, still watching me closely. "Rita, give—I'm sorry, what's your name, gorgeous?"

"Lulu," I reply, starting to feel uncomfortable.

"Give Lulu an hour off," he says, but Rita shakes her head.

"Not happening," Rita says, and then she turns her gaze to me and says only loud enough for me to hear, "Watch yourself, Lu."

Flirting with customers is normal. Build a light, friendly camaraderie with them, and they tip well.

But I only have eyes for Rome, and I suddenly feel like I crossed a line I shouldn't have.

Except I didn't.

"I didn't do anything wrong," I murmur back to her.

"Didn't say you did. But that guy is rich, powerful, and doesn't take no for an answer. Be careful."

I nod and deliver his drink to him. "Have a good evening."

He nods, slaps a hundred on the bar, then walks away. I let out a long breath.

"I *barely* flirted with him," I say to Max as he stops by me to fill a glass with water. "And that was only because I was in a good mood."

"Babe, flirting is the name of our game. But some of the customers take it a little far. That guy, Aaron Pierce, is one of them. Have you heard that name, or are you too new to Vegas?"

"Too new."

Max nods. "He's the mayor."

My eyes just about bulge out of my head. "Of the *city*?"

"Yep." Max gives me a stern look. "Smile, say hi, ask what they'd like to drink. Be cautious with compliments unless you'd like to go to the playroom at some point."

"I'm not here for that," I reply, shaking my head.

Something tells me that would be a hard no from Rome, and unless it's with him, it doesn't interest me.

"That's a good boundary to set right away." Max nods.

"Do you play? On your nights off?"

"Fuck yes," he says with a laugh. "But it's not for everyone, and that's okay. If you were into it, I'd invite you in."

I blink at him in shock.

"I hate to break it to you, but you're sexy as fuck, Lu," Max growls next to my ear. "So if you ever change your mind, the offer stands."

I lick my lips and offer him a smile. "Good to know."

He winks and walks away to take another order.

Max thinks I'm sexy as fuck. Hmm. Can't say that doesn't give me confidence. However, I have a strong feeling that Rome would not like that one bit.

The night gets busy, and I'm starting to feel more self-assured with each order that comes in. Rita is definitely right about the clientele. They're all loaded and know what they want. A few hours in, I turn around and see that Scarlett has sidled up to the bar.

"Well, hey! Do you want a drink?"

Scarlett wrinkles her nose and shakes her head. "No, thanks. Mr. Alexander asked me to come take you on an official tour since you haven't seen everything yet."

I glance over at Rita, who nods. "You're good to go."

Excitement courses through me. I admit, I'm curious to see the playroom, just to see what all the fuss is about. I've heard so much about it.

But when Scarlett loops her arm through mine, she leads me to an elevator.

"Aren't we going to the playroom?"

She winks as the doors open for us and leads me inside. "Abso-fucking-lutely. But first, we're going up. We'll work our way down."

"I've been to the penthouse," I reply.

"What?" Her voice screeches at a decibel only dogs and aliens can hear. "You *what*?"

"I've been to the penthouse," I say again. Scarlett starts to jump up and down, still holding my arm, jostling me.

"Girl, you'd better start talking. Mr. Alexander *never* lets anyone on that floor. Ever. It's forbidden. It's even part of our on-boarding paperwork. Even though you need to have your palm programmed in to get up there, it's outlined just so no one tries. Did you get in trouble or something?"

"He took me," I reply and bite my lip. How much do I tell her? I don't think I should tell her about my father or the guy who came to take me back to him. Or being drugged.

"He took you to his penthouse," she echoes softly as we reach the tenth floor and the doors open. She takes my hand and pulls me out of the elevator before the doors can shut on us. Sure enough, just like Rome said, a big guy dressed in all black stands next to the elevator.

Scarlett pulls me to the side and turns to face me. "Did he fuck you?"

"No. But he slept with me."

Her blue eyes widen, and she's watching me like I'm a mythical creature.

"And he had personal shoppers come in with racks of clothes for me."

Her eyes skim down my body and back up again.

"Was this dress one of them?" she asks.

"Yeah."

"It's killer. Shows your curves off perfectly. I'd kill for your tits."

I smirk and check hers out. She's in red leather tonight. "I thought the same about you the first time I saw you."

"Aw, you're sweet. But let's circle back. You slept with Mr. Alexander in his penthouse."

"I think I'm living there now."

Scarlett lets go of me and backs away two steps as if she's afraid to touch me.

"What? What's wrong?"

"Holy. Jesus. Christ." She shakes her head. "Wow. I'm so happy for him. And for you. This is awesome. I'm totally jealous because he's hot as fuck, and so ... mysterious. And I'll bet that man can do amazing things in the bedroom. Also, he's always been so kind to everyone on staff but never *too kind*, if you know what I mean."

Scarlett has diarrhea of the mouth. It's amazing.

"And I know he's into some shady shit that is none of my business, but who cares? He's the best boss, and I love you to death. We're already besties. I want you guys to work out."

Besties.

I've never had a bestie.

"Um, thanks. It's really new."

"Obviously," she says with a laugh and takes my arm again. "You just got here. But sometimes, when it's right, you just know."

I nod because that's exactly what it was.

What it *is.*

And I love that she gets it, and she's happy for me, and she's not asking weird questions. Scarlett is one of the most genuine girls I've ever met, so I don't doubt her sentiments at all. And knowing she considers us besties is awesome. I haven't had many friends growing up, and her enthusiasm is infectious.

But the most telling is that she's happy that Rome is happy. That speaks volumes about the man. Rita and Max show him the utmost respect, as do his men. So I'm with Scarlett. I hope that this will be right because even though I've only known him for such a short time, he's been nothing but kind and ... respectful.

"Where are we?" The color scheme up here is different. Soothing, with blues and greens and glittery ceilings that look like diamonds.

"The spa," she says with a grin as she leads me into a lobby with water features that tinkle in the air, and when I look in the pond, huge koi fish are swimming around. It's magical. "So in addition to this whole building being Mr. Alexander's home and the club, it's also a full-service hotel with apartments. There's a west and an east wing. The west side is mostly the hotel, the restaurant, and a casino over there that Mr. St. James owns called King of Spades."

"Who's Mr. St. James?" I ask her.

"Carson? He's around a lot."

"I've met him," I confirm, and she nods and keeps talking.

"We have clients from all over the world, and when they come to Vegas to play at the club, they stay here on-site. Well, most do. They don't have to, but it's so fancy and nice that most take advantage of it."

I nod, enjoying the way it smells of jasmine and orange blossoms. Just being here in the lobby is relaxing. The two women behind the reception desk smile at us.

"The spa is open all the time?"

"This is Vegas," Scarlett reminds me. "Everything is open all the time. Okay, so the floors between this one and the penthouse are all apartments. A few of the staff live here on-site, too. Like Rita, Loveland, um, some of Mr. Alexander's security. People like that. The east side, which is connected by the coolest sky bridge in Vegas, is the hotel. You don't have to be a member to stay there, but you *do* have to be a member to come to the west side. The hotel has its own spa and workout center over there."

"Interesting," I murmur.

"Plus, as part of our membership package, we can take advantage of the spa and the gym, which I'll also show you. We get a killer discount on services. You *have* to get a massage from Kathy. You'll never be the same. And we have some of the best aestheticians in the country. My skin doesn't glow like this all on its own. We'll have a girl day up here soon."

Just the thought of that excites me.

"I've had plenty of massages, but I've never been pampered with a whole girl day. I'm in."

Twenty-Two

ROME

"I've never been pampered with a whole girl day. I'm in."

My firefly's face lights up, and I rub my hand over my chest as I lean forward, taking everything in. I've been listening since they left the bar, following them through all of the camera feeds from the comfort of my own office.

I don't mind that she confided in Scarlett. I want her to make friends, and based on Scarlett's reaction, I need to give the woman a raise. She's loyal, and I reward loyalty.

I'll arrange for a day in the spa for both of them.

"Do you like to work out?" Scarlett asks Eloise as they walk back to the elevator.

"Define *work out*," Eloise replies with a smirk. "Because not really. I mean, I'm on my feet a lot, and I like it. But no, I've never been to a gym. I wasn't allowed to."

Scarlett frowns at her as she presses the button in the elevator for the next floor down, and I switch cameras.

"What do you mean?" Scarlett asks.

"Well, I wasn't allowed to leave my house much. Just for classes, and if I volunteered. Going to the gym wouldn't have been allowed even though my father totally fat shamed me every chance he got."

Rizzo's going to meet a painful death.

"Dude, you're *beautiful*," Scarlett says, and I can tell that she squeezes the arm she's been holding. I don't love someone else touching my firefly, but I'll allow this. Eloise looks at ease. Not only that, but Scarlett's telling my firefly the truth. She is beautiful. Sexy. "People suck. I didn't know that Loveland was such a sizist."

"*Sizist?*" Eloise asks.

"You know, someone biased based on size. So I'm totally bisexual. I love *people*. Male, female, trans, I don't really care. Sexy is a state of mind, an attitude. A persona, if you will. And it comes in all shapes and sizes. I mean, look at you."

I narrow my eyes as the elevator stops, and they step out, and I shift cameras again.

"Your curves are *amazing*. You have to know that you father was so, so wrong. You're a bombshell. And you have all that gorgeous dark hair and green eyes, and yeah, I get why Mr. Alexander wants to keep you."

Eloise snorts, and it's fucking adorable.

Yeah, I want to keep her. I am keeping her.

Twenty-Three

LULU

"Okay, now you're just being nice. I think besties are supposed to say stuff like this."

Scarlett laughs and leads me into the gym. There are treadmills, rowing machines, ellipticals, and other machines that I wouldn't know how to use. There are also tons of weights and a room with yoga mats rolled up and stacked on the side.

"I mean, sure," she says, "it's my job to make sure you feel good about yourself as your bestie, but I am not a liar. So don't listen to Loveland, or your father, or anyone else. I think you're awesome."

I grin at her. "I think you're awesome, too. Are you going to make me work out?"

"Duh." Scarlett rolls her eyes. "If I have to suffer, so do you. But we can reward ourselves with a protein smoothie after our workouts."

"I guess that could be a thing. Do you live here, too?"

"No." She shakes her head and leads me around to

where the smoothie bar is. It's staffed now, even after midnight. It must be available around the clock as well. "I would *love* to, but I'm not a manager or anything. I share a house with four other women about thirty minutes from here."

I wrinkle my nose. "That's far away."

"It's not so bad. It's a really nice house, and we all have our own suites. But yeah, it's a bit of a commute. I'm not complaining, though. If I was ever worried, I know that Mr. Alexander would have someone get me home, not that I'd ask."

I could imagine him doing that. It's no wonder his staff revere him. I'm just about to ask Scarlett about her housemates, because you never know, one day I might need to find something similar, but she asks another question.

"So have you met Mr. Alexander's security? Specifically, Luke?"

I blink over at her. "Yeah, I have. Why do you ask?"

"Oh, no reason." She bites her lip and won't look at me.

I pull us to a stop. "No way. There's a reason."

She shifts on her feet.

"He's hot. I've done scenes with Luke in the playroom, and I like him *a lot*. But I don't think he likes me back. Not in that way, anyway. We fuck a lot, but that's it."

"What do you mean, you do *scenes*?"

Twenty-Four

ROME

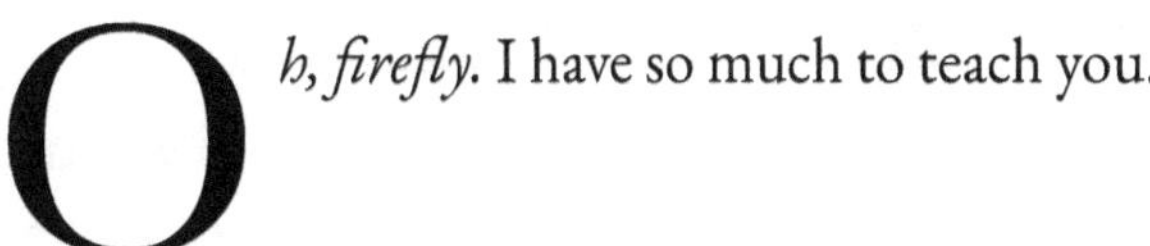

Oh, firefly. I have so much to teach you.

Twenty-Five

LULU

"I'll show you," Scarlett says with a knowing smile. "Now that you've seen all of this, we'll go back downstairs. We'll start our workouts first thing after our shifts tonight."

"You want me to work out at six in the morning?"

"I mean, unless Mr. Alexander is giving you a different kind of workout, yes." She smirks and hits the button for the elevator.

"Are you from Vegas?" I ask her.

"Nah, I'm from Nebraska." She shakes her head. "It's so *boring* there. I wanted bright lights and excitement. So I came here when I turned eighteen and found this job about a year later. I'm never leaving it. I'll be old and wrinkled and still working in the playroom."

I giggle at the thought, and then we're back on the lounge level. I wave at Rita as Scarlett leads me to the heavy double doors that open to the playroom, and when she pulls it open, I step inside and feel my breath catch in my lungs.

Oh my God.

The black-and-gray color scheme does *not* carry into this space. It's white. White tile floors, white wallpaper with gold designs in it. Flowy, transparent fabric hangs from the ceiling, giving the illusion of rooms. The stage is dark and empty right now, but I can't help but wonder what kinds of shows they put on in here.

The furniture is all in jewel tones. Purples, reds, yellows, and greens. I don't even know what half of it is, because I've never seen anything like it.

But then there are also couches, stools, and benches. There are two beds in opposite corners of the space, and there are pillars throughout the room where couples are fucking.

A *lot* of sex is happening in here.

Music pounds around me, which fascinates me because I don't hear the music in the lounge. The playroom must be soundproofed.

Scarlett leads me to the right.

"We're going to make a circle," she yells into my ear, "through the whole space, so you can take it all in. Then we'll walk down the hall of privacy rooms."

I can only nod as she leads me to the corner with the first bed. A woman is lying in the middle of red satin sheets on her back, all four limbs secured with ropes to the corners of the bed. She's naked, and two men, one on either side, are playing with her, running huge peacock feathers up and down her skin.

"They're just beginning," Scarlett tells me. "They'll progress with different instruments until they get to the pain part."

"The pain?"

"Sure. She's here to test her limits, and George and Adam are the best. They'll keep her safe, check in with her often, and the second she uses a safe word, it's over. This is just one kind of scene I was telling you about."

"Have you done this?" I ask her.

"Of course." She winks at me, and we stay to watch.

It's not sterile-looking, as far as decor goes. Ruby-red drapes frame the bed, giving it a rich tone that feels intimate.

The men switch from feathers to soft makeup brushes, the kind I'd use for my blush. They circle her breasts, down her stomach and over her pussy, then down her legs.

Next up is a riding crop, and now I shift on my feet.

But they don't slap her with it. They glide it over her skin, up and down her body. One of them does give her breast a little slap, and she gasps, then smiles.

Is that normal? For women to like that?

"Over here is the spanking bench." Scarlett gestures for me to keep walking, and my eyebrows climb. "It's what it sounds like. You bend over, and someone spanks you. Or you're the spanker. Both are fun."

I notice there are restraints on it, and I frown.

"You get tied down while they spank you?"

"Sometimes, but you don't always have to be. They're there for whoever wants to use them."

"I don't want to be hit." I shake my head adamantly. "No, thank you."

"A hard limit." She nods approvingly. "I like it. No spanking bench for you, then."

I'm so out of my element. The two brief sexual encounters I've had did *nothing* to prepare me for this. Watching these people be so unabashedly open with their sexuality almost makes me jealous. That they're not shy about being naked, about making noise and taking what they want is something I admire and respect.

I don't know that I could do it.

Could I?

I imagine Rome kissing me, touching me, pushing me up against one of the pillars, and my core tightens. But letting him get me naked here?

I don't think so.

The entire time we've been in here, I feel like his eyes are on me, but I haven't seen him in the room. That doesn't mean he's not watching. I know he is. I can *feel* his eyes on me.

Scarlett leads me past a couch where two men are fucking one woman. She's straddling one of them, and the other is behind her, and all three are writhing like it's the best night of their life.

Against a pillar, a man has another man bent over, gripping the wood tightly, as he's fucked from behind.

There's so much to see everywhere. So much movement and noise and music. I try to keep my face impassive because I don't want anyone to feel like I'm judging them.

Because I'm not. I think it's awesome that this place exists.

But there's a lot here that I don't want to do.

Breath play? I don't know about that.

Definitely no spanking or whipping.

Being tied up actually looks kind of hot.

"Shibari," Scarlett whispers to me as we approach a man working with different colored ropes with his partner. "That's what it's called."

"I kind of like it," I admit, and she smiles with a nod.

The guy wanders over to me and lets me touch the ropes, winking at me. They're so soft. And the knots he's made all up and down her body are beautiful.

He returns to his girl and continues. She's kneeling, her hands behind her back, watching him closely. She's panting. Her eyes are dilated so wide, all I can see is black. And I can see why. Yeah, that's hot as fuck, and I wonder if Rome can do that.

After we make our way around the room, she leads me through another set of doors and down a hallway, but it's not really that simple. It's so beautiful down here. The floor is mustard yellow, and the walls are papered in a gorgeous purple design. The music is muted a bit here, but I can still hear it.

"Most of the rooms are private," she says. "Members can book them ahead of time. Sometimes they ask one or more of us to join them or bring their own partners."

"Not all of the rooms are private?" I ask her.

"Some are voyeur rooms." She grins.

"Isn't that what the playroom is?"

Scarlett laughs and wraps her arm around my shoulder. "I guess so, but this is different. Basically, people are engaging in things in the room, with the guise that it's just for them, but there are windows for people to watch. Like here."

A small crowd is gathered around the window that looks into an opulent room. There's a king-sized bed, and in the center of it, a woman is on her hands and knees, and a man is fucking her from behind. One hand on her throat, one on her ass, pounding into her, and she's screaming his name. Her hair falls over her face, and he gently brushes it aside. He leans over her, kisses her neck, and whispers something into her ear that has her grinning as if in anticipation of whatever he's suggested.

It's hot as hell.

By the time we're finished in the privacy hall, I'm so worked up, I can hardly breathe. My thighs tremble, my lips are parted, and I'm breathing hard.

I need Rome.

I want him like I've never wanted anyone before, and I need him to soothe this ache that Scarlett's tour has brought out inside me. I feel like I'll die if he doesn't do something about this *right now.*

"Do you know where Rome is?" I ask Scarlett as we walk out and into the lounge.

"I think probably his office," she says, pointing toward the elevator.

But I'm already striding away, not even glancing at the bar as I go in search of the man who has called me his own. Who has brought me into his home, into his work-place, into his ... playroom?

The man I want with every breath within me.

My man.

I nod at the guard by the elevator, then press my palm to the glass reader and the button for the third floor, needing to get to Rome. Hoping he's alone, I also hope he's okay with me attacking him in there.

I hope I don't get fired.

Yet at this moment, I don't really care if I do. Because all I can think about is getting to the man who has totally taken over my universe.

I don't bother knocking on the door, and when I push inside, Rome glances up from his computer and lifts an eyebrow.

"Were you watching me?" I ask him as I move to lock the door, but the mechanism flips before I can reach for it.

I whirl back to him and see his finger on a button on his desk. Then all of the windows magically go cloudy, so we can't see out, and no one can see in, and I take a deep breath in.

"Every minute," he confirms. "You're gorgeous. And what did you think of my club, firefly?"

I lick my lips and lean against the door. I want him, but I also love the way he's looking at me right now. His blue eyes dance up and down my body, and when they find my eyes again, I smile at him.

"It's fucking amazing, Rome. I love it."

His eyes darken.

"Your face is so expressive," he says as he stands from behind the desk and circles it, moving toward me. "Not judgmental."

I shake my head.

When he's standing right before me, his thumb brushes over my lower lip.

"You liked the voyeur room."

I don't answer him.

"You hated the spanking."

"I've been hit enough."

His jaw clenches at that. God, he's sexy. He's in a white dress shirt, with the sleeves rolled on his forearms, showing off that ink. His hair is perfectly styled and makes my fingers itch to mess it up.

"What was your favorite part?" he asks.

"The ropes."

He hums deep in his throat and brushes his nose down my neck before looking at me again.

"Why are you in my office, firefly?"

"Because I'm so turned on," I admit, staring at his lips.

"And?"

My gaze whips back up to his. "And I needed to find you."

God, that makes me feel vulnerable, but it's the truth.

"Oh, firefly. That was the right fucking answer."

Twenty-Six

ROME

"Did watching all of that turn you on, beautiful?" I brace my hand on the door above her head and lean into her, brushing my nose down her soft cheek. Her hands glide up my chest, but she doesn't respond. "Answer me, Eloise."

"Yes."

Her voice is breathy and small, so I pull back to look into her gorgeous eyes. There's lust there, but something else as well that I can't put my finger on.

"What's wrong?" I brush my thumb under her eye, over the apple of her cheek. "Talk to me, firefly."

"What—" She swallows hard, and her brows quickly pull together before relaxing again. "What's wrong with me that I'm so turned on by—"

"Absolutely fucking *nothing* is wrong with you." And I hate that she'd question it for even one second. She pulls in a shaky breath as I pepper kisses on her neck. "It

146

should turn you on to see others enjoying themselves. To know that what they're doing is consensual and safe and that they're getting exactly what they want and need, even if it's not something that you yourself would enjoy."

Her hands move farther up into my hair, and I pause. It's a knee-jerk reaction. Aside from my barber, no one has touched my head in years.

But when she pushes her sweet fingers into the strands, it feels like heaven, and I resume kissing her jawline.

"You're so fucking beautiful," I tell her again. I can't stop telling her because it's true. "So sweet. This hair ..."

I push her thick, dark locks over her shoulder, exposing more skin for my lips, and lightly nibble on the fleshy part of her shoulder before I sink my teeth in and mark her.

"Your skin is so fucking soft," I continue, moving back to her neck, hovering over her pulse point. "And I can't wait to sink inside you."

She whimpers, pushing her stomach against my already hard cock, and I can't help but grin against her neck.

"You like the sound of that, do you?"

"Yes." Her breathy responses are going to be the death of me.

"Me, too. But right now, we don't have time for me to lose myself inside you. Once I get inside that sweet little cunt, I won't want to leave for a good long while. I'll bet you're tight as fuck."

My hand glides down her side, and I bunch the skirt of her dress up so I can ghost my hand up her soft-as-fuck thigh.

Christ, I can't wait to push my face between these soft thighs and devour her.

And suddenly, a wave of jealousy rolls through me at the thought of *anyone* enjoying her like this.

"How many men, Eloise?"

I'm watching her face, wanting to see every reaction as my fingers move up, and I find her panties soaked as fuck.

"Wh-what?" she stammers.

"How many fuckers have been here before me?" The thought of it sets me on edge. The idea of *anyone* seeing her like this makes me want to kill someone. "Tell me."

She scowls. "No."

"Wrong answer," I whisper against her cheek and push the tip of my finger over her slit, over the panties. "Tell me how many have had the privilege of touching your sweet little pussy."

She shakes her head, but I nudge my finger inside her panties and lightly brush her hard clit, and she gasps.

"If you don't tell me, this stops right now."

"Don't stop."

"How many?"

She whimpers, swallows hard, then says, "One."

Fuck. One?

But then I'm reminded that her father ruled with an iron fist, and it's a wonder anyone was able to get their hands on her.

Was he selling her to a man expecting a virgin? Fuck the bastard.

She's mine.

I push my finger inside her wet heat. She tips her face forward onto my chest and groans deeply while her tight muscles pulse around me.

"Fuck, baby. You're *so tight.*"

"Please don't stop." She's circling her hips, sucking me in all the way to my first knuckle. I can't wait for it to be my cock.

A second finger joins in the fun, and she groans again.

"Rome."

"That's right. Say my name, firefly. Who's finger-fucking you up against this door?"

"Rome." She tips her face up to look at me. "You are."

I nip at her chin, and I *know* she wants me to kiss her.

But I love edging the fuck out of her.

So she can't have that quite yet.

"Fuck, you're soaked. Did you need me to take care of this for you, Eloise?"

She nods, and her jaw drops into an O when I cover her clit with my thumb and brush back and forth. My hand is soaked from her, and I'm so tempted to unfasten my slacks and take her right here.

But then I feel her quiver, her cheeks flush even more than they already were, and her eyes go glassy.

"There it is." I can't take my eyes off her perfect,

expressive face. "That's right, take it, baby. This is what you needed, so you take it. Come for me."

She cries out with it, not caring in the least if anyone can hear her.

They can't.

Her body jerks, her pussy clenches down hard, and she falls apart with her orgasm.

"Stunning," I murmur as I kiss her neck and pull my hand free of her, then lift my fingers to my lips and taste her.

So fucking sweet.

She blanches as she watches me lick every drop as if no one has tasted her before.

"Did he not do this for you, Eloise?"

She bites her lip, breathing hard, those gleaming eyes pinned to me, and shakes her head.

"Good. This is mine. Only I get to taste you." I step back far enough to make sure she's straightened out, then I close the gap and kiss her forehead. "Now, you'd better get back to work."

She huffs out a breath. "At least I'm not fired."

"Are you kidding? That was worth a raise." I wink at her, then open the door. "Go on. Have a good night, firefly."

She looks like she wants to say something, but she just offers me a smile and walks away. As she gets to the end of the hallway, I hear her mutter, "Holy fucking shit," and it makes me chuckle as I leave the door open and return to my desk.

Three texts are waiting for me from Luke that I ignored while I was getting my little firefly off.

Totally worth it.

> L: Ten minutes.

> L: Need you down here, boss.

> L: We have a problem.

I shove my gun in its holster, grab my suit coat, and hurry down to the loading dock. It's a ten-minute walk from my office, and when I get there, I snarl.

"Oh, good. You finally fucking showed up." That's not Luke.

My second watches me with rage-filled eyes. He has three semi-automatic weapons trained on him. Three of my men are dead. The others are also held at gunpoint.

"What. The. FUCK!"

Mendoza, the new head of the cartel since his father died last month, grins, showing off a gold tooth.

What a fucking tool.

"We're going to change our terms."

"I've done business with your family for a long fucking time, Mendoza," I reply, ignoring the snick of more guns being cocked and turned my way as I casually walk toward the man. "The terms have been mutually beneficial."

"I'm the head now," he sneers. "And I've decided that it's *not* beneficial for me."

Fuck you.

But I keep my face bland. "What would you like the new terms to be?"

His eyes gleam. He's such a greedy fuck. "I'm raising the price by one hundred percent."

I simply tip up an eyebrow and let the statement hang in the air for a moment.

"Let me get this straight. You delivered my product, but rather than make the transaction as agreed upon and then setting up a meeting with me at a later time to discuss further business dealings like a respectful head would do, you came to *my* dock, killed *my* men, and have changed the terms."

Mendoza tips his head to the side as if he's thinking about it.

"That's right."

I shake my head and walk to Luke, staring him in the eyes, and have a silent conversation.

There are eight of Mendoza's men here, all with weapons drawn. I have myself, Luke, and four other men.

The odds are excellent, given that my men are highly trained in hand-to-hand, but I don't like that they're not armed.

"I want you to toss your gun aside," Mendoza thinks to add, and I smile at him, knowing that the look on my face makes most men piss themselves.

Mendoza's men shift, share a look, and we use that moment to strike.

I draw my weapon and kill four of his men immediately, while Luke snaps the neck of one, and the other four of my men wipe out the rest.

Mendoza's eyes are wide. The whole altercation took less than ten seconds.

And now he's alone, unarmed, and *fucked*.

"If you kill me, you'll start a war," he says, lifting his chin.

"You just did that all on your own," I reply, holstering my gun. "Now, to repay me for this inconvenience, you're leaving the product here free of charge."

His face goes beet red as rage fills him.

I don't give a fuck.

"And this will be the last time you sell anything not to only me but also to anyone else in Vegas. You're done in my city."

"We've had this territory for three generations—"

"I don't fucking care," I roar over him. "Your father was an honorable man. He was a pleasure to do business with. Now I have to deal with a sniveling, greedy, entitled piece of shit like you? No. I don't do business like that. Get the fuck off my dock and don't come back to Vegas, or you won't leave alive."

I turn my back on him, further disrespecting him, and walk to Luke.

"Call Sven," I tell him, irritated that I just ruined yet another suit with blood spatter. "Get this cleaned up, and make sure he leaves town immediately."

"On it," Luke says with a nod, frowning down at the four we lost.

"Make sure their families are paid."

He nods again. "Will do."

Before returning to my office, I go up to the penthouse and shower. After I change into a clean suit, I return downstairs, where I plan to sit at the bar and fluster my firefly.

Instead, I run into Loveland. I haven't seen much of her since the other day in my office, but when she catches sight of me, she pauses. Her eyes widen, but then she lifts her chin and approaches me.

"We had a problem in the playroom," she says.

What the fuck is going on tonight?

"What kind of problem?" I ask her.

"Mr. Sanderson brought his own flask in. Apparently, he's not a fan of the two-drink rule."

My eyes narrow. "Where is he?"

"He was escorted out. I informed him that his membership was revoked, and he wouldn't be getting a refund."

"Did he hurt anyone?"

Her eyes soften just a bit. "No. He was obnoxious, lewd, and annoying. But he didn't get his hands on anyone."

I nod and walk past her. "Good."

"Rome."

I turn back and lift an eyebrow.

"I hope she's worth it."

I step back to her so I can talk low in her ear.

"She's worth everything. And you'll do good to remember to mind your own fucking business."

I leave her and decide to make a pass through the playroom, just to make sure that everything is okay.

I glance at the bar in the lounge and see Eloise

smiling as she passes someone a martini. She glances my way, and her smile widens. But when she sees me reach for the playroom door, that smile dims a bit.

Don't worry, firefly.

I'll make it clear to her later that she's the only one I'll have my hands—or anything else—on for the rest of my life.

Twenty-Seven

LULU

"See you tomorrow," Scarlett says with a sleepy smile. "I'm gonna go pass out for the next twenty-four hours."

"You're not working tonight?" I ask her.

"Nope. I'm gonna sleep and eat and do some laundry. Do you work tonight?"

"No, actually. I'm going to get some sleep, too, and then I'm going to cook."

Scarlett's eyebrows climb. "What are you going to cook?"

"I haven't decided yet." With a smile, I pull my phone out and pass it to her. "Give me your number, and if it sounds good to you, you're welcome to come eat with me."

She pauses. "I can't come up and eat at the penthouse."

"Why not?" I frown at her.

"Because I'm not allowed to be up there."

"I live there," I remind her. "And you're my bestie. I'm inviting you."

She takes the phone from me and plugs in her number. "Please just check with Mr. Alexander first, okay?"

"If it makes you feel better, I will. But it'll be fine. Go get some rest."

With a smile, I get into the elevator and press my hand to the glass for the penthouse. I came up right after work to change into the only leggings and T-shirt I have before going back to the gym to work out with Scarlett.

My muscles are going to ache tomorrow.

I step off the elevator and smile at the guard standing there and then smile again at the one in front of the penthouse door. There's only one, so Rome isn't home yet.

Which is kind of good. I need a shower and a little time alone.

I didn't like that he went into the playroom earlier, which is totally stupid. This is *his* club. Of course, he makes the rounds and walks through the place. It doesn't mean he's touching anyone, or having sex, or even checking them out.

But yeah, the green-eyed monster appeared for the first time in my life.

I kick out of my shoes and carry them to the bedroom, where all my things are, but then I frown. I don't know that Rome is okay with me being in his personal space. I know he said I'm living here, at least until things are settled with my father, but that doesn't mean I'm living *here.*

I venture out and down the hall and find a guest room that is obviously rarely used. But the bed is nice, and it's a good-sized space with an attached bathroom, so I decide to make this my home base.

I transfer most of my clothes to the closet and then the few toiletries I have to the bathroom, then check out the kitchen downstairs before I shower and go to sleep.

I wasn't kidding when I said I could permanently squat in this kitchen. It's a chef's dream with at least a square mile of counter space. Gorgeous white marble countertops and a huge island make the room so bright. The cabinets are light wood and stocked with all the tools I'll need, including a gorgeous pasta maker just like Iris's. *Yes.*

The six-burner gas stove is something I see in my sleep, and the fridge is enormous.

I could easily cook for twenty people at a time.

With a little shimmy, I pull out my phone and make a list of grocery items I want to stock the shelves and the fridge with. I'm going to bake brownies later, and I'm going to make pasta from scratch with homemade marinara and meatballs. Maybe even some bruschetta, but I'll need to bake some bread if I do that.

I shimmy again and then head up to my new bedroom to take a shower and get cozy. I don't know where Rome is, or when he'll be home, and I don't want to text him and bother him when he's working, but I need to send this shopping list to someone.

Luke.

I decide to send it to Luke.

Me: Rome told me I should make a grocery list. Here it is. If anyone has any questions, I'm happy to answer them. Thank you.

I send it off and then start the water in the shower, and while that heats, I wipe my face with makeup wipes and brush out my hair so it doesn't tangle as much when I wash it.

The hot water feels divine on my weary muscles. There's even a handheld nozzle that I take down, set on blast, and press to my lower back.

I'm *tired*. I'm used to being on my feet a lot, but not for long shifts behind a bar. It'll be good to have a night off.

Although I do plan to be on them in the kitchen all day. Does that count? I don't know.

With a smirk, I hang up the nozzle, then shave my legs, wash my hair, and step out to dry off.

After moisturizing my face, I find a blow-dryer—the expensive kind—in a drawer and use it to dry my hair, which takes half the normal time with this awesome appliance.

When I step out of the bathroom, wrapped only in a towel, I jump when I see Rome leaning in the doorway.

And he looks *pissed*.

Twenty-Eight

ROME

I want to take my firefly to bed and lose myself in her for several hours before we curl up and fall asleep for the majority of the day. I got word from my men that she went to the gym this morning with Scarlett, and she's since gone back to the penthouse. The thought of her being in my home fills me with satisfaction.

Mine.

After our encounter in my office, the night went to shit. I'm ready for the distraction of a gorgeous woman.

My gorgeous woman.

"Get some rest," I say to Luke as we ride up in the elevator. "Be at my place by six this evening."

"I just got a text from your girl," he says, surprising me.

I narrow my eyes. I don't like Eloise texting Luke unless it's an emergency.

"What did she say?"

"It's a grocery list." He turns the phone so I can see it. "What do you want me to do?"

"Send someone out for the fucking groceries," I reply and stare at him like he's stupid. "But from now on, requests will come through me."

He smirks and nods, and the elevator stops at his floor. "I'll take care of it. See you later."

When the doors close again, I take a deep breath. It seems I need to have a talk with Eloise.

I stride over to my door and nod at the two men standing there.

"Some groceries will be delivered later. One of you can come in and put the cold stuff in the fridge."

They nod, and I step inside and close the door, then stop and listen.

I don't hear her bustling around downstairs, and by the way the air is still, I can tell that she's not down here.

She's in bed.

As I climb the stairs, I shed my suit coat and tie. I unbutton my shirt as I walk into the bedroom and toss the garments on a chair in the corner.

But Eloise isn't here.

With a frown, I walk to the bathroom.

No Eloise.

I kick out of my shoes and listen. Then it occurs to me that her things are no longer in my bathroom, and with my temper starting to rise, I move to the closet.

Her clothes are gone.

If she'd moved out, my men would have told me.

Then I realize that a shower is running. With a scowl, I walk out of the bedroom and down the hall to the guest suite that's never once been used—who the fuck am I going to invite over?—and realize that she's moved into it.

What the fuck?

I hear the shower kick off, so I lean against the doorway, waiting for her.

She's murmuring to herself. After a few moments, the blow-dryer kicks on, and still, I wait.

Eloise emerges from the bathroom, wrapped in a white towel, her dark hair loose and still a little damp around her shoulders. Her face is clean of makeup, and she looks so goddamn fuckable.

But she stops short when she sees me and bites her lower lip.

"Hi," she says tentatively.

"Hello, Eloise." Her brows pull together in an uncertain frown at the coldness in my voice. "Why are you in here?"

She glances around and licks her lips. "Because I didn't know if you wanted me in your space, so I—"

I push off the doorjamb, and she stops talking.

"You what?"

"I found a guest room." The words are quieter, and her gaze falls to my chest. She likes the ink. But I want her eyes on mine.

"I don't want you in this room," I tell her as I close in on her. I wrap my hand around her throat loosely and guide her backward against the wall, holding her there. Her pupils blow wide.

"Wh-where do you want me?" God, that breathy voice of hers when she's turned on takes me out at the knees.

"In *my* bed. In *my* room." *Our bed, our room.* But she's not quite ready for that yet. "I want you with me, firefly."

"I don't want to be in your way."

She doesn't want to be in my way? Many men—and women—yield to me daily. It's what I expect and demand. But this is different. And if I know anything about Salvatore Rizzo, this is the product of his abuse. His utter control. His cruelty.

How can I show her that I'm not like him? That she has a choice, but that I hope she chooses what I want?

I lean in and brush my cheek against hers and whisper in her ear, "I want you in my way."

I tug the towel loose and let it pool around her feet, and then I push my hand between her legs and growl.

"You're already wet. Why are you so wet, Eloise?"

She swallows hard against my hand. I fucking love that I can feel her pulse, her swallows, her breath.

"I—" She gasps when my finger slips between her lips and circles her entrance.

"Tell me."

"I can't talk."

I grin against her cheek. "Yes, you can. Why are you so turned on?"

She swallows again and moves her hips as if she's seeking more, but I pull my finger back, denying her.

"Because you looked sexy with just your pants on, leaning on the door, with your arms crossed and your muscles tight, and you looked so mad."

"Making me mad turns you on?"

She shakes her head. "It's just ... *God*, please touch me."

"I will." I brush over her clit so lightly, she whimpers. "I'll give you what you need. Tell me the rest."

"I don't know how to explain it."

I dip my head down and pull one nipple between my lips, making us both groan.

Christ, she's delicious.

"I just felt excited when I saw you like that."

It's all she can give me now, so I push two fingers inside her, continuing to suck on her nipple, until she cries out, clinging to me. Those little hands dive into my hair again, and her orgasm washes over her faster than I expected.

"This isn't your room," I say as she pants, coming down from the high. "And that's the second time you've come on my hand and not my cock or my mouth."

Picking her up, I march us out of the bedroom and down to *our* room, where I lay her on the bed. I stretch out over her, brush the hair off her face, and press my lips to her cheek.

"Rome," she whispers as her fingers dance up and down my back. Christ, her touch ignites something in me that I didn't know existed.

"Yes, firefly."

"I really, *really* want you to—"

Before she can complete that thought, I cover her lips with mine, and she whimpers in relief. I don't often kiss women on the mouth. It's too intimate, too *close*. But this might just be my new kink.

Kissing Eloise.

Her lips are soft and plump, and when I lick across them, she opens up for me beautifully, letting me in.

I sink into her, devouring her, exploring her. My pelvis settles against hers, and she rubs against me, soaking my pants as I kiss the fuck out of her. I can't stop. Touching her, feasting on her mouth.

Fucking delicious.

My life is too dangerous to bring something so fucking good into it.

Yet I know I'll never let her go.

Her hands roam down to the waistband of my slacks, and she pushes under them, wanting me naked.

Happy to oblige her, I reach down and unfasten them and work them off, then return to her, brushing my mouth over hers gently.

"Better?" I ask her.

"So much better," she agrees and claims my mouth once more, wrapping her arms around my neck as her legs open wider and pull up around my hips. My cock lies heavily in her wet slit. "Maybe about to get even better?"

I chuckle. "Are you ready for my cock, firefly?"

"*Yes.*"

I reach between us and rub the head, along with the metal there, over her clit, and her eyes widen.

"Holy shit, what's that?"

With a smile, I lick over her lips. "It's going to make you lose your fucking mind."

I slip the head inside her and pause, then growl.

"So damn tight."

She makes a strangled noise in the back of her throat but pushes her hips up in invitation.

"Don't stop."

"I'm going easy," I inform her. "I don't want to hurt you."

"It's okay. Hurt me. Fuck, Rome, just—"

I shove inside her, making her cry out, and then pull back out and do it again.

"Is that what you want?"

She nods, her head thrown back.

"Eyes on me, Eloise."

Those green eyes open and fly to mine, and I love how her pupils are dilated and her breaths are coming faster.

"More," she whispers.

"You like it rough, baby?"

"I didn't know I did until right now."

And that sets fire to every cell in my body. I can't hold back. I couldn't if I tried, and I'm a man who has control in all things. I push into her, harder and deeper, but I want more.

I grab a pillow and lift her ass off the mattress, then

shove the pillow under her, and it gives me the leverage I need to be even deeper.

"*Rome.*"

"That's right." I sink my teeth into her neck, fucking her hard, and she's clutching onto me as if she's scared that I'll pull away.

Not a fucking chance.

I push up onto my knees and take her in. Tits bouncing with every thrust, her soft stomach so fucking gorgeous and begging for my hand.

So I cover it and press the pad of my thumb over her clit, and she arches her back, pushing even harder onto my cock, convulsing around me.

"Fucking come," I growl, and watch as her skin flushes. Her hands fist in the sheets, and her gaze stays pinned to mine as she hurls over the edge into an orgasm so damn strong, she takes me with her.

I rock into her, my cum filling her, and feel nothing but ... *bliss.*

That has to be what this is. There's no other word for it.

I cover her once more and kiss her cheek, her neck, and over to her lips where I brush back and forth, gently, as we both catch our breath.

"This is *our* bed," I say against her lips. "And *our* room. You'll be here with me. Understood?"

She nods and licks her lips, brushing my own in the process.

"You'll also text grocery requests and anything else directly to *me.*"

Her brows pull into that frown. "Okay. I didn't know what to do."

"Now you do." I kiss her again. "Just ask me if you don't know, baby."

"Okay."

I roll us onto our sides so my weight is off her.

"That was—"

"Fucking incredible," I answer. I love the tender smile I get in return. *Genuine. Happy.*

"Your piercing ... you're right. I can't explain how good that was."

"I'm glad, firefly. It's all yours now."

A blush covers her face. Then she goes quiet.

"What?" We're still connected—*I don't want to leave her heat*—but I can tell something's on her mind. Even though I should have fucked all thoughts from that pretty little head.

She takes a breath.

"I want to invite Scarlett here. She's my friend."

"That's fine."

"She was scared."

I frown. "Why?"

"Because it's drilled into new employees that this is off-limits."

"Ah." I brush her hair over her shoulder. Christ, I can't take my hands off her. "If she's invited, it's okay. Would it make you happy if I offered her an apartment here?"

She blinks rapidly. "You'd do that?"

"She's your friend. If she wants it, I don't have a

problem with it." My firefly's eyes fill with tears, and I frown. "Hey, what's this for?"

"I'm not used to ... any of this."

"Any of what?"

"Being listened to. Cared about. Feeling like I have a voice and a choice."

"You have anything and everything you want." I kiss her forehead. "Now, we have one more thing to discuss for now."

"Okay." She sniffs and brushes her sweet fingertips down my cheek.

"If you don't want to get pregnant, you'd better get your birth control figured out. I don't plan to ever fuck you with anything between us."

Her eyebrows shoot up in surprise, and I grin before kissing her, then pulling away to use the bathroom.

"Rome—"

"It's not up for discussion," I add. "Although, the idea of you pregnant ..."

Her eyes startle at that. Inwardly I do too. Just having someone I care about makes me more vulnerable. *But a child?*

That could bring me to my knees.

But the thought of having children with my firefly fills me with warmth.

"But are you ... clean?"

I turn back to her. It's a valid question. She knows I run a sex club, and she saw me go into the playroom last night.

"Yes, I'm clean. I'd never put you at risk."

She still has questions, but I know she won't voice them.

"And Eloise, when I go into the playroom, it's not to play with other women. I'm just doing my job, making sure everyone who comes through my doors—either staff or clientele—are completely safe."

She nods. "Understood."

Twenty-Nine

LULU

Is it just me, or are things moving ... fast? Fast actually feels like a mild term. It's really more like supersonic. I didn't even know Rome a week ago, and now, I live with him, we've had the most amazing sex of my life, and he just told me that he's not afraid of getting me pregnant.

These should be red flags.

Yet I can't bring myself to feel like it's wrong.

The timer dings, signaling that it's time to knead my dough and get it in the oven. I've been baking and cooking for the past two hours. My sauce is already simmering. It's best if it can simmer for a full day, but this will do just fine. When I woke up, Rome was still out cold, and I didn't want to disturb him, so I slipped out of bed and went to the guest room to pull on clothes. When I got to the kitchen, I was excited to find that the groceries had been delivered while we slept.

At least, I think it was while we slept and not while

Rome had me screaming down the building with the best orgasms of my life.

Is *that* why I'm so quick to agree to this supersonic relationship? Because I'm so attracted to him, and his pierced dick does magical things to me?

To be fair, I was into it before I discovered how talented he is with his dick, pierced or not.

With the bread in the oven, I cross to the fancy farm sink and wash my hands, and then I take stock of what I still need to do.

But when I turn around, I find Rome standing on the other side of the island, leaning against the countertop, watching me.

He's in a white T-shirt and lounge pants. I've never seen him this casual.

"Hey." I smile at him and wipe down the countertop with a sponge. "You were sleeping well."

"Did you not sleep well?" he asks with a frown. Christ, I love his voice. It's so deep and ... *sexy.*

"I slept like the dead, actually. I just woke up and knew I wouldn't get back to sleep. Plus, this is my one night off, and I don't want to waste it."

His eyebrow kicks up, and he looks almost irritated. "You can work any night you want."

"No." I shake my head firmly. "I work for Rita."

"And Rita works for me."

I smile at him as I find a cutting board and knife, then pull tomatoes and basil out of the fridge, grab a head of garlic, and start chopping.

"But *I* work for Rita," I counter. "And she sets my

schedule. I don't want special treatment. I love the job, and I'm not complaining at all."

"It didn't sound like you were," he says, crossing his arms over his chest. Holy shit, do the tattoos look good. They're down both arms, and his T-shirt hugs his biceps like a second skin, and it all makes me a little sweaty.

"I'm just ready for a night of downtime, that's all. It's been a crazy week, and I feel like I haven't had a minute to just breathe since I sat down at that breakfast with my father. Everything was scary. Not just that day or the days since, but for *years*. And it feels good to take a breath."

I realize I've finished chopping the tomatoes, and my eyes fly up to his.

"I might have said too much."

"Never." He circles the island and wraps his arms around me from behind, pressing his lips against the top of my head. "I hate that you lived in fear for even one minute. Someone will pay for that."

I sigh and lean back into him, enjoying his strength, his warmth. *Nothing* feels better than being held by Rome. "I don't need someone to pay for it. I just don't want to live that way anymore."

I feel his breath in my hair as he rubs his lips lightly back and forth. "You'll never live that way again. What are you making? It smells fucking amazing."

I smile and tip my head back to look up into his icy-blue eyes. "This is for bruschetta. I have bread in the oven for that, too. But I'm making homemade pasta for dinner, and the sauce is simmering. I should have asked you if you have allergies or if there's anything you hate."

"I'll eat whatever you make," he says before he kisses my forehead. "Do you have everything you need?"

"Your kitchen is well-equipped. I love it."

"I've never used it." He smirks and hugs me before letting me go. "I'll be heading to work at around six."

"This will be done before then," I assure him. "I'd like to invite Scarlett over to hang out here with me tonight."

"I don't have a problem with that. When she arrives, have one of the guards outside go down to get her."

I nod, relieved that Rome is so laid-back. Most men in his world are hard and cruel. Uncaring. Certainly not affectionate and happy to do a woman's bidding.

"You have an odd look on your face," he says, watching me.

"If you hadn't told me that you're part of organized crime, I'd never have guessed. I've spent my whole life in that world, and you are *not* like them."

"Explain." His eyes narrow, and his jaw firms, but he doesn't look angry. He looks … *concerned.*

"You're not hard and angry. Mean. Vicious. I'm not afraid that you're going to hurt me just for the fun of it."

His jaw works. "I need to get something straight with you. I'm *not* a good man, Eloise. I *am* hard and angry, and I can be vicious. I have no qualms about taking someone's life."

"But it's because they're the bad guys. Not just randomly, or because you enjoy it."

He tips his head to the side. "Don't romanticize me. I'll treat you well every moment of every day, but few others get that luxury. No, I don't enjoy hurting women. Killing is a part of most of my days. People fucking fear me because I need them to. *I* am the bad guy, firefly."

I nod slowly, taking it in as I stir the bruschetta mixture, then place it in the fridge so all of the flavors can marry.

Next, I get started on the pasta.

"Just because you haven't seen it doesn't make it nonexistent," he finally says.

"But I prefer not to see it." I clear my throat. "I'm not innocent, Rome. I've seen my fair share of death. My father thought it was funny to murder the men who betrayed him in front of me."

He lowers his hands, and they fist on the island, but I keep talking.

"He's a sadistic bastard." I shake my head and open cupboards. "Do you have a stand mixer with attachments?"

"I have no idea."

"Hmm." I walk into the pantry to look and don't see it at first, but then it catches my eye on a corner shelf, high up. "Aha! Found it."

I'm able to grab it with my right hand, but it's too heavy for my left since I can't reach all the way above my head. I almost drop it, but suddenly, Rome's there, helping me.

"Whoa," he says, taking it from me. "Don't do that again."

"Sorry, I can usually manage, but when something is

high up, I have issues." I demonstrate how far I can raise my left arm. "This shoulder doesn't work well."

"Why the fuck not?" he asks as he sets the mixer where I point on the counter.

"It's been dislocated too many times."

I turn to walk away, but then I'm spun back around, and Rome's fierce eyes glare down at me.

"Say that the fuck again."

I lick my lips. Jesus, I just say *everything* around this man. He's like a truth serum. But who else have I ever been able to tell? No one on my father's payroll would have given a shit. Iris *hated* how I was treated, and sometimes she'd make sure to hold me when I couldn't hold in my pain. But she also needed to keep her job, and the walls had ears, so she would never have been a true confidante.

I had no one, and I hadn't realized how lonely my life was until I came to Rapture.

Is that why all of this is coming out of my mouth? *Because I've never had a soul to tell?* Because I could never divulge to anyone that I lived with a narcissistic monster who treated me so despicably?

"My left shoulder has been dislocated a lot, and I never had physical therapy for it. So I can't reach up, and I can't lift heavy things above my head. But I'll just get a step stool—"

"Fuck the stool. Who dislocated ... let me guess, your piece-of-shit father?"

I lick my lips again and give him a jerky nod. "If I

made him mad, he grabbed my arm and pulled it behind my back. Hard."

Rome paces away from me, then turns back my way. "What else?"

I frown. "What do you mean?"

"I want to know every fucking thing he did to you. I saw the bruises. And now I know about the shoulder. What else, Eloise?"

"I have a scar"—he growls—"on my low back from a knife. Mostly, it was slaps, though. Once in a while, he'd punch me, and once I was on the ground, he'd kick my ribs. That's what you saw. Those are fading nicely and don't hurt anymore."

"Anything else?"

I reach out and take his hand, giving it a squeeze before I resume my place at the island to make the pasta. "Mostly, it was psychological. I've seen men tortured, hacked up, bled out, all of the things."

"When did he start doing that to you?" His voice is hard and low.

"I was young." I blow a piece of hair out of my face, thinking it over. It was just before my mom died. "Probably eight or nine."

"Christ," he whispers.

"Yeah, some girls went to dance class, and I watched men lose their fingers. He never made me be the one to do it, but that's because he loves it too much. He always said it was because my idiot of a mother never gave him a son, so he didn't have a proper heir, and I'd be expected to be it instead.

But let's be real, I was never going to inherit anything. Women aren't dons. Whoever he made me marry would have taken over the family. He just liked hurting me. Watching people die tore me up until I was in my early teens, when I learned how to turn my brain off and disassociate."

I shake my head as I mix the eggs and flour by hand. This is my favorite part. I *love* getting my hands dirty in the kitchen.

"Why did we start talking about this?" I ask with a frown.

"You prefer not to see it," he says, reminding me.

"Ah, yes. You can tell me you're a bad man, and when you're not with me, you're running drugs, or cleaning money, or whatever the hell it is that you do. And in the process, men die, because they're stupid and disloyal and make poor choices. But if it's all the same to you, I'd rather just work my amazing bartending job, cook in this stellar kitchen, and be with you whenever I can have you. Just *please* be careful."

I get the idea that Rome would rather I be forthright about what I want here. This is so new, and maybe I'm a new shiny toy to someone like him and will be discarded despite his words of adoration. But the anger I saw tear through him at what my father has done? I can't deny that was gratifying. I know Rome's also a violent man, and I can hope he's a man of his word, and truly someone I can trust.

I've never known a man I can trust.

This is his home, his world, and therefore his rules, but I hope he'll respect mine while I'm here.

"I have two rules, Rome: don't ever raise a hand to me and if you're going to fuck other women, be discreet. Those are the deal breakers for me."

He circles back around to me, and his hands frame my face.

"You're with me, and that puts you in danger. There's nothing I can do about that. I wouldn't leave this life if I could, and I can't."

"I know that."

"But you're always safe with me. There are reasons it's important to me that you're safe. No one will ever raise a hand to you in anger. Unless death comes knocking on our door, I'm happy to shield you from ever seeing blood being drawn again. I just need to know that if anything were to ever happen, you could protect your-self if I couldn't get to you."

"I can shoot, and I know some basic hand-to-hand, although not much. I have a good aim when stomping on an instep or kneeing someone in the balls."

His eyebrows climb.

"My father's men got a little too friendly."

"Jesus."

"I'm not a delicate flower." I grin and boost up on my toes, intending to kiss him, but I'm still not tall enough, and my hands are still covered in sticky pasta dough. "Hey, come down here."

"Not yet. That second statement about fucking around on you? That's not going to happen. I don't want anyone else, and when I'm committed, I'm fucking committed."

"It's been *days*, Rome." I shake my head, but he holds me firm. "Seriously, it's been such a short time. This might not work out between us."

"It doesn't matter how long it's been. I *know*. There will be no one else for either of us ever again."

I let out a shaky breath before he presses his lips to mine twice and pulls away.

"You're unbelievable, Eloise."

"No, I'm not." I turn back to my dough. "I'm just a product of what I survived."

"Unbelievable." He drags his hand down my ponytail and kisses my temple. "I have some work in my office."

"Okay." I smile at him as he leaves the room. Once the dough is ready to go, I wash my hands again and text Scarlett.

> Me: I'm making a huge dinner! Wanna come over to eat and hang this evening?

The dots dance on the screen as I open the fridge and pull out a bottle of water, uncap it, and take a long sip.

> Scarlett: Did you talk to Mr. Alexander?

I smirk and reply.

> Me: Yes, and he's totally cool.

Scarlett: Then hell yes! Can I head your way now so we can hang while you cook?

Me: Get your sexy ass over here.

Scarlett: Be there in about 30.

By the time Scarlett texts to let me know she's downstairs, I have the pasta ready to go in a boiling pot and the brownies in the oven.

I open the front door and smile at the guard there.

"Hey, my friend Scarlett is downstairs. Would you please bring her up?"

"Sure thing," he says, and I close the door.

I pad over to the office and see Rome typing away on his keyboard.

"Come here, firefly," he says without looking up at me.

Following orders, I walk behind the desk, and the next thing I know, I'm in his lap, and he's kissing me like his life depends on it.

My God, this man can kiss.

He's a master at it. His lips are soft yet demanding. His tongue is just right, exploring my mouth without trying to choke me out.

When I come up for air, I say, "What was that for?"

"Been wanting to do that since I woke up in that bed alone," he says, drifting his knuckles down my cheek.

"The next time I'm too wordy, just shut me up and kiss me."

"No way." He rubs his nose against mine. "I like it when you talk to me, baby."

Good because I can't stop telling him everything.

"Scarlett's on her way up," I inform him. "I was just letting you know."

He checks the time, then pats my ass and helps me to my feet. "I need to get ready for work. My men will be here shortly."

"It's a good thing I made so much food."

"You don't need to feed everyone, Eloise."

"Need to? No. Want to? Yes. Are you going to tell me I can't?" I set my hands on my hips and grin while he growls low in his throat and shoves his hands through his hair.

"It seems I can't say no to you for much. But I don't want them getting used to it. I'm not sharing you with the whole fucking building."

I laugh and rub my hand up his chest. "Of course not."

The doorbell chimes, and I pad through the door of the office, but suddenly, Rome is at my side.

"You check the security cameras," he says, showing me the screen next to the door. "*Always,* even when you're expecting someone. And you better only have women up here. My men will be instructed to shoot any men on sight."

"That's ... crazy. Besides, it's just Scarlett."

"This is when I put my foot down. You will always check, Eloise. Do you hear me?"

"Okay, I hear you. How do I do that?"

He shows me which buttons to push, and a picture of the hallway comes up. Sure enough, there's the guard from earlier along with Scarlett.

"See?"

"Never open this door without this step. I'm deadly serious."

There's no humor in his face.

"I promise, Rome."

He nods once, then opens the door. Scarlett's ready with a big smile, but it dims a bit when she sees Rome. I can tell she's full of nerves.

"Oh, hi, Mr. Alexander."

"Welcome," he says, gesturing for her to come inside. "I hope you two have a good evening. I've booked out the spa for both of you tonight, starting at eight."

We both stare at him in shock.

"You did?" Damn, the man is swoony.

"Yes. Enjoy it. Get pampered." He kisses me on the head, nods at Scarlett, then goes upstairs.

"Holy shit," she whispers to me. "One, I've never seen him dressed like that. And two, he kissed you in front of me."

I bite my lip, grinning.

"And three, he's treating us to the *spa!*"

I laugh and take her hand, leading her into the kitchen.

"Best night ever," I tell her, offering her some bruschetta. "Here, eat this to start, and tell me what you think."

"Oh God, it smells so good in here. Do I smell brownies?"

"They're in the oven for dessert."

"What else are you making? Show me everything."

I take ten minutes to show her the sauce, the pasta, the breads, and all the things I've been sweating over this afternoon.

"Okay, really. Eat this and tell me if it's good."

She takes a bite of her appetizer and closes her eyes. "Marry me. Leave the hot, rich guy and marry me, Lu."

"I heard that," Rome says, walking into the room while finishing with his tie. He drapes his jacket over the back of a stool and picks up some bruschetta of his own.

"You'll understand when you take a bite of that," Scarlett assures him, not sorry in the least. She looks so adorable in her skinny jeans and a slouchy black sweatshirt that shows off one shoulder. Her bra is lacy and blue, and her hair is in a high pony, off her clean face. There's no makeup in sight.

I think she's gorgeous.

Rome takes a bite, and his eyes fly to mine. "Wow."

"Okay, you guys are just inflating my ego." I get to work dishing up three helpings of the pasta and pass them around. This sauce is my specialty. "Here you go."

"We can't go to the spa," Scarlett says around a mouthful of pasta, shaking her head. "We have to spend the night at the gym because I'm eating *all of this*. Oh God. Are you a chef or something?"

"I took culinary classes." I shrug and look at Rome, who's staring at me while he chews. "And I had a great housekeeper and cook at home growing up. Oh, and I made homemade vanilla ice cream to go with the brownies."

Rome's eyes narrow.

"What's wrong?"

"Absolutely nothing."

I tip my head to the side, but before I can ask him anything, Luke comes through the door, followed by Julian, Mateo, and Carson, along with who I assume are their seconds-in-command.

The penthouse is suddenly filled with huge, scary, dangerous, and beautiful men, all armed to the gills.

"Holy shit," Luke says, taking in the spread.

"Grab plates," I tell them all. "There's plenty here."

I rattle off what everything is, and no one has to be told twice. Rome looks irritated.

"Don't get used to this," he grumbles. "She's not doing this for you assholes all the time."

"Wow, pretty bartender," Carson says with a wink. "You did this for me?"

"Not for you," Rome counters, and I laugh.

"I did this," I confirm.

I realize that Scarlett has gone quiet, and when I look over, I find her and Luke eyeing each other. The tension between them is palpable.

The attraction is absolutely not one-sided.

"Is it poisoned?" Mateo asks, eyeing the sauce.

"You're the one who drugs people," I counter, holding my chin up.

The others laugh, and Rome winks at me.

"Christ, I'm moving in here," Carson says. "Leave him for me, pretty girl. I'm better in bed."

"I will fucking *end you*," Rome growls, but Carson just laughs and pats Rome on the back.

Their dynamic is fascinating. They're obviously all good friends, joking with each other. It's nothing like what I saw in my father's home.

But then again, my father doesn't like anyone. He definitely doesn't have any friends.

I notice that Julian and Mateo continue to watch me with cool, untrusting eyes, and I can't say I'm surprised. Rome knew who Salvatore Rizzo was, which means these men do too. I'm an unknown commodity here, getting close to their friend, and they definitely think the worst of me. My father trusted no one, so I can imagine that's a standard trait with men like these. Yet I have a deep sense of ... relief. Despite my niggling doubts, Rome means a lot to me. I can see myself staying. Living here. With him. In this life, no matter the risks. And these men? They'll protect Rome at all costs, and that's more important than them liking me.

Hopefully, I'll prove my loyalty ... and maybe win them over through their stomachs too.

"I have brownies and ice cream," I announce, getting up to pull everything out for dessert.

"We're leaving," Rome says. "No brownies for them."

"I made a shit ton," I counter. "Of course, you're all going to eat it. You don't tell an Italian woman no when it comes to food, Rome Alexander."

The room goes dead quiet. No one lifts their forks to their mouths.

All eyes are on Rome while he stares at me.

No one speaks to him that way.

My stomach quivers a bit in apprehension. Did I take it too far? Should I be more submissive when his friends are around? I forget that he's a boss, and his men and friends are here, and I just got sassy.

Shit, I don't know what to do!

But Rome's mouth twitches into a half smile, and he crosses to me and kisses my forehead.

"You heard my Italian woman. Eat her food."

"I'm sorry," I whisper, so only he can hear. "I didn't mean to sass you in front of them."

"You're fine, firefly." He smirks and reaches for a brownie of his own. After scooping some ice cream on top, he takes a big bite. "This is fucking good."

When the men are done eating, they all smile and wave at me, but I know that no one would dare touch me.

And I'm okay with that.

"I'm Spider," a big, bald man says. He has face tattoos and a piercing in his lip, but his smile is nothing but friendly. "Carson's second. Thanks for dinner."

"You're welcome. Be careful tonight, guys."

They shuffle out the front door, but Rome hangs back. When they're all gone, he pulls me into his arms, with Scarlett our only audience, and kisses the hell out of me.

"Thank you," he murmurs against my lips.

"You're welcome."

He backs away and turns to leave.

"Have a good time at the spa, ladies."

And with that, he walks out. Scarlett stares at me in awe.

"Did that all just happen?" I ask her.

"I think so." She swallows hard. "Um, you had all of the Kings of Vegas in this kitchen, eating dinner."

"Yeah. They're kind of goofy. And intimidating." Or, you know, terrifying. Scarlett's reaction is much more natural than mine. Am I immune to danger now? "And Luke has it bad for you, my friend."

She blinks at me. "What? No, he doesn't."

"He couldn't take his eyes off you."

"No way. My tits aren't even out, and I'm not wearing makeup or anything."

"I don't think he cares about that at all. He likes you back."

She worries her bottom lip. "Can I have another brownie?"

With a laugh, I get us each another. "We can eat the rest of the pan."

Thirty

ROME

"**Y**our girl can *cook*," Carson says as we walk out to the waiting SUVs.

"Flirt with her again, and you're fucking done."

The fucker smirks. "Come on. You know I wouldn't do anything. I like her for you."

I glance his way. "I'm so relieved that I have your blessing. Are you ready to go intimidate my woman's piece-of-shit father now?"

The humor leaves his face, and what replaces it is pure wrath.

"Always. Let's do this."

The four of us are traveling in separate SUVs, as usual. Rizzo agreed to meet with us, but we're in the middle of a goddamn war, so we need to be ready for anything. We have an army of forty men going with us, and I trust each of them implicitly.

"Our guys are in position and ready," Luke informs

me once I'm in the back seat of my black SUV. "Rizzo is there. He has eight men with him."

"That's it?"

Luke shrugs. "Seems so."

I shake my head and feel the fury pulse through my veins as every word my firefly said to me earlier in the kitchen runs through my mind.

He didn't just abuse her.

He fucking tormented and tortured her for twenty-three years.

I'm not simply going to kill him. That's too good for that piece of shit. No, I'm going to keep him alive for a good long while and make him beg for death. Even then, I won't give him peace.

He'd better enjoy every day of his freedom because it's coming to an end soon.

We stop outside of the warehouse that we use for meetups like these. Our army has instructions to surround the area, with fifteen men coming inside with us. Just because Rizzo has eight at his side doesn't mean he hasn't given similar instructions to his own men.

We could be walking into an all-out battle.

I check both my sidearms and the knives on my belt before stepping out of the vehicle.

Julian, Mateo, and Carson are ready as I join them, and the four of us walk through the doors side by side.

Rizzo leans negligently against a crate, his arms folded over his chest. His dark hair is slicked back, and his eyes are hard and calculating as our men file in behind us.

"So much for a friendly meeting," he sneers.

"We don't have a friendly relationship," Julian reminds him, taking the lead. Rizzo thinks we're here because of the man's attack on Julian's port. We don't plan to tell him about Eloise's whereabouts. "You made sure of that when you killed my men and stole from me."

Rizzo shakes his head. He's not quite fifty, less than ten years older than any of us, but he likes to talk down to everyone around him.

He's annoying as fuck. I want to send one of my knives right through his throat. It would be so easy. So fast.

Too fast.

"Now, Julian, I didn't know the port belonged to you."

"That's a crock of shit," Mateo says with a scoff. "The entire West Coast knows. You thought you could swing your dick around and get away with it."

"Did you get my package?" Julian asks. Suddenly, weapons are cocked and pointed at us.

I grin.

This is the part I enjoy. Threaten me. Fucking threaten me and see where it gets you.

"Listen." Rizzo holds his hand up, and his men stand down. "I got your message, Julian, and you have my apologies. Like I said, I didn't know it was your shipment."

Carson growls.

Mateo scoffs.

But Julian and I simply stare.

And Rizzo's eyebrows pull together, just long enough to show that he's rattled.

"I want my diamonds back," Julian says. "With interest. And I want your men off my turf."

Rizzo doesn't speak for a moment, and then says, "I can agree to that, with a condition."

"I don't really think you're in a position to demand conditions," Mateo mutters, but Rizzo keeps talking.

"My daughter is missing," he says, and my hands ball into fists. "The last I knew, she was here in Las Vegas."

"The last you knew?" Carson asks, tipping his head to the side.

"The man I sent to collect her has gone missing," Rizzo replies. "And there has been no news. That was days ago."

"Send men into our city without talking to us first, and bad things happen," Mateo says.

"I was trying to rescue my daughter," Rizzo says. "I love her so much and just want her home with me."

My jaw is clenched so tightly, it's a wonder my molars don't break.

"It sounds like she might not want to be found," Carson says, and Rizzo licks his lips.

Everyone is terrified of Carson.

"Maybe she skipped out with your man," Julian suggests, knowing it'll piss me off.

"She's a foolish girl," Rizzo replies, shaking his head. "I'm ready for her to be married, and she needs to come home. So I'll pay your interest if you help me find Eloise."

Her name in his mouth makes me feral.

I could kill him and all of his men right now. It's nothing less than he deserves.

But Julian still has his product and money to collect.

"I want the goods and the money within twenty-four hours," Julian says. "Once that's delivered, we'll see what we can find out about your daughter. She may not even be in our city."

"I suspect she is," Rizzo replies.

"Why?" I ask, speaking for the first time. "Why do you think she's in Vegas?"

He watches me for several long moments. "Call it a hunch."

I don't buy it.

He knows something. Once Julian has what he needs out of this asshole, I'm taking him out.

"Twenty-four hours," Julian repeats, and the four of us turn to walk out of the warehouse.

"Oh, one more thing," Rizzo says, catching our attention. "If I find out that one of you has touched her, that she's not pure as fucking snow when she's delivered back to me, I'll kill all of you."

Carson smirks.

"No," Mateo says in a low voice so only I can hear, so I don't raise my weapon and take him out.

Without answering, we leave and climb into our vehicles, then drive away. To say my fury is barely controlled is an understatement. The piece of shit who not only beat his daughter but sold her was right fucking there. Pretending he loves his "foolish" daughter. I could have gotten justice for my firefly. It can't come soon enough. Christ, she survived *that.*

We reconvene at Julian's mansion since it's the closest, and once inside, we sit in his living room with some whiskey. This room is massive, but it's lived in and not ostentatious. Julian built this place about five years ago, and we've all spent plenty of time out here, especially when we want to get out of the city.

"He knows more than he's saying," Mateo says, staring at me.

"Do we have a problem?" I challenge my friend.

"Maybe. I'm not convinced that your girl isn't a fucking plant. I don't care how well she cooks or how good her pussy is—"

"For fuck's sake," Julian grumbles.

"She could be a goddamn spy, and you know it."

I shake my head, impatience seething through me. "She's not a goddamn spy. I've seen the bruises her father put on her. She's told me about what that fucker put her through. She's not trying to get information for him."

"She could be lying," Julian points out.

"Okay, I'm going to side with Rome on this one," Carson says, shaking his head. "That girl is no plant. I really don't think he knows where she is. He sounded almost desperate."

"And not because he loves her," I add. "Eloise told me about his plan to marry her off, but that she didn't know the man. Had never heard his name before. Whoever it is, Rizzo clearly needs her for an alliance of some kind."

"Did she tell you the name?" Mateo asks, but I shake my head.

"No. Just that she ran because she didn't trust that they'd be any better to her than her father had been. If she was a fucking *plant*, she wouldn't have been living in that piece-of-shit motel. She wouldn't have been so goddamn terrified." I watch Julian and Mateo, and I can see that they agree with me, but they still don't trust her. "What do you need to know to trust her?"

"I need Rizzo to die and to see her reaction to that news," Mateo says simply.

"Well, as soon as Julian gets what he needs from the asshole, that's the plan," I tell him. "Because after what he put Eloise through, he doesn't get to live one minute longer than necessary."

Before the conversation can continue, Julian's son, Elliott, walks into the room with his fiancée on his arm. He's in a tux, and Natasha looks beautiful in a floor-length gown the color of her eyes.

Sapphires.

Her blond hair is swept up and away from her face, and she's holding Elliott's hand.

She won't look any of us in the eyes. That's not unusual.

"Hey, everyone," Elliott says with a smile. "Natasha and I were just headed out to the Wish Upon a Star Gala. We're going to bid on some silent auction things and dance, right, babe?"

Natasha's smile is forced, but she nods. "It should be fun."

I glance over at Julian, who watches his son cooly. Julian has had to buy Elliott's way out of jail a few times, yet the idiot continues to be reckless. His gambling habit will end up getting him killed, even if his father *is* Julian Stavros.

But recently, Julian approved the engagement between his son and Natasha Ivanov, the daughter of Sergei Ivanov, the head of the Russian Bratva. The alliance would be good business for both families.

However, based on how tight Natasha's smile is and the way she looks like she wants to run away from Elliott, my guess would be that she's not thrilled by the union.

"Have a good evening," Julian says with a nod. The couple walks through the door and out to Elliott's Range Rover.

"She doesn't look thrilled," Mateo says.

Julian's eyes narrow. "They've only just met a few weeks ago. They're getting to know each other."

"When's the wedding?" I ask him.

"Next month."

We nod because there isn't anything else to say. This is how things work in our world, whether we like it or not.

"We have other business to discuss." Mateo changes the subject. "And Carson's not going to like it."

"I don't like much," Carson reminds us. "Just say it."

"Adam Damien," Mateo says, and Carson stands to pace. "I haven't had eyes on him in our city, but there have been rumblings."

I watch Carson, aware that this hits a particularly sensitive nerve for him.

For all of us, really.

Adam Damien is why Carson spent the better part of a decade in federal prison.

He's also the reason the love of Carson's life is dead.

Damien's why Carson is as deadly as he is. The reason he's filled with revenge and wrath despite none of that bringing Rina back.

Nothing can bring her back.

"If he steps one toe in this state," Carson growls, "I will skin him alive."

"I'm just putting everyone on the offensive." Mateo shakes his head. "The man's a fucking ghost, but I've been hearing things."

"Keep listening," Julian suggests. "And keep us informed."

Thirty-One

LULU

"Best night *ever*," Scarlett says with a sleepy smile as we stride toward the elevators. We just finished getting rubbed, buffed, and polished all over, and we're as limp as the cooked pasta I served earlier.

"So good," I agree. "I wonder if I could talk Rome into this once a month."

"I'm pretty sure you could talk him into it whenever you want," she says with a chuckle as she presses the button for the elevator.

The doors open when it stops on our floor, and I'm surprised to see Luke standing inside.

"Ladies," he says with a nod, but he only has eyes for Scarlett.

"Is Rome back, too?" I ask him.

"I just dropped him off at the penthouse," he confirms. "I'll ride up with you and make sure you make it safely."

"I can ride along," Scarlett says, and I press my lips together.

Atta girl! Get some one-on-one time with the sexy mobster.

She winks at me, and once we're on the top floor, I step out, make sure the guards are at the door, then nod back at Scarlett and Luke.

"Bye, guys."

They wave, and before the doors shut, I see Luke make a dive for Scarlett. I can't help but giggle and do a little happy dance as I stride over to the door.

"Miss," one of the guards says with a nod as I press my palm to the plate, unlocking it.

"Have a good night." I step inside, then shut and lock the door the way Rome told me to.

A light is on in the kitchen, but no one is down here. Rome must have left it on for me.

He's so considerate for being a self-professed bad guy.

After kicking off my flip-flops, I pad barefoot up the stairs and into the bedroom. I can hear the shower running in the en suite, but when I cross the threshold into the bedroom, the water cuts off, so I crawl up to sit in the middle of the bed.

I don't have to wait long before a naked, still damp Rome saunters out of the bathroom. He's headed for the closet, but he stops dead in his tracks when he sees me sitting here.

Holy Christ on a cracker. Every inch of him is perfection. All that inked skin. The muscles. The blue eyes and the dark hair.

And that pierced cock does, indeed, make me lose my fucking mind.

"Did you have fun tonight?" he asks.

"Too much fun." I grin at him. "I'm so relaxed, I think I could sleep for a week. Scarlett and I both thank you."

"You're welcome." Rather than cross to the closet, he sinks his knee into the mattress and crawls his way over to me, urging me onto my back.

"We ran into Luke in the elevator," I inform him as I cup his cheek. "And I'm pretty sure Scarlett's staying with him tonight."

Rome blinks at me. "I don't know if I need to know that information."

"You don't. But I'm sharing a little gossip about my best friend with my man."

I bite my lip and grin at him.

"Because I know you'll be discreet, and I can trust you."

He nods and leans in to brush his lips over mine. "Yeah, firefly. You can trust me."

"I know. Did you have a good evening?"

"It was productive."

I smile and snuggle into him. "That's pretty vague."

"But accurate." He pushes his hand into my hair and drags his fingers through it, making me sigh. "Your hair is so fucking soft."

"I don't know what they put in it, but it's magic."

"Smells like ..." He buries his nose in my locks and inhales. "Fucking heaven. Christ, I could devour you."

His hands pull on my leggings until they're down my legs and tossed over his shoulder. Next, my T-shirt is discarded, and I'm lying here naked with Rome's magical hands moving all over my skin.

"Love the way you touch me," I murmur against his lips. "You have great hands."

My own hands are roaming up and down his sides as he braces himself over me, kissing me, and his gaze finds mine.

"I don't usually let people touch me," he admits, and my hands immediately drop away.

"I'm so sorry."

"No." He shakes his head and takes one of my hands, kisses it, and returns it to his side. "*You* can touch me all you want. You have unlimited access to me, Eloise. But this is new for me."

He doesn't like to be touched, but he trusts me enough to put my hands on him at will?

"Why me?" I ask softly, dragging my fingertips up and down his back.

"My body knows you," he says with a slight shrug. "It's the only way I can explain it. It's familiar. Which is crazy because I'm twenty years older than you, and I'd never seen you a day in my life before last week."

My eyes sting because that's how it felt for me, too. As if my whole body just *knew* him. Although I had no clue there were twenty years between us.

I'm also so curious. Has he suffered in the past, and that's why he doesn't want to be touched?

"Why don't you like to be touched?"

He shakes his head and kisses me, and I resign myself to not getting the answer to that question tonight. And that's okay. He'll tell me when he's ready.

His hand glides down to my breast, and he gently rolls his thumb over my nipple until it's a hard, aching bud. My legs scissor, my core looking for a release only he can give me.

"Do you know what I've realized?" he asks, peppering kisses along my neck.

"What?"

"I've never had my face in your gorgeous cunt."

I almost choke on my own tongue, and he grins as he kisses his way down my torso, to my stomach.

I have a slouchy, poochy stomach. I've always been self-conscious about it, but Rome kisses it and keeps moving as if it's a beautiful part of me.

As if he's not at all bothered by the extra pounds that I carry and have been shamed for all of my life.

And the fact that someone as absolutely freaking *gorgeous* as this man thinks that I'm sexy, too? Well, that's an aphrodisiac all by itself.

Rome works his way between my thighs, but suddenly, he whips us around so he's on his back, and I'm hovering over him, my core lined up with his mouth.

"How in the hell did you do that?"

He chuckles. "Lower yourself down here, firefly."

"I'm pretty sure I'll get assassinated for smothering you," I reply, shaking my head.

"Then *don't* smother me. Come on, I'm hungry."

I huff out a surprised laugh, but keep myself up on

my knees, hands braced on the headboard to keep my balance.

"Rome, this isn't going to work."

"Eloise, look at me."

I drop my chin and look down at him. His hands drift up and down my thighs soothingly.

"Christ, this is one amazing fucking view." He swallows hard. "Baby, I want to taste you. I'm telling you to sit this absolutely breathtaking pussy on my fucking mouth. *Now.*"

"But I'm—"

"If you say anything other than perfect, I won't let you come." His eyes flash up at me. "You're perfect, firefly. If I wanted you any more than I already do, I'd spontaneously combust. Now, be a good girl and lower yourself down for me."

I take a steadying breath, then squat over him. Rome cups my ass cheeks as he feasts on me, stealing my breath away.

Holy God, I'm going to die.

It's a good thing I can hold this headboard because I'm quite sure Rome just sucked my soul out of my body. I can't stop myself from rocking over him as he licks my clit with just the perfect pressure. When he presses two fingers inside me, I start to see stars.

"Rome," I mutter, thrashing my head from side to side. "Please."

His fingers move faster, and then they shift, and it feels like every muscle in my body is shuddering. I can't control the shaking in my legs.

"Oh God. I'm going to fall."

He chuckles, but his arms are like bands around my hips now, keeping me in place, and he doesn't stop.

I try to lift, but he's too strong.

All I can do is succumb to this incredible orgasm, and before I've had the opportunity to catch my breath, Rome slips out from under me and pushes into me from behind, making me cry out again.

"God, you're so goddamn *beautiful*," he growls against my ear as he thrusts into me, harder and harder, setting a punishing rhythm I can't get enough of. "You taste like sunshine. Your skin is the softest silk, and the noises you make drive me out of my fucking mind."

His words, his hard cock, and that metal in the tip shove me right over into another climax that has tears streaming down my cheeks.

"Fuuuuuuck," he groans. "Your pussy was made for me, baby."

He presses his mouth to my spine, and then he's coming apart. I can feel rope after rope of hot cum splashing inside me. I'm surrounded by him, and I love it. *It's so surreal.* Mind-blowing that I bring this man to orgasm through my own. *How is that possible?*

We're panting, sweating, and a complete mess when Rome finally pulls out of me, and I collapse onto my stomach.

Holy fuck.

"Come on, I'll clean us up," he says, catching his breath.

"It's okay. I'm gonna just lie here." I wave a hand in

the air, and he laughs. But then I'm airborne and being carried to the bathroom.

"When did you get pierced?" I ask as he sets me on the vanity and turns on the water. As it warms, he grabs a washcloth, then leans in to press his lips to mine. I can taste myself there, but it doesn't bother me at all.

"A long-ass time ago. Fifteen years easy." He gets the cloth wet, then gets to work cleaning me up before he does the same for himself. "And before you ask, yeah, it hurt."

"I wasn't even going to ask because *duh*. Of course, it did."

He kisses my forehead before tossing the cloth in a hamper. "You like it."

"I do. I like the ink more." My fingers trace over the angel on his chest.

"You do?"

"Hell, yes. The ink's one of the things I first noticed. Even though you were in a suit, so I could only see the neck and hands." I kiss his knuckles, and then he's carrying me again, his hands under my ass, my arms wrapped around his neck, as he takes me back to the bed.

When we're all wrapped up in each other, ready to sleep for a while, I sigh and tighten my arm around his waist in a hug.

If anyone had told me a month ago that I'd run from my father's home and find life-altering joy in the arms of a man twenty years my senior—a badass criminal with an enormous heart—I would have asked them what drugs they were on.

Yet, miraculously, wonderfully, I landed in this man's life. He adores my curves, he showers me with kindness, and he fucks like a man starved for me.

"I'm really happy I found you."

He kisses the top of my head. "Me too, firefly."

Thirty-Two

LULU

"**D**id you miss me?"

I've just passed a glass of champagne to a pretty blonde when the voice comes from my right, and my back is immediately up.

The mayor.

I turn to him and offer a polite smile. "Good evening. What can I get for you?"

"Oh, come on. Don't pretend we aren't friends. You'll hurt my feelings." He sticks his lower lip out in what I'm sure he thinks is an adorable pout when, in reality, he looks like an idiot.

The mayor is young, likely in his late thirties, and he's handsome. Strawberry-blond hair and ocean-blue eyes with a little scruff on his chin. He's trim and fit, and frankly, I don't understand why he thinks he has to be smarmy. I'm sure plenty of women here would happily fuck him.

But that girl isn't me. Even if I didn't have Rome, the hottest man to ever live, I wouldn't want the mayor.

I don't answer. I simply tilt my head to the side, waiting for his order. We've been busy tonight. The lounge has been full, every seat at the bar and each table around the room spoken for all evening, and I've enjoyed the vibe. The energy has been up. The people have been friendly and happy to be here. There's been no inappropriate flirting.

Until now.

This guy is such a creep.

"Would you like a whiskey neat?" I ask, remembering what he ordered last time, and his eyes gleam with predatory satisfaction.

Fuck. I should not have said that.

"See? I knew it. Yes, that sounds great. Pour yourself one and come sit with me at my table."

I turn to grab the whiskey, but I reach wrong with my left arm, and the bottle almost drops out of my grasp.

"You okay?" Max asks with a frown.

"The mayor is here," I mutter, and his face clears. He glances over my shoulder and nods.

"I can take it."

"I've got this," I assure him as I pour the drink. "But don't go far, okay?"

"I got you, babe." He winks and resumes filling his own drink order when I turn to deliver the mayor's request.

He takes a sip, eyeing me, then smacks his thin lips together. "You make one hell of a drink, Lulu."

"I literally did nothing," I remind him. "It's straight from the bottle. But I'll give Macallan your well wishes."

I turn to give another customer my attention, but the mayor's hand is suddenly around my wrist, holding me in place against the top of the bar.

"You're going to want to remove your hand," I tell him coldly.

"Or what?" He smirks and leans closer to me. "Do you know who I am, little girl?"

"Yes. I do. And I don't care."

His eyes go ice cold, and I know without a doubt that if we were alone, he'd backhand me. I know that look well.

Asshole.

"Take an hour off and come with me to a privacy room."

"Not today or any other day, *Mayor* Pierce."

Suddenly, a large knife is plunged into the wood of the bar, less than a quarter of an inch from where the mayor holds me, and he jerks back, releasing me.

Julian.

Julian's dark gaze is on mine, and I give him a small nod, confirming that the man was touching me without my consent.

At least, I *think* that's what he was silently asking me. I don't know these guys well enough to read their minds yet, but I'm grateful he's here.

"There's a rule at this club," Julian says in a hard, tight voice, leaning closer to the mayor and making the man break out in a thin sheen of sweat. It's actually fascinating to watch the man go from feeling powerful to being afraid. "No touching unless a person has consented to it."

"You got it all wrong," the mayor says, forcing out a laugh. "Lulu and I always flirt. It's our thing. Tell him, baby."

"I'm not your baby," I reply as I take a step back and find both Rita and Max there.

"I've told you before," Rita tells him. "Lulu isn't going to a room with you. Ever. And from now on, you won't order drinks from her either."

"Oh, come on. You're all being ridiculous. It was just harmless flirting. She's a beautiful woman. What's the problem?"

"The problem is I told you no," I reply, and Julian nods at me, making me want to smile at the praise.

But it only lasts a moment.

"Jesus, try to be nice to the hired help, and they lose their shit. I paid to be here, and you work here. As far as I'm concerned, I'm entitled to fuck whoever I want."

"And you're done." Julian signals to two of the security guys, and when they join us, he says, "Escort Mr. Pierce out. He's not welcome to return."

"Hey! This isn't your business," he says, practically spitting on Julian, who simply glares at him.

If it were me, I wouldn't want Julian glaring at me.

"Should I call Rome?" I ask Julian.

"He's conducting some business right now," Julian replies with a quick shake of his head as security takes the mayor by the arms and escorts him out. "But he'll be filled in right away."

Rita pats my shoulder, and I glance down into her concerned face.

"I'm sorry," I whisper.

"You didn't do anything wrong, honey," she replies with a nod. "He crossed the line. He'll pay the consequences, even if he's the fucking mayor. Rome will see to it."

A chill runs down my spine.

Does that mean he'll kill the mayor?

I turn my attention to Julian, and the question must be written all over my face because the smile he gives me in return isn't reassuring.

It's menacing.

"Don't worry about it," he says in a low voice. "Do you need anything?"

"I'm fine." I clear my throat, then turn to another customer and get back to filling orders. Nothing the mayor did rattled me too badly until he touched me. When he grabbed my arm, I just froze. It's the same arm my father would grab, and I was waiting for the white-hot pain that always came with it. I should have shaken him off, and I would have if Julian hadn't stepped in. But for a heartbeat, my body froze, and I didn't like that.

A few things have become clear to me in the past couple of days. First of all, I really need to seek out some physical therapy for my shoulder. I'm fairly sure that with some exercise and help, I can get the strength and mobility back.

The other is that I'd like to take some self-defense classes. I believe Rome when he says that he'll never let anyone hurt me again, but I shouldn't freeze up every time a man touches me in a way I don't like. I want my *fight* reaction to kick in, even if it's just to pull myself away and look for someone in security.

I need to build my self-confidence, and I think classes will help with that. Maybe Scarlett will take one with me. I wonder if there's a class in the gym here on-site? It's worth asking.

A couple of hours pass by without incident, and I'm feeling better. Julian only stayed at the bar for maybe thirty minutes, and then he was on his way.

Things have mellowed out considerably as members have drifted into the playroom or privacy rooms, and I really want to find Rome.

I need a moment. A hug.

I've been able to stay focused on making drinks and ensuring our guests are happy, but the mayor's anger, so familiar and horrifying, has also shown me that deep down there are many other scars and bruises than the eye can see. *And I hate my father even more.*

It's Rome's arms I want wrapped around me, making me feel … safe.

Does that make me a needy girlfriend? Maybe, but he owns the place, and it's only for a few minutes.

"Rita, do you mind if I go find Rome for just a minute?"

She smiles over at me. "Not at all. We're good here. Go take an hour if you want it."

"I don't know if I'll need that long, but thanks."

I untie my apron, fold it up, and stow it in a drawer for when I return, then head over to the elevators.

But when I get to his office, Rome isn't around, and no one's guarding his door.

I sigh and feel my shoulders slump, then pull my phone out of the pocket of my black dress and decide to send him a text.

If he didn't want me to contact him, he wouldn't have given me a phone, right?

> Me: Hey! I have a quick break and was looking for you. Nothing urgent. Are you in the building somewhere?

It says that the message is delivered, but after thirty seconds of staring at the screen, there's no sign that he's replying, so I shove the phone back in my pocket and ride back down to the lounge level.

Before I return to the bar, I turn to the extravagant doors that lead to the playroom. Maybe he's inside, checking on things, and can't hear his phone?

With a deep breath of courage, I open the door and step inside, and I'm immediately met with music and lots of people.

My eyes skim the area, but I don't see Rome. I do see Julian sitting on a couch with a woman kneeling in front of him, giving him one hell of an enthusiastic blow job. His hands are fisted in her hair, guiding her up and down his shaft, and I look away.

I don't really want to watch Rome's friends have sex.

Instinctively, I make my way over to where that same man from the other night is working with his ropes again, but this time on a different woman.

Shibari.

Even the name is sexy.

The man offers me a small smile, then turns all of his attention back to his partner. I cross my arms over my chest and *watch*.

Thirty-Three

ROME

That came in twenty minutes ago.

I pick up the blowtorch that sits on the workbench of the cell. Luke's eyebrows climb. "So soon?"

"She needs me," I say as I flip it on. "So his time just shortened."

The man whimpers and shakes his head.

"Come on, boss," Rocky pleads as blood streams down the side of his head where his ear used to reside. "I swear, I didn't know."

"You didn't know." I nod, processing what he's telling me. "You stole one hundred grand of my money, and *you didn't know* that was a problem for me?"

"It was fake," he says, and I shake my head as if I can't

figure out how he could be so stupid. "And I was going to replace it."

"How? By printing more from *my fucking printers?*"

I set the blowtorch under his bare foot and listen to him howl. The rest of his crew is standing by, watching, to prove a point.

Don't fucking steal from me.

I let go and look around at the other ten men who work on the printers. They're stony-faced. A few look a little green like they want to throw up, but they've held it together so far.

"This is what happens when you betray me," I tell them calmly. "I pay you well. If you need more, you come to me, and we'll talk. Because if I find out that you've taken what's mine—"

I pull my weapon from behind my back, then turn and shoot Rocky between the eyes.

"You die. Painfully."

"Yes, boss," they reply.

"Get to work," I bark, and they disperse, off to the printing room.

"I thought you'd play longer," Luke says as he joins me.

"Eloise is looking for me," I reply.

"I wondered if she was upset," he says, and I turn all of my attention to him.

"Why would she be upset?"

"Christ," he says, shoving his hand through his hair. "I thought Julian would have told you."

My heart thuds faster in my chest. "You'd better fucking explain."

"The mayor was a slimy asshole," Luke says, blowing out a breath. "He wouldn't take no for an answer. Julian stepped in, got the asshole kicked out, and I assume you'll be revoking his membership."

"Immediately. Was she hurt?"

"No, he just grabbed her wrist, but she didn't invite it, and I hear it rattled her for a second."

Fuck.

"Get him to the graveyard," I say, pointing at Rocky. "I'm going to go find her."

"On it," Luke says, and I leave the cell, pull my suit jacket on, and ride the elevator up to the lounge level.

When I get to the bar, there's no Eloise.

"If you're looking for your girl, I saw her go into the playroom about fifteen minutes ago," Rita says with a wink.

The playroom?

If anyone has a finger on her, they'll die.

I've already killed one man tonight. What's one more?

I walk inside, and as my eyes adjust to the dimmer light, I skim the area for my firefly. I've almost walked a complete circle when I spot her.

And I grin.

Oh, baby.

She's standing, legs spread just a bit, hip cocked, arms folded over her chest as she watches Jason work his ropes around Beth. For Beth being such a tiny woman, he's done a lot of work on her already. And based on the way Beth's eyes are dilated, and the way she's breathing fast, she's sitting happily in subspace.

And my firefly is entranced.

I want every person in here to know that she's mine. And I want to have some fun with her. No one gets to see her bare except for me, but that doesn't mean I can't make her come with an audience.

I press up behind her, my chest to the back of her head and wrap my arms around her, holding her close.

"You might want to be careful," she says without looking up at me. "My man could walk in at any minute. He's kind of scary. You don't want to piss him off."

I lean down and press my lips to the shell of her ear. "That's one, firefly."

"One what?"

"One orgasm you don't get to have."

She sighs and leans into me, not concerned at all, but I'm not lying. At some point, I'll deny her, and I can't wait.

Edging is one of my favorite kinks.

Jason nods at me but continues tying his knots over Beth's thighs. The design he's working on is intricate and beautiful. I'd love to do something similar to Eloise.

"Can you do that?" she asks, leaning back so I don't have trouble hearing her above the music in the room.

"I can do this," I confirm and feel her take a quick inhale when Jason wraps his soft, red rope beneath Beth's crotch, just to the side of her pussy. "You really love this."

"It's so pretty," she breathes and covers my arms with

her hands, holding me to her. "The different colors of the ropes, and the way he knots them. It's like a dance. I wish my arms could do that."

Beth's arms are behind her back, and the ropes are looped from the top of her shoulders to her wrists, where they're tied together.

"I could put you in other positions," I say against her ear and pull one arm from her chest, so I can drag my hand down her side and under her skirt at the back. I'm directly behind her, so no one can see her ass as I push a finger under her underwear and find her *soaked*. "Fuck, firefly, you've just been standing here and you're turned on."

"I can't look away," she admits with a thick swallow, and I push the finger inside her, making her moan low in her throat. The music is loud, so only I can hear her, but I notice that people are looking at us.

Because I *never* play in here. I've never taken a partner to fuck, to use my ropes on, to experiment with. But if my firefly gets off on watching Jason and Beth work this scene, I'm going to fucking enjoy it with her.

And everyone who sees will understand that she's *mine*.

"Rome," she says as she tips her head back on my shoulder, but she's still watching Jason. Beth's eyes are glassy and round as she stares straight ahead as if she can't even see us. She's so far under Jason's spell that he's all she knows right now, and that's exactly how it should be.

"He's working her beautifully," I murmur in Eloise's ear. "Taking his time with her, making sure the rope slides over her skin before he knots it. She's on fire for him, isn't she?"

Eloise nods, and I turn my hand so I can reach her clit, making her jerk in my arms.

"Can you see how wet she is, firefly?"

"Yes."

"She's dripping down her pretty thighs. I wonder which part does it for her? Is it the feel of his hands skimming over her skin?"

Eloise pops her ass out, silently begging me to fuck her harder, to press on that magical rough patch inside of her pussy to make her come apart.

And I will.

Soon.

"Oh, look. He's kissing her shoulder. Has he been kissing her between knots like that, baby?"

She nods and licks her lips. "Yeah. And touching her."

My girl loves touch.

I press my lips against her neck and start to work her harder.

"Rome, people are watching."

"Good."

She glances up at me now, her eyes wide but not scared or apprehensive.

No, those emerald eyes are full of lust.

"I've got you covered, firefly. They can only see what I want them to see. And I don't share this pussy with anyone."

She bites her lip and goes back to watching Jason,

who has just crisscrossed his rope over Beth's stomach, leaving her navel bare.

I can't wait to do this to my firefly.

The sooner, the better.

Her fingernails dig into my arm, through my suit jacket, and then she's coming apart, squeezing the ever-loving fuck out of my fingers and making me hard as stone.

And when she's finished, I lick my fingers clean before wrapping that arm around her once more.

Jason lifts Beth into his arms, and now that the scene is over, he carries her to a private room, where he'll likely fuck her and then shower her with aftercare.

Jason is one of the best Doms in this club.

Eloise spins in my arms and hugs me around the middle, then tips her little face up so I can kiss her.

Which I am fucking happy to do. With my finger under her chin, I slant my lips over hers and deepen the kiss until we're both breathing hard.

"Wow," she whispers. "I just wanted a hug."

"Are you okay, firefly?"

"Yeah. The mayor's an asshole, though."

I narrow my eyes on her.

"Julian handled it."

I'll thank my friend later and have him help me send a message to the mayor of our fair city.

Suddenly, Eloise frowns and looks at something behind me, to my left.

"Something's wrong over there."

I let go of her and turn to follow her gaze and watch

as a man pulls back with a bullwhip and cracks it across a woman's back.

She's strapped to a Saint Andrew's cross, her back showing, and there are at least a dozen bleeding wounds down her back.

"Some people are into this, firefly."

"No," she says, shaking her head. "She's saying something. Oh my God, it's Scarlett."

Eloise runs to the cross, to the front of it, and sees Scarlett's face.

"She's screaming her safe word!"

The man pulls back as if he's going to whip her again, and I wrench it from his hand as I signal for guards to get their fucking asses over here.

"Get him in the cell," I tell them and recognize that this is the same piece of shit who ignored Beth's safe word last week. Why he's here, I don't know. Loveland should have informed him that his membership was revoked.

What the fuck?

"She's into it! She doesn't know what she's saying," he cries as he's dragged away, and I get to work unbuckling Scarlett as Eloise reassures her that she's safe now.

"We're here," Eloise says soothingly. "Oh, sweetie, we're here. It's okay."

"He wouldn't listen," Scarlett cries as I unbuckle the last shackle. She falls against me, her legs giving out on her. Careful not to touch her back, I lift her in my arms and hold her by the ass, her legs wrapped around my waist.

"Loop your arms around Rome's neck," Eloise says, helping her. "It's okay, sweetheart. It's okay now."

Scarlett is sobbing. I don't like holding a naked woman in my arms who isn't Eloise, but Scarlett can't walk on her own, and her back is so fucked up, I can't wrap her in something.

"It's okay." Eloise's eyes shine with tears. She gives me a knowing look that tells me she understands my discomfort but also knows that I'm taking care of her friend, and this is not in any way sexual. "Where can we take her?"

"We have an infirmary," I reply and gesture to another guard. "Call Dr. Asgood and get her here ASAP. We'll be in the infirmary."

"Yes, sir," he says with a nod, pulling out his phone.

"You have a doctor on standby?" Eloise asks, and I simply nod as I stride toward the small room we've made into an exam room for the few moments like this, or if one of my men needs to get stitched up.

There are three beds inside, and I set Scarlett down on the edge of the nearest one so her feet dangle off the side. Since she can't lie down, I grab a blanket and cover her front with it.

She hugs the blanket to her, still crying.

"I said *okra* over and over again. I hate that fucking vegetable." She wipes at the tears on her cheeks and the makeup that's run down her skin. "He wouldn't stop."

"Did you agree to the whip?" I ask her softly.

"No, that's not my thing," she says, shaking her head. "He asked if he could use a riding crop and a flogger. I told him I'd safe word when it was too much, and he agreed."

Motherfucker.

I squat in front of her and hold her face in my hands. My rage has a heartbeat, sending heat through my body. That asshole is going to pay dearly for what he did to this woman. "Scarlett, look at me. I'm so fucking sorry, honey. That should not have happened to you."

She shakes her head and starts to cry again.

"I'm going to handle this. I have a doctor coming to take care of you."

Her lips quiver, but she nods. "Thank you, Mr. Alexander."

"You never have to thank me. It's my job to make sure you're safe, and I failed you tonight. It won't happen again." I kiss her on the head and stand, then pull the guard aside.

"Michael," I say to him. "Let Rita know that Eloise won't be finishing her shift, then get her upstairs to the penthouse. When the doctor arrives, make sure she can get right in to see Scarlett and has everything she needs. Keep me apprised of what's going on in here."

"Yes, boss," Michael says with a nod. "If anyone asks, where will you be?"

"The cell." I turn back to him. "Oh, and have someone bring me that bullwhip."

Thirty-Four

LULU

I watch Rome leave the room, and after he gives me one last look and reassuring smile, I turn all my attention to my best friend. She may be a new friend, but she's damn important to me, and I'm going to make sure she's okay.

It's the blood that I can't get over. Christ, she's a mangled mess, and I hope with all my heart that Rome makes that fucker pay.

"Lu," Scarlett says with a sob as she wipes her tears on the blanket she's clinging to, covering her naked breasts. "God, it hurts. How do people do this for fun?"

"It's not my thing either," I assure her and brush some sweaty hair off her face and tuck it behind her ear. I grab a bottle of water off a nearby tray, crack it open, and offer it to her. "You need to hydrate."

"I didn't know him," she says, shaking her head when I offer her the water. "I'd never seen him before. And he seemed so ... *normal.* He was nice, and handsome, and said he'd never played with the flogger before and wanted to try. That he wouldn't let it go past me getting a little pink. We discussed it at length, and I clearly explained my boundaries."

"You heard Rome. You didn't do anything wrong, Scarlett. And has anyone suggested turning the music down a bit in the playroom? It's so loud that it's hard to hear a safe word if you're not standing right next to someone."

"He heard me," she says. "He told me to shut up. But yeah, it does get loud in there sometimes. I've mentioned it to Loveland, but she blows me off on the regular."

I really don't like that woman.

Why wouldn't Scarlett's boss listen to her? She and I got off to a rocky start, but she's worked here for years, which means Rome trusts her. I can't imagine Rome would allow his staff to be treated poorly by one of their managers. That's just not him.

"I didn't even want to work tonight," Scarlett admits with a soft voice. Her eyes meet mine. "Luke and I ... last night was really great. It doesn't feel right to fuck other people, but this is my job, and Luke knows that. I felt weird about it anyway."

"Hey." I kiss her forehead. "It's going to be okay."

The door opens, and a petite woman in her fifties with curly white hair in expensive clothes bustles in and frowns when she sees Scarlett's state. Another woman follows her, around the same age, with blond hair.

"Miss Lulu," Michael, the guard, says. "I was given

instructions to take you to the penthouse when the doctor arrived."

Scarlett clings to my hand, and I shake my head. "I'm not leaving her."

"But Mr. Alexander—"

"Is certifiable if he thinks for one minute that I'll leave her here by herself after the trauma she's just been through. I'm not going. And I'll deal with Rome myself later."

Michael swallows hard, obviously not wanting to go against Rome's wishes.

"I'll text him," I say, and Michael's shoulders drop a little in relief.

"I'm Dr. Asgood," the doctor says with a soothing, calm voice to Scarlett as I type out my message. "And this is my assistant, Cheryl. We're going to take care of this, Scarlett."

> Me: I'm not going to the penthouse. I'm not leaving Scarlett. Michael will stay with us here. I'm not in danger.

I tuck my phone away and turn my attention to my friend.

"He made me count," Scarlett says after a hard swallow.

"How many times did he strike you?" Dr. Asgood asks, looking at Scarlett's back but not touching her. Her eyes are sharp, and they flash with anger at the destruction in the flesh.

"F-f-fourteen," Scarlett replies.

"The wounds are drying, so we need to get you cleaned up. It will hurt. I'm sorry for that, but I'll give you a sedative and some pain medication to take the edge off."

Scarlett bites her lip and watches me with pleading eyes.

"I'm not going anywhere," I assure her, and she nods. "I'm right here. You and me. We've got this, babe. Let's talk about something happier while they clean you up. Maybe we should go shopping for something extra beautiful in a few days when you're feeling better."

"Shoes," Scarlett says, and winces when Cheryl places the IV in the crook of her elbow. They get some fluids going, and Cheryl injects something into the line.

"This is the medicine," Cheryl tells Scarlett. "It's going to take the edge off the pain for you. You might feel a little sleepy, too. There's also an antibiotic in here, in case there's any kind of infection."

"Okay," Scarlett breathes. "Am I okay here on the edge of the bed?"

"That's perfect," Dr. Asgood replies. "You can lean on your friend if you need to."

"I'm an excellent hugger," I say with an encouraging smile while dragging a stool over to sit in front of her. "Seriously, tell me where you need me."

Scarlett nods, and the eyes that held some fear and pain soften a little as the medicine takes effect.

"What kind of shoes do you want to look for?" I ask her as the doctor and Cheryl lay the supplies out behind Scarlett and get to work. "Heels? Sneakers?"

"Both, I'm not picky." She hisses with the first contact of the cloth on her back. "Oh shit, that fucking hurts like a bitch."

"I know, sweetheart," Dr. Asgood says. "I'm so sorry. We're going to work carefully but quickly. Hang in there and let me know if you need a break."

"Breathe with me," I encourage Scarlett. "Take a deep breath."

"If I ever have a baby, you have to be in the room with me," she says, watching my face and taking a deep breath. "You'd be really good at that."

"Do you want babies?" I ask her, trying to keep her distracted.

"Maybe. Someday. I think I have to quit this job. I can't go back into that playroom, Lu."

"You don't even have to think about that right now." I brush my fingers over her forehead and frown because she feels warm. "Does she have a fever?"

"She might," the doctor confirms. "It's a normal response to this kind of physical trauma and fear."

"How is it that I've known you for such a short time, but you're the best friend I ever had?" Scarlett asks, her voice slurring. "Maybe we're soulmates. It doesn't have to just be for romantic relationships, you know."

"I totally think we're soulmates," I confirm, and notice the two women behind Scarlett share a smile. "What's your favorite comfort food? I'll make it all for you after you get some sleep."

"Cheeseburgers," she says. "With greasy fries. And a chocolate shake."

"I can make you all of that. Should we watch some chick flicks, too?"

"Yeah." She winces again, and it makes my stomach clench. God, I hate this for her. "Or some reality TV. *Housewives of Beverly Hills* or something?"

"I'm down for that."

"Can you text Luke for me?" she asks with a whisper.

"Of course."

I pull out my phone and bring up his contact.

"What do you want me to say?"

"Just that I've been hurt, and I want to see him. I don't even care if it makes me sound like a whiny baby."

"Dude, I had a guy just piss me off earlier and went hunting for Rome so I could get a hug. You can bet your gorgeous ass I'd be begging for him right now."

Scarlett smiles softly. "You two are the cutest."

I punch out a message to Luke.

> Me: I'm with Scarlett in the infirmary. She's been hurt and would like to see you when you're free.

"There. Message sent."

"Thank you."

Thirty-Five

ROME

I walk into the cell and find four of my men flanking the piece of shit from the playroom.

"Strip him down to his underwear and tie him to the ceiling."

The man wails in terror, but I don't give a fuck. Once more tonight, I remove my jacket, roll up my sleeves, and settle in to torture a man.

While my guys work on getting him ready for me, I call Luke.

"Hey, boss," he says.

"You need to get back here." I sigh and look at the ceiling. "Scarlett's been hurt. She's in the infirmary with Eloise and the doctor. I have the asshole with me in the cell."

"The fuck?" Luke's voice is hard, and I feel for him. If the tables were turned, I'd burn the world to the ground for my girl.

"She was whipped."

"WHAT THE FUCK?"

"Get back here. I'll get him started for you."

I might be the boss, but Scarlett is Luke's girl. I've watched him watch her for months. I didn't need my firefly to fill me in on their relationship.

I have eyes.

And I know my second-in-command.

But just because I'll let Luke finish this fucker doesn't mean I won't have a little fun in the meantime.

"Do you know who I am?" I ask as I step toward the idiot and glare at him.

"No."

"Well, let me introduce myself. I'm Roman Alexander, and I own this club." I slap him hard across the face. It's humiliating, and it stings.

And I enjoy it.

"You came into my club and broke my rules. Twice. And now you're going to pay for it."

The door of the room opens, and one of my guys passes me the bullwhip.

"What's your name?" I ask the man strung up before me.

"Emilio."

I snap the whip but don't hit him.

Emilio flinches like the pussy that he is.

"I'm going to hurt you, Emilio. Now, we have some business to discuss. First of all, you ignored the safe word at the spanking bench last week. And I'm warning you, if you lie to me, you'll only make this worse for yourself."

"I didn't mean to," he says, sweating.

"That's the wrong answer." I slap him again and grin when blood spatters out of the side of his mouth.

"I did," he confesses.

"Good. See, I don't allow that bullshit here. Loveland revoked your membership for that, yet you're back in my establishment."

"She didn't," he says, and that gets my attention.

"Explain." My voice is hard.

"She gave me a warning and told me not to do it again. But she didn't kick me out."

Loveland is done.

"So you got your warning and came back here and did it again anyway. But this time, you took a whip to a woman who expressly told you *not to* do that." I weigh the whip in my hands. It's the best quality. Heavy. Thick. And fucking brutal. "You tore up her back."

His eyes flare with satisfaction at that statement.

"You're a sadist," I continue, watching him closely. "If you'd have simply told Madam Loveland that, you would have been introduced to like-minded people, Emilio, and all of this would have been avoided."

He licks his lips, eyes moving back and forth like he's trying to decide what to say next.

"That's not what I want."

I stop and stand directly in front of him, about ten feet away.

"You don't want them to know it's coming," I guess, and he stares back at me. "You're a predatory piece of shit."

"If she didn't want me to hit her, she shouldn't have—"

I don't let him finish that sentence. I strike the whip over his face, slicing it in a diagonal from his right eye to the left jawline, and he howls in pain.

"Didn't see that coming, did you?" I get in his face now. "How did that feel?"

"Please," he whines, and I spit on him, then turn away.

"I wonder how many times Scarlett said *please*."

I wonder how many times my mother said that word. Cried. Screamed.

I clear my throat and strike again, this time over his chest, and the long slash immediately starts to bleed.

"Weak motherfucker," I mutter, shaking my head. "You might as well get used to this. We're just getting started."

Thirty-Six

LULU

"Just a little more," Cheryl croons to Scarlett, who is no longer whimpering, but the tears still spill down her cheeks. She's clinging to my hands, and we stopped chatting about ten minutes ago.

She just couldn't think anymore.

I suspect she's disassociated herself from it all, and I totally understand where she is. I've been there myself.

It's the only way to get through the pain.

Suddenly, the door is pushed open, and Luke runs in, his face a mask of fear and fury. He glances at her back, and his jaw clenches as he walks in front of her. I scoot aside so he can squat in front of Scarlett.

"Oh, baby." He gently frames her face in his huge hands and brushes his thumbs back and forth on her cheeks, wiping the tears away. "Scar? I'm here."

She blinks, and when her eyes find Luke's, her face crumples again, and she leans into him.

"Shh, I'm right here. I'm so sorry."

Scarlett fists her hands in his shirt and clings to him as he brushes his hands up and down her arms.

"We're done cleaning you up," Dr. Asgood says with a sigh as she takes her gloves off and tosses them in the trash. "You'll need to have them cleaned once a day. They should heal within a few weeks, but if you have questions or concerns, just call me. Luke has my number."

"Okay," Scarlett whispers, then turns her gaze up to Luke. "Will you please drive me home?"

"You're staying with me," he informs her and kisses her so tenderly on the forehead, I almost feel like I'm intruding. "You're going upstairs to my place, baby."

Scarlett sighs in relief as Luke turns to me.

"I have to go to work for a bit," he informs me. "But will you please go with her?"

"Of course. I'm stuck to her like glue." I glance at Michael. "Will you go with us up to Luke's apartment?"

Michael nods.

"I've got her," I say to Luke, who obviously doesn't want to let go of Scarlett. His face is full of misery, and I feel awful for both of them.

"You're safe," he croons against the top of her head. "I'm sorry, baby."

"I'll be okay." Scarlett smiles up at Luke, putting on a brave face. "Thanks for letting me crash at your place. I'll head home tomorrow."

"No." He kisses her tenderly. "You won't. You're with me now. We'll talk about it later, babe."

Luke walks us to the elevator and makes sure we're

safely inside with Michael. As the doors close, he winks at Scarlett.

The ride up only takes a few seconds, and then Scarlett leads us to the second door on the right. She punches in a code—I didn't know she had the code to his door—then pushes inside, and I follow her.

"I'll be right outside," Michael assures us before closing the door behind him.

Luke's apartment is not what I was expecting. It's big and bright, with cozy furniture and amazing artwork. Lots of blues and grays fill the space, making me wonder if he did this himself or hired a decorator.

"I can't lie on my back," Scarlett chokes out. "And I don't know why I can't stop crying."

"Because you were scared, and it fucking hurts." I take her hand and link our fingers. "You can sit on the couch, with your shoulder against the back for support, and I'll rig up some pillows for you to lean on in the front so you can drift off."

She bites her lip and nods. "Thank you. I'll be better tomorrow."

"I think you're doing great now. But I need to know that this is where you want to be. If you want to come up and stay with me in the penthouse, I'll take you up there right now."

"No, this is perfect." She squeezes my hand and smiles softly. "I feel safe with Luke. And something is starting between us."

"Well, I can see that for myself. He was so *swoony* back there. He cares about you a lot."

"You don't think it's just about the sex?"

"No way." I shake my head as I arrange cushions and pillows on the couch. "He was so mad and worried. His face just about broke my heart. And he calls you Scar!"

"It's kind of cute," she agrees with a soft smile. "Almost as cute as firefly."

"I still have no idea why Rome calls me that. He's done it since the very beginning. I asked him, but he wouldn't say."

"Well, whenever he tells you, I want to know, too." She winces as she tries to settle herself onto the couch. When she leans forward on the cushion I stole from a nearby chair, her eyebrows climb in surprise. "Hey, this is comfy. How did you know to do this?"

"My dad used to like to dislocate my shoulder." Her jaw drops, and I shrug. "I got good at figuring out ways to get comfortable. Hopefully, this is the last time either of us has to do this."

"I hope you're right," she says with a deep sigh.

"Are you still hurting? I can give you something." The doctor sent us away with some oral pain meds, but Scarlett shakes her head.

"No, I won't do anything stronger than ibuprofen. I have a sister who's addicted to pain meds, and I refuse to go down that road."

I sigh as I sit next to her and lean my head back against the couch.

"Oh shit!" I sit up straight, startling her. "I never told Rita I'm not returning for my shift."

"I'm quite sure she knew when she saw Rome carry

me out of the playroom with you right next to me," Scarlett says.

"I didn't even notice that," I confess. "I was too busy worrying about you."

Scarlett reaches over and tucks my hair behind my ear. "You're a good friend. Lulu."

"So are you. I wonder what our guys are doing right now?" Rome mentioned something about the cell, but I have no idea what that is.

She bites her lip. "We probably don't want to know."

Thirty-Seven

ROME

The puddle of blood beneath Emilio is quite impressive, but I need to slow down so the piece of shit doesn't bleed out before Luke gets here. He should be here by now, but I suspect he probably swung by the infirmary to check on Scarlett.

It's what I would do.

The door opens and in walks my cousin. He glances at me, and I see the rage.

Murderous rage.

Emilio isn't leaving here alive.

Without a word, I pass Luke the whip and step out of the way. I gesture for the other men to leave the room, leaving only Luke and me here.

"Please," Emilio whispers right before Luke hits him. "You can call my boss. He'll pay you to keep me alive."

Luke pauses. "Who the fuck is your boss?" he growls.

"Damien."

Luke's gaze whips to mine.

What the fuck?

How did one of Damien's men get membership access to my club?

Luke doesn't say another word. He whips the man over and over again, circling him. He strikes him from behind, from the side. On the head, the ass, over his dick. He's stopped screaming, and now the only sound is the crack of the whip against flesh that might as well be ground beef.

"He's dead," I say after a particularly brutal gash on the neck makes Emilio bleed out the rest of the way. "Luke."

But he takes one more lash before he drops the whip, heaving.

Luke turns to me.

"I'll send some of our men to take him to the grave-yard, but I'm not going with them. I need to get upstairs to Scarlett."

Under normal circumstances, Luke would *never* presume to tell me how anything was going to go, and he'd follow my instructions to the letter.

But tonight, he's my friend. My cousin.

"Did you see her?"

"On my way here," he confirms with a nod. "He fucked her up."

"He did. I assume you'll be keeping her with you?"

He nods again.

"Permanently?"

"Yeah. She's mine."

I smile at him. "Good. I like her. I was going to offer her an apartment here since she and Eloise are so close."

"She's with me," he says, shaking his head. "She doesn't need her own place."

"Understood." I clap my hand on his shoulder as we leave the room, and he looks at me with surprise.

No, I never initiate touch.

"Are *you* okay?" I ask.

"No, I'm pissed as fuck. Look, I get that she loves her job, but I'm not okay with anyone else touching her. I'm trying to be cool about it. I know I'm an asshole, and a piece-of-shit human, but she should have what she wants, even if it's fucking other men in the playroom. And I know that something like this won't happen again, but I don't want *anyone* putting their hands on her."

"I get it," I assure him. "I feel the same way about Eloise. Listen, Scarlett's going to be out of the game for a while. Given her injuries, she may not want to come back, and if that's the case, that's fine with me. But I might have a new position for her soon."

We step into the elevator.

"What position?"

"One that I need to make available first. I'll talk to Scarlett about it when she's ready. But she wouldn't be in the playroom anymore. Not like she has been."

Luke blows out a breath. "Here's to hoping that's what she wants."

I take out my phone and type in instructions to have Emilio's body disposed of and the cell cleaned.

When we reach Luke's floor, we step out of the elevator and find Michael standing guard at the door.

"They're inside." He sighs. "Boss, I tried to take Miss Lulu upstairs, but she basically told me to go fuck myself and refused to leave Scarlett. I stayed nearby and made sure they were safe."

I nod. And then smile. My girl is made of steel, and although I'd be furious at the *why*, I'm glad too. She needs that strength to be my girl and live in my world. "I should have known. Thank you. We've got it from here."

Michael nods and strides away.

"Your girl scares everyone," Luke informs me before he punches in the code to his door. "It's pretty impressive."

I chuckle and follow him inside, and what we find has my heart stuttering in my chest.

The two women are on the couch. Scarlett is held up with cushions, so her back isn't being crushed, and she's dead asleep.

Eloise sits beside her, facing her, brushing her fingers lightly through Scarlett's blond hair. She's crooning softly to her.

"You're so pretty," she says. "Everything's going to be okay. Our guys handled it. You just sleep now."

Yeah, baby. We fucking handled it.

I step closer, and my firefly turns her head toward me and smiles softly.

"Hi," she whispers. "Luke, come take over."

She gingerly stands, and Luke sits where she was and leans in to kiss Scarlett's head.

"I can come clean her wounds tomorrow," Eloise offers, but Luke shakes his head.

"I've got her," he says, but looks at my girl. "Thank you, Lulu. I owe you one."

"Nah. She's my friend. She'd do the same for me."

I pull her into my side and wrap my arm around her shoulders, bury my nose in her hair.

"Come on, firefly. It's time for you to go home."

"Yeah, let's go home. I'm hungry."

I look back to say goodbye, but Luke's focus has already shifted, and he's crooning to a sleeping Scarlett.

When Eloise and I walk into the penthouse, she kicks out of her shoes, then immediately walks into my arms, presses her head to my chest, and holds on tight.

"Holy shit," she says. Her voice is quivering.

"You held it together for her," I murmur, running my hands up and down her back. "You can let go, baby."

She sniffs against me. "That fucking sucked," she says, holding on tight. "Tell me you hurt him."

I kiss her cheek and her forehead. "We hurt him."

"Good."

I won't lie to her, but I also won't always give her all of the information. She doesn't need to know that we basically tore that son of a bitch apart. She's seen enough of it in her young life.

"I want to take self-defense classes," she informs me. "Do you offer them here?"

"This conversation took a turn I wasn't expecting." I tip her chin up so I can see her face. "I'm your self-defense, firefly."

"I know, but I think it would help my self-confidence. When the mayor touched me ..." I growl low in my throat, but she keeps talking. "I froze. I didn't like that."

"I'll make arrangements for you," I tell her and brush my knuckles down her soft cheek. "Did he mark you?"

"No, he was just *such* an asshole. What is it with men not taking no for an answer?"

"I've never had this issue in my club in the decade I've owned it," I confess to her. "And it's pissing me off."

I also suspect that it's Loveland's fault.

I'll deal with her tomorrow.

"You said you were hungry?" I ask her.

"Yeah."

"We could order in."

"I'm going to make mac 'n' cheese."

I grin at her. "That actually sounds really good. I have a box in the pantry, I think."

The way she turns her nose up at that is adorable.

"That's disgusting. Do you know how many preservatives are in that? No, babe, I'm making *real* mac 'n' cheese."

Babe.

I think that's the first time she's called me anything other than my name.

"Why do you look like that?" she asks.

"Like what?"

She tips her head to the side. "Gooey."

I laugh and take her hand, leading her to the stairs. "I'm *never* gooey."

Thirty-Eight

ROME

"I thought we were going to the kitchen," she says.

"We will. I need to do something first."

She doesn't ask any questions. Maybe she can feel the need coming from me. I lead her into the bedroom and immediately turn to her, unzip the back of her sexy-as-fuck dress, and let it pool around her feet.

She's in lacy black panties that make me growl low in my throat, and when my eyes find hers, they're wide and still full of anger, fear, and lust.

This woman feels *everything*.

How could her father hurt her? How could *anyone* want to hurt her?

"Come here." Without hesitation, Eloise steps forward and pauses in front of me. I love the trust she shows me every day. "Undress me."

She catches her bottom lip in her teeth and her little fingers unfasten the buttons on my black shirt, and when she's finished, her mouth opens on an audible inhale as her green gaze flows over my skin, eating up the ink in front of her.

"What is this for?" she asks, brushing her fingertip over the angel on my chest.

"My mom."

Her eyes fly up to mine, but she doesn't press for more. She leans in and presses a sweet kiss there, making my breath catch.

She's so fucking precious.

She unfastens my belt, then my pants, and when I'm standing before her in just my red boxers, she pauses.

"I'm not naked, firefly."

"I know." She takes a deep breath and lets it out slowly. "I'm just enjoying this. I like it very much that you let me touch you."

I reach out and push my fingers into her thick, dark hair. "I've come to crave your touch."

She steps into me, works her hands into my boxers, and nudges them over my hips and down my legs.

"Same," she whispers and drags her hands over my abs and up my chest. "I know you can be a brutal man, but you're only ever so good to me."

"That will never change." I frame her face and lower my lips to hers, gently brushing them back and forth before I remove the black lace from her body, then lift her and lay her on the bed. "I will never let you go, Eloise."

She smiles softly and pushes her fingers into my hair. "Good. I plan to stay right here. With you. For as long as you'll let me."

Forever. She's staying for-fucking-ever. That's what I mean when I say I'll never let her leave.

I nibble my way down her chest and over to each perfect breast. Her tits are magnificent. They fit in my hands like they were made for me, and her pink nipples pucker beautifully when I brush my tongue over them.

Her legs scissor, and her breath hitches, making me smile.

"I have to deny you one orgasm," I remind her. Her eyes snap open, and she stares at me in horror.

"I thought you were kidding."

With a wolfish grin, I shake my head. "I never joke about that. It's one of my favorite things."

"Making me suffer makes you happy?"

"Not suffer." I shake my head and kiss down to her navel. "Yearn." I kiss that belly button. "Need." Drag my tongue around it in a circle. "I want to push you right to the edge and bring you back down again."

"That sounds horrible."

I chuckle and spread her legs, opening her wide for me, and shake my head as I take her in. She's already so wet, her pink pussy swollen and practically begging me to fuck her.

"Christ, you're gorgeous."

I wrap my arms around her thighs, hold her down with one arm over her lower stomach, and *feast.*

Her back tries to bow off the bed, but I hold firm, and her hands immediately sink into my hair, holding on tight.

"Oh God," she moans.

I circle my tongue around her clit, and down through her lips, already swollen with desire. She's *so wet,* and I lap at her, wanting every single drop.

"Rome. God, I love it when you do that."

I know.

Pressing two fingers inside her, I look up and watch as her mouth opens and her bright emerald eyes meet mine.

"You're perfect," I tell her. "So fucking perfect."

The way she responds to me is unlike anything I've ever experienced. She doesn't go through the motions just for the sake of it. She's genuine. Her sounds, the way her body moves, everything is because she needs this, not because she's trying to impress me or wants something from me.

She's such a fucking breath of fresh air.

Her walls start to quiver around my fingers. Her thigh muscles tighten under my arms, and just as she's about to lose it, I pull away entirely.

She tries to cover herself with her own hand to get herself off, but I move fast, capturing her wrists and boost up over her.

"No."

"Rome—"

"No." Careful not to wrench her left shoulder, I press just her right arm over her head and the other one flat at her side, restraining her. "You'll come when I say you can come, Eloise, and not a second before. You're not in charge here."

She whimpers and lets out a shallow breath. "Can I at least touch you?"

"I don't know." I drag my nose down her jawline and kiss her neck, soaking her in. "Are you going to be a good girl?"

"Probably."

I huff out a laugh, then bite the fleshy part of her shoulder, but I release her left arm, and her hand immediately finds my side and drifts up and down.

My cock is heavy against her core, moving back and forth in her wetness, and her legs lift higher around my hips in invitation.

"You feel so good on me," she whispers sweetly, and that's all I can take. "And that piercing against my clit is *everything.*"

I grin against her neck and rub it over her nub again, making her gasp. But I need to be inside her.

I need her.

I reach between us to guide the head of my dick to her entrance, and I ease into her carefully, unwilling to hurt her.

There's a time and place for pain.

Tonight isn't it.

"Fuck, what are you doing to me?" I push all the way inside her and hold steady, trying to rein in my emotions. Tonight was a shitty night ... but this woman makes everything good.

Her heart is too good for my black soul.

But I know that I can never live without her. Now that I've had her, she's *mine.*

"Please, Rome." She pushes up to kiss my chest. "Please move."

I pull my hips back, sliding out to the tip, then slowly push back in again.

"Nothing can ever happen to you," I whisper.

"Nothing will happen," she assures me, bringing her hand to my face. "I promise."

Her hips move with mine, and we settle into a rhythm that feels so good, it shouldn't be real.

"Please, can I come?" She doesn't take her eyes away from mine as she asks. There's no way I'd deny her anything right now.

"Fall apart for me, firefly." I brush my lips across hers, then sink into her, and she tightens around me. Her arm, her legs, her pussy, all clench me to her, and she moans against my lips as she falls over the edge.

My spine tingles as my own climax works through me, filling her perfect pussy up with my release, and then I roll us to the side so I don't smother her as I hold her to me, cradling her close.

"Are you okay?" I drag my lips back and forth over her forehead and feel her sigh.

"I'm so okay." She breathes in deep and nuzzles against my chest. "Hungrier now than earlier."

Her stomach growls, making me grin.

"Let's clean up and go downstairs."

"Okay." But she doesn't move away. She tips her head back and smiles softly up at me. "You're ... *incredible.*"

Christ.

I kiss her nose and her forehead. "Come on. Before I can fuck you again, I need to feed you."

She grins and pulls away. "You have that backward. *I'm* going to feed *you*."

Before I can smack her ass, she rolls away and hurries into the bathroom. I stay right where I am and watch her go.

Because what a fucking view.

This woman. This kind, loyal, and sexy-as-fuck woman. I had no idea I *needed* her until she walked into my establishment with her bright smile and sweet heart. Her strength. *I love her strength.* I loved watching her care for Scarlett tonight, refusing to leave her side. *I love her loyalty.* I love that when confronted with something that unnerved her, she dealt with it, but then sought me out.

I love ... that she needs me. *Needs* me.

I'm in love with her.

Fuck.

I'm in love with Eloise.

Thirty-Nine

LULU

I've just set a pot of water on the stove to boil for the pasta, and I fetch a few blocks of cheese from the fridge so I can shred them and turn back to the island, where Rome is sitting, watching me.

He's only wearing a pair of black lounge pants. His torso is bare with all those delicious tattoos on full display just for me.

"Did you do that on purpose?" I ask as I set the shredder on a plastic cutting board.

"Do what?" he asks, his face void of any emotion at all.

I let my eyes move over his body, taking in the ink and his muscles and bite my lip because *damn*. When my gaze returns to his face, he's smiling at me.

"You did it on purpose," I confirm with a laugh. "Not that I'm complaining."

He leans his elbows on the counter and rests his chin

on his hands. "You're wearing my shirt, firefly. I didn't have a choice."

I glance down at the black button-up that I grabbed from his closet before coming downstairs.

"You have about a hundred more just like it. It's comfortable, and it smells like you." I pull the collar up to my nose and take a deep breath. "I could live in this thing."

"And I'll be fucking you in it before we go to sleep." God, the way he says the word *fuck* should be illegal.

It makes me want to just lie down and spread my legs for him. Right now, I want to circle this island, climb in his lap, and let him hold me.

Just hold me.

Because nothing feels better than being in Rome's arms, and after everything I went through tonight with Scarlett and the mayor, I could use some snuggles.

But first, we're hungry.

I lift an eyebrow and resume the task at hand. "Well then, maybe I should wear your clothes more often."

He smirks, and his eyes move down to my cleavage, which is clearly visible because I didn't button the shirt up all the way.

"Before this moment devolves into me bent over this countertop, I have questions for you," I tell him, and his eyes climb back to mine.

"You can ask me anything."

I reach for my water and take a drink, eyeing him. "You're mysterious. A little confusing."

"How so?"

"You're a major player in organized crime," I say as simply as if I'm saying that he sells used cars for a living, "and you likely kill people without a second thought. In my experience, men like you don't have soft spots."

"Is there a question in there somewhere?"

I laugh and start shredding some cheese. "How did you come to own the club? I can tell that it isn't simply a front for you. It's not just a way to do your nefarious business."

"*Nefarious.*" He hums. "I like that."

"You care about it," I continue. "You care about the people there. I could tell before, but after what happened to Scarlett tonight, it's more obvious than ever."

The humor leaves his eyes, and I wish I could take the words back. But I want to know. I'm falling in love with him, and I need to know what makes him tick. What makes him the man that he is.

I want to know everything, not simply how good he is in bed or how protective he is of me.

"If I answer questions, you answer questions," he says.

"That's fair. I'm down for that. Start talking."

"First, you're the only person in this world who can make demands of me. I want you to be aware of that. No one else *tells* me to do anything."

"Not even Carson, Julian, or Mateo?"

"We don't give each other orders," he says, shaking his head.

"Wow, I get to touch you *and* boss you around."

He blinks. "No. You can make requests, firefly."

I grin at him. "I know, I'm only kidding. Okay, please talk to me."

He takes in a breath and watches my hand run the cheese up and down the grater.

"My mom was a sex worker," he says at last, and that has me pausing, surprised. I don't know where I thought Rome came from, but I guess I assumed his family had a history in organized crime, like mine. "I don't know who my father was. Likely a john. She probably either couldn't afford birth control, or it simply didn't work."

I resume shredding, not wanting him to stop. His voice is level, matter-of-fact, and I can see he's not looking for pity. But I can also see this is a difficult conversation for him by the way he fists his hands on the counter.

"So she was a single mom," I say, reaching for another block of cheese.

"She was. And she was really good at it. I never wanted for much. Don't get me wrong, we were fucking poor. I wore a lot of secondhand shit. But I never missed school or a meal, and I knew she loved me. We had fun together. She wasn't a junkie or into drinking, but she was young. Only fifteen when she had me. She ran away from home because her father was an abusive piece of shit. I never met them."

"Doesn't sound like the kind of people you'd want in your life anyway." I turn to find the water at a rolling boil, and I pour the macaroni in, give it a stir, and turn back to the cheese.

"No. I never really knew what she did for a living. She worked mostly at night and had a neighbor stay with me while I slept."

"So she could have worked any kind of night job, as far as you were concerned."

"Exactly." He nods, and his shoulders relax as if he just now realizes I'm not judging his mother for her choices.

"Do you look a lot like her?" I ask.

He stands and walks to an end table in the living room. He opens a drawer and pulls out a framed photo, then brings it to me.

The woman smiling out at me is *gorgeous*. And yes, Rome looks so much like her. Those ice-blue eyes and dark hair. The skin tone. The smile that sets my soul on fire.

"She's beautiful," I say softly with a smile. "And you definitely favor her."

He nods and looks down at the photo, kisses it—my ovaries explode—then puts it away.

"She was murdered," he says, his voice gone cold, "when I was sixteen. Sex got too rough, and they fucking strangled her."

I set the cheese down and grip the edge of the counter, watching him.

"They threw her body into a dumpster because they were afraid of getting caught."

"Fuck," I whisper, shaking my head.

"Took three days before someone found her behind one of the resorts. So yeah, I care about the people who work for me and the members, too. Sex work shouldn't be scary. No one should worry about their safety. Many people do this for a living by choice, not because they *have* to, and I've given some of them a safe place to do that. I don't allow drugs here. Everyone is screened often for substances and STDs, and members are rigorously vetted. I do a lot of shitty things, Eloise. I kill people. Fuck, I killed two tonight alone. I print fake money, I run drugs and weapons, and aside from you, I don't give a fuck about much. But no one gets hurt in my club without me making it right."

I swallow and then walk over to him.

"She deserved someone like you looking out for her. I'm sorry there wasn't anyone back then." I place a gentle kiss on the ink on his chest that represents his mom. *You raised an amazing man.* His swift intake of breath is all the reaction I get, which is perfectly fine.

Heading back around the island, I pick up another block of cheese.

"What happened to you after your mom died? You were still a kid."

He nods. "I discovered, or the authorities did, that I had an aunt. My mom's sister. Luke's mom."

My eyes widen in surprise. "Luke's your cousin?"

He nods again. "I moved in with them. Luke's a couple of years younger than me. When I switched schools, I met Julian and Mateo, and we hung out pretty much all the time. Julian's dad was a crime boss, Greek, and the three of us went to work for him. Luke followed."

"Thank you for telling me all of that," I tell him. "And I'm sorry about your mom. I know how it feels to lose her."

He shifts on his stool. "What happened to yours?"

"You don't know?" I frown at him, surprised.

"Should I?"

I scoff at that and turn to wash my hands, gathering my thoughts. I check the pasta and see that it still has a few minutes to go.

"My father is a piece of shit," I say as I wipe my hands on a towel. "That's not news. I was about eight, and I heard him screaming at her. He did that a lot too. I think they'd gone to some wedding or party, and he was angry because he thought one of the capos was looking at her."

I shrug and grab some butter and milk out of the fridge.

"Maybe the capo *was* stupid enough to do that, who knows? I doubt it just because most of them seem to be scared of my father, but I wasn't there."

"And you were a child," Rome adds quietly. His arms are crossed over his chest, and he looks pissed as fuck.

"Was I ever really a child?" I wonder, tapping my finger on my lips. "Maybe, when I was a toddler. Anyway, whenever he'd go on one of these tirades, I'd usually hide in my room under the covers. But this time, my spidey senses were tingling, and I *knew* something horrible was going to happen. So I crept down the hall to the landing that overlooked the living room, and I knelt in the corner, making myself as small as I could."

I clear my throat and take another drink of water.

"The thing is, my mom wasn't like yours," I tell him, meeting his eyes. "She wasn't much better than my dad. I mean, she would hug me, and she never hit me or anything, but she wasn't a good human. I caught her fucking the gardener a couple of times."

He raises an eyebrow at that.

"She wasn't discreet. Maybe she wanted to get caught. Perhaps she knew that if she got caught, Dad would kill them both, and she saw that as the only way out of her shitty life."

"Maybe the capo *was* checking her out," he says.

"Probably." I blow out a breath and look at something over his shoulder, seeing what happened in my mind's eye. "But I'm quite sure she thought he'd put a bullet in her head and call it a day."

"That's not what he did."

"No." I shake my head and turn to drain the pasta. Not giving it time to cool, I pour it into a big bowl and start to fold the cheese in so it'll melt. "He tortured her. It was gross and painful. Horrifying."

"Please, Salvatore!" He laughs and hits her with the bat again, tearing open her scalp...

"And you sat there and watched."

"He knew I was there. At one point, he glanced up at me and smirked."

"That motherfucker."

God, his voice is hard and frightening. If that's the

last sound his victims hear before he kills them, they might die of fright before the bullet hits.

"He spread a rumor that another family kidnapped her and tortured her. Even had her body dumped somewhere and everything."

"How is it possible that you came from all of that, yet you're the sweetest, most amazing human on the planet?"

I bark out a laugh at that and finish stirring in the last of the cheese.

"I think you're biased."

"I'm not," he says. "I've seen so many shitty people in my life that there's no way I could count them. You're so *good*, Eloise. You're kind and gentle."

"Because I've been on the receiving end of the opposite of that all my life, and I won't ever do that to someone."

I dish us both up some dinner even though it's almost morning and pass him a bowl.

"But, Rome, I *can* be ruthless. I'm capable of hardness. I can feel it inside me sometimes. Like tonight. I hope the man who hurt Scarlett is one of the two you killed today because he doesn't deserve to breathe."

"He's no longer breathing," he confirms, watching me with those intense blue eyes. "Now, get over here, firefly."

I circle the island, and he pulls me to him, right between his legs, and holds his loaded fork up to my mouth.

I take the bite. "Mmm. That's actually really good."

Shoving some into his own mouth, he nods. "Excellent."

"Better than the box?"

He laughs and kisses my forehead. "Much better than the box."

Forty

ROME

Eloise whimpers next to me, waking me up. She's already in my arms, curled up against my side, but her beautiful face is puckered in a frown as if she's in pain or dreaming about something awful.

"It's okay, baby," I whisper and kiss her forehead softly, not wanting to wake her but needing to soothe her.

I check the time and drag my hand down my face. We've only been asleep for about four hours. We both worked last night, and I need to get down to my office now. I shouldn't have come up to bed at all, but I wanted to be close to her.

I needed her.

In the past week since Scarlett was whipped, Eloise and I have grown even closer while settling into a routine. It's completely unexpected. We work, we fuck, we talk, and we sleep. Not always in that order. I'm not a chatty man, and I don't confide in people. But with my firefly, the words just come. I don't shy away from her questions.

I trust her.

That puts me on edge, yet is also something I want to lean into. I know she comes from a piece of shit. Mateo and Julian are still wary, worried that she could be spying on my operation for her father.

But there's no way in hell.

Eloise settles into a sweet sleep once more, and I press my lips to her head before I ease out from under her and get dressed, then leave the penthouse and make my way down to my main office.

The building is mostly empty at this time of day. The cleaning crew is taking care of making sure everything is sanitized and ready for tonight. Employees won't start rolling in until around eight this evening.

But I asked Loveland to meet me at noon. I don't give a fuck if she's been to bed yet.

After that night a week ago, I wanted to fire her on the spot, but then I decided to sit back and watch her. I'd grown too complacent over the years where Loveland was concerned. That was my mistake.

One I won't make again.

I gave her specific, seemingly insignificant tasks to see to, and she didn't do even one of them. I told her I wanted a new policy implemented for new members. It hasn't been done. I asked for a list of names of any members who have received warnings in the past year. She hasn't delivered. It seems she believes that she can do whatever the fuck she wants around here, and she's going to pay for that.

I've just started looking through emails when there's a knock on the door, and Loveland walks into the office. She's still wearing the same white dress she wore for work last night.

"It's not like you to call a meeting so early in the day," she says as she sits across from me and crosses one long, thin leg over the other.

I lift an eyebrow and stare at her for a long moment until that casual, comfortable look in her eyes is replaced by fear.

"You've been running the playroom the way you see fit for a while now," I begin.

"I'm the manager," she says simply. "That's my job. To run it for you so you don't have to."

"To run it *for me*," I repeat and lean back in the chair, feigning relaxation. "To my specifications."

"Of course."

"To the letter."

She tips her head to the side. "Yes."

I nod and turn the laptop next to my desktop around so she can see the screen, watching her eyes as she takes it in.

"That's Mr. Deluca."

I don't say a word, waiting.

"He's a newer member," she continues. "We vetted him about three months ago."

"*We?*" My voice is granite, and she starts to breathe a little faster.

"Yes. Don't you remember him?"

"Oh, I remember him. But I didn't vet him, Sarah." I only use her first name when I'm pissed, when she's in trouble.

And once upon a time, when I fucked her.

Her pupils blow wide.

"This sack of shit hurt my girls." She squirms in her seat. "And you know it. I told you to revoke the membership and make sure he didn't come back."

"I did."

"Lie to me again." It's said in a challenge, and she bites her lip.

"Look, it was the spanking bench. I talked with Beth, and she said he didn't leave marks or break the skin."

I want to fucking rip her heart out of her throat.

"He ignored her safe word."

"He didn't hear it."

I slap my hand on the desk, making her jolt. "He. Ignored. Her. Safe. Word."

"We're all human," she says with a negligent shrug. "He fucked up and assured me he wouldn't do it again."

"That wasn't your call to make."

She starts to argue but then thinks better of it. Shutting her mouth, she glares at me.

"He came back a week later and whipped Scarlett so badly, she's still recovering."

"She should have used her safe word."

I lean forward, and with a menacing voice, I say, "She did."

I hit play, and the security footage from the playroom

starts to roll. Scarlett is tied to the cross, her face in view as Deluca whips her, and her face is a mask of horror, pain and terror.

Loveland swallows hard, but doesn't cave.

I make her watch every strike of the whip. By the time number fourteen is delivered, Loveland is sweating.

"Does that look consensual, Sarah?"

"I don't—"

I hit another key, and the next photo to pop up is what happened to Deluca when we were finished with him, and Loveland's eyes fall away.

"This is what happens when fuckers don't follow my rules."

I slam the laptop shut and stand, and she closes her eyes.

"What makes you think for even *one* second that you can run things your way, Sarah?"

"I made a bad judgment call," she says, her hands twisting in her lap. "Like I said, we're all human, and I made a mistake."

"Yes," I agree. "And according to Scarlett, who is still in enormous pain, thanks to you, when she requested you lower the music in the playroom so it's easier for members to hear each other talk, you laughed in her face and ignored her completely."

"Rome, the members haven't complained—"

"A member of *your* staff suggested something to change for the benefit of both staff and members alike, and you fucking ignored her."

"Rome—"

"You're done." Taking her by the hair, I pull her out of the chair. "You have six hours to pack your shit and get the fuck out of my building."

She spins, her mouth agape. "I don't have anywhere to go."

"I don't give a flying fuck. You're fired." I shove a stack of bills into her hands. "That's the last of your pay. I'll send two of my men up to make sure you're out in six hours."

"I can't find a new apartment in six hours, Rome."

I get in her face, my nose almost touching hers. "I DON'T GIVE A FLYING FUCK!"

She jumps, and then she backs up to my office doorway.

"Can I have twenty-four hours?"

"No. Get the fuck out."

I pick up my phone and call Luke.

"Don't you ever sleep?" he asks, his voice drowsy.

"Send two men to Loveland's apartment to make sure she packs her shit and is out by six. Not a minute more."

"Yes, boss."

He hangs up, and I sigh, rubbing my hand over my face.

I'm quite sure that piece-of-shit Deluca paid Loveland off. She's lucky I didn't take her to the cell and interrogate her.

And I'm glad she's gone.

Just as I'm about to head back upstairs, my phone rings with a call from an unknown number.

"Alexander," I growl into the device.

"Have you found my daughter?"

This motherfucker.

She's asleep in my bed, and I fucked her six ways to Sunday less than a half dozen hours ago.

"No," I reply, clipped. "My men haven't seen her."

"It's been more than a week since I asked you to handle it," he barks.

"Have you forgotten who you're speaking to?"

Rizzo clears his throat. "I'm sure she's in Vegas. I want her home. If your men can't find her, I'll send my own."

"If any of your men set foot in my city, I'll execute them."

"You'll never find them," he says. "They'll be in and out."

"Don't fucking push me, you sack of shit," I snap, but my voice is bland. "You're lucky we didn't kill you when you paid Julian back. I told you we'd be on the lookout for your kid, and if we see her, you'll be contacted."

I hang up and take a breath.

I can't wait to fucking kill him.

Forty-One

LULU

Ouch.

I moan as I turn over in bed and feel like my abdomen is being squeezed from the inside out.

Opening my eyes, I see that Rome is no longer in bed with me, and by the feel of the cool sheets, I'd say he's been gone for a little while.

I could use a hug.

Because I'm pretty sure I'm starting my period, and my periods *suck.*

I climb out of bed to go to the bathroom but stop short and stare in horror at the blood on the sheets. It looks like something out of a horror movie.

"Shit."

No.

No.

Fuck. I can't let Rome see that. He'll ... he won't like that at all.

"Eloise, what the fuck!"

Oh God.

"I'm sorry, Dad. I was just about the change the shee—"

Whack.

I double over in agony. I hate him. I hate him so fucking much.

"Clean this fucking mess up, you stupid, fat bitch."

Slap.

"I'm sorry," I whisper, grasping my cheek, which is no doubt as red as my soiled sheets.

I flinch, remembering my father's brutality.

It's over now, Lulu. You're safe now.

Taking a deep breath, I pad into the bathroom and see that I have blood on my legs and I'm leaving drops on the floor. I pick up the pace and use the toilet, rush to pull on panties and sweats, along with an oversized T-shirt, but I don't have any pads or tampons.

Maybe in my purse?

I scramble downstairs for my handbag and open it, rummaging around, but come up empty-handed.

My last period ended the day before I left my father's house, and it didn't occur to me to get supplies.

"Rome?" I call out, in case he's in his office or somewhere else in the penthouse, but it's still.

He's not here.

And I absolutely *refuse* to ask one of his foot soldiers to go to the pharmacy for me. No. Definitely not.

I can get it myself, but I'd better hurry because I'll bleed through my clothes quickly.

I know from experience.

I'm the girl with embarrassing period stories from high school.

Lucky me.

With my bag slung across my body, I slip my feet into the flip-flops I have by the front door, unlock it, and step out.

"Miss?" the guard asks.

"Hey. I'll be right back. There's no problem."

He watches me for a second, then nods. I hurry to the elevator.

I say the same thing to a couple more guards. The pharmacy is just down the block. I'll be back before anyone knows that I'm gone. Hopefully, the pharmacy has a restroom I can use while I'm there. Otherwise, I might alarm the guards when I return with blood on the crotch of my sweats.

I shiver at the thought and push outside into the sunshine. I take a deep breath of fresh air, and it occurs to me that I haven't been out of Rome's building since he brought me here from that shitty motel.

To be fair, the building I live in is massive, with everything I could need or want right there. Restaurants, coffee, the spa, the gym, my job, and my home are all packaged up nice and tidy in that building, and I kind of love it.

But I need fresh air and sunshine. This feels good, and if it didn't feel like my uterus was trying to plan a coup to escape my body, I'd be damn happy.

I make my way down the block, my face turned up toward the sun. It's quiet on the streets of Las Vegas at this time of day. It's just after noon, and I assume most of the tourists are sleeping off last night's shenanigans in their hotel rooms. A few people walk past, but very few. And I have to admit, it's nice. Much like the week I've had.

Rita, the most understanding boss in the world, was so understanding when I went back in for my next shift. I felt like I'd let her down, leaving her high and dry in the middle of a shift to take care of Scarlett, but thankfully, she was good about it. Her concern for Scarlett was genuine and empathetic, and it made me like her even more.

Max, understanding Rome and I are a couple has backed off with his flirting—probably a wise choice given who my man is. Work is ... fun. Challenging, and for the most part, an awesome experience.

Each day, I've made sure that Rome's men are fed, much to his chagrin. But I know from the way he kisses me—hard—as he thanks me that he's quietly happy with how I care about his men. After feeding them, I've spent time with Scarlett.

Her dressings are changed regularly, but she's still in so much pain. I don't envy that. I now know what her comfort foods are and which movies are her faves. Rita even joined us one afternoon on her rare day off to watch *Sweet Home Alabama*. She's like a protective older sister, which is something I've never had.

It's almost like I've found a brand-new family. Not to

mention, a gorgeous, sexy man, who I'm falling in love with.

I've never been happier. I've never felt safer.

I walk into the pharmacy and make a beeline for the feminine products with a basket. I choose a couple of boxes of what I need, then walk down the pain reliever aisle, grab my favorite bottle, and stop by the seasonal candy.

Armed with all my supplies, including chocolate bars and nacho-flavored corn chips, I approach the checkout.

Once I've paid for everything, I cringe at the exhausted-looking woman who just took my money.

"Can I use your restroom?" I ask her and point at the tampons. "It's an emergency."

"I'm not supposed to let you," she says, "but I get it. Been there. Sure, it's through that back door and immediately to the right."

"Thank you." My shoulders sag in relief as I gather my bag and hurry to the back of the store.

I'm going to go back to the penthouse, stay in bed all day, and read a book.

ROME

I'm going to curl up around Eloise and breathe her in. I have a call out to Julian, Mateo, and Carson to figure out how and when we can take Rizzo out.

I want him dead.

But first, I want him to suffer.

In the meantime, I need to touch my firefly.

I approach the penthouse, nod at the guard, and walk inside. It's quiet. She's still asleep.

Good.

My woman works her ass off. Rita told me just yesterday that she's never seen anyone work harder than my Eloise, so I'm glad she's still sleeping soundly.

I strip out of my suit coat but come to an abrupt halt in the doorway of the bedroom, and my heart rate climbs.

Blood.

There's blood on the sheets.

"Eloise!" I call out and run for the bathroom, but she's not in there.

There are drops of blood on the floor.

Panic wants to set in, but I ruthlessly push it back and rush back to the bedroom as I dial Eloise's number. Her phone starts to ring beside the bed.

She doesn't have her motherfucking phone?

I run out of the bedroom and check every room, coming up empty, and then, with red fury covering my eyes, I pull my gun and step out of the penthouse, take the guard by the throat and push the weapon against his temple.

"Where. The. Fuck. Is. She?"

"She said she'd be right back," he says, his eyes round. "I thought she was going to find you."

I growl. "When did she leave?"

"Maybe ten minutes ago? She seemed fine. Said she'd be right back."

"Was someone with her?"

He frowns. "No. Of course not."

I push him away and call Luke as I rush to the elevator.

"Yes, boss?"

"My office. NOW!"

Luke's running to my office as I get there.

"Eloise is gone," I say, and type quickly on my computer, bringing up the security feeds. "She was bleeding. I don't know where she went."

"She didn't let you know—got it," he says when I glare at him.

We both watch Eloise make her way through the building. She looks tired. Like she doesn't feel good. At one point, her hand is over her stomach, yet every guard she comes across, she smiles, and says she'll be right back.

"Where the fuck did she go?"

In horror, I watch as she waltzes right out the fucking front door.

"Every one of those men is going to die."

"Boss—"

I punch the heel of my hand on the desktop and stand.

"Why didn't she have a four-man detail with her?" I demand, getting in Luke's face.

"Because we didn't know she was going anywhere," he replies calmly. "She's supposed to text, and the guys meet her at the door. She knows that. It's her protocol. Not that we've ever had to use it because she doesn't go anywhere."

"I want every man we have to meet me in the penthouse so I can give orders. I'll be up there in case she comes back."

Luke nods and starts making calls. Less than five minutes later, I'm standing in the foyer of my home, barking orders.

Every guard who let her leave looks green.

They should.

This will be their last mission.

"She's been gone for twenty minutes," I say, pacing back and forth. I can't even think about the blood upstairs without wanting to lose my goddamn mind.

Christ, she has to be okay. "She's injured. I don't know how badly."

"Did someone call her?" Luke asks, frowning. "Why would she leave if she's hurt?"

I blink at him, then sprint upstairs to get her phone. Why didn't I think of that?

Unlocking her phone, I look back on her call log and texts, but it's only myself and Scarlett there. Nothing in her deleted box.

Dammit.

Shaking my head, I return downstairs and slip her phone into my pocket, needing something of hers on me.

I need her. I'm going out of my fucking mind. I've never felt this helpless, this goddamn scared in my life.

"No calls," I tell Luke, who looks as grim as I feel. "I want you all to canvas the area. She can't have gotten far."

"Unless she jumped in a cab," one of the men says, and I rub my hand over my mouth.

Christ.

Where the fuck did she go?

I feel like I'm about to lose control when the mechanism on the front door engages. The door opens, and Eloise steps inside.

She stumbles to a halt when she sees all of the men. Her eyes go wide as they search for me, and when she finds me, her shoulders sag in relief.

"Oh good, you're okay," she says.

I gnash my teeth together.

"Out!" I shout, my eyes pinned to hers as my men file out, with Luke being the last to leave. He pulls the door closed behind him, and it's just Eloise and me, staring at each other.

"Have you lost your beautiful mind?" My hands fist at my sides. I want to rush to her, kiss the fuck out of her, and pull her to me.

I also want to spank her ass until it fucking glows.

"I had to go to the pharmacy," she says, frowning as she swallows. She winces.

"What happened? If you're hurt, you call me, and we take care of it."

For the first time since she walked in, I notice the bag in her hands.

"Don't go upstairs," she says, shaking her head. "Just stay down here, okay?"

"Too late. Do you know how fucking terrified I was? What the fuck happened?"

"Stop yelling at me."

"No!"

I stomp away from her and will my heart to calm the fuck down. She's fine. She's safe.

Her father doesn't have her.

"I have to change my clothes," she says. "I'm a mess. I wasn't fast enough."

"Fast enough for what, Eloise?"

She shakes her head and moves for the stairs, and I follow her. I want to touch her. I want to keep her right next to me every minute of every day to make sure she doesn't slip away again.

"Rome, this is embarrassing. Let me be alone in here."

"Absolutely fucking *not.*" I follow her in, and my gut roils at the sight of the blood on our bed. "What happened, baby? Why are you bleeding?"

"Because I'm a woman!" She spins and stares at me like I'm stupid. "You've fucked me bare like a rabbit, but there were no takers, and I started my period, and it fucking *hurts*, Rome. I didn't have even one tampon to my name, and I was *not* going to ask someone else to get them for me. I had to go to the pharmacy!"

Jesus. Christ.

"I was bleeding like a goddamn faucet, and I had to hurry. And I wasn't fast enough not to ruin my underwear and these sweats, and I need to change because it's gross, and then I'm going to order in food and change the bed so I can just lay there all day and wish I was dead. Okay?"

I walk to her and yank her to me, crushing her against my chest. "No. It's not fucking okay. You *never* leave this building without a guard with you. Never, firefly."

"I was gone for twenty minutes, and I don't want your goons watching me pick out pads and chocolate. That's too intimate."

I kiss the top of her head and breathe her in. "Then I'll go with you. But you won't do that to me again. Do you hear me?"

"Rome." She sniffles, and it's almost my undoing.

"Don't cry."

"I love that you're holding me and not yelling anymore, but I *really* need the bathroom and to change my clothes. A shower. Please."

"Christ, you scared me." I kiss her once more and let her go. "Go handle what you need to. I'll take care of the bed."

"No!" She shakes her head almost frantically. "I'll do it. Please don't."

"Hey, I've seen blood before, you know. Although, this gave me a bad moment that I don't want to repeat, knowing that it's yours."

"Please. I'll change them. I'll take care of it."

I take her face in my hands and frown down at her. "Baby. It's okay. The bed, not you leaving."

She tries to shake her head, and *now* her eyes are full of fear.

"Why are you scared?"

She licks her lips. "Bad things happen when you ruin the bedsheets."

He's going to suffer so fucking badly.

"Not in our house, firefly." I kiss her forehead gently, keeping my hands tender as I hold her face. "You're safe here, remember?"

She nods. "Okay. I need the bathroom."

I release her, and she hurries to the closet, gathers clean clothes, and then disappears into the bathroom. She shuts the door, and I hear the water start.

I blow out a breath.

Fuck.

I don't want to repeat that. She just took ten years off my already short life.

I turn to look at the bed, and my stomach clenches again. I strip the sheets off the mattress and throw them away, then find a clean set in the linen closet and dress the bed. I'm just pulling the pillowcase onto the pillow when the door opens, and Eloise walks out, her eyes on the bed. Her shoulders slump.

"I'm so sorry."

"Come here."

She walks right into my arms and clings to me. "I didn't think about taking anyone with me. I just didn't want someone to go *for* me. Definitely not. And I knew the pharmacy was just down the block, and I would be fast."

I interrupt her by tilting her chin up and kissing her gently on the lips. "I know, firefly. But just because it's embarrassing for you doesn't mean it's not dangerous. Remember the world you're now part of because of being with me."

She nods.

"I didn't think it was a big deal. Nothing's happened with my father or his men in a while."

She doesn't know.

"Do you want to rest in here or down on the couch with the TV?"

"Downstairs for now."

I pick her up and carry her, and she doesn't giggle. She doesn't argue. She just curls up against me and wraps her arms around my neck.

"Baby, you really don't feel good."

"I know it's not sexy. I just have horrible periods. I always have. With everything that's happened since the last one, I wasn't counting the weeks, and it snuck up on me."

I gently set her on the couch, but I sit in the corner and guide her between my legs, so she can lean back on my chest. I drape my arm down her torso, between her breasts, to rest on her stomach.

"Is this okay?"

"Yeah, it's warm, and that feels good. Well, shit."

"What?"

"I forgot to buy a heating pad. I'll just—"

"You won't go anywhere," I growl into her ear. "I'll get you a fucking heating pad."

She relaxes against me. "Thank you. I didn't mean to make everyone fuss. Why were your guys here when I got home?"

I turn her so I can look into her eyes. "They were here because I was arranging a goddamn search party for you, Eloise."

"What? Why?"

"You don't get it. Because you *left*. There was blood upstairs, you were nowhere to be found, and you didn't have your phone. I was out of my fucking mind."

She cups my cheek. "I'm sorry. I forgot my phone. I just needed to take care of it."

"*Always* call me. Always. Even if you're on your way out the door, you call me. And text for your protection detail. Promise me, Eloise."

"I promise." She sighs. "It was nice to get some fresh air, though. I hadn't realized that I hadn't been outside in like two weeks."

"We have a rooftop area," I inform her and kiss her head. "You can go up there whenever you want."

"Oh, I like that." She yawns. "I'm so damn tired. I'd better nap if I'm going to work tonight."

"You're not."

She snorts. "Yes, I am. I can work. I'll just take some meds."

"No."

She starts to argue, so I turn her around to lie on me, stomach to stomach, and I take her chin in my fingers.

"Listen very carefully. I own this business. You're miserable. You will *not* work tonight. You'll stay here, and you'll rest."

She sighs and bites her lower lip, but I pull it back out with my thumb.

"I don't like calling out sick," she admits. "This is my first real job, and I want to do well. I want Rita to know that she can count on me."

I kiss her lips lightly. "She knows that already. And she'll understand. We have one more thing to discuss."

"Okay."

"I want to put a tracking device in you."

Her eyebrows climb to her hairline. "What? What the hell do you mean *in me?*"

"It's subdermal," I reply and brush my thumb under her eye, over the dark circles there. "And that way, if *anything* ever happened, I could find you."

"That feels a little unhinged, Rome."

I simply lift an eyebrow. "It'll make me feel more at

ease. I would have known exactly where you were when I was losing my shit earlier."

"It'll hurt."

"Yes." I kiss her nose. "I'll try to make it as painless as possible for you, but it won't be comfortable."

"Will the doctor do it?"

I shake my head. "No. I will."

She chews that pillow of a bottom lip. "I have one condition."

I'm not used to being questioned. "What?"

"You have to have one, too. Of the two of us, you're the one doing dangerous shit. If you can see where I am, I need to know where you are. If you won't agree to that, then it's a no-go for me."

This woman. God, I love her.

If anyone else demanded something of me, I would have glared so hard that they would have run from me. But not this woman.

"I need to know where you are."

For her ...

"I'll do it."

Her eyes flash with surprise.

"You will?"

"I'll do pretty much anything for you, firefly. Now, settle in and get some rest."

Eloise lies down, her head on my chest, and snuggles in. "If you don't want to be trapped under me while I sleep, you should move now."

"I'm not letting you go, baby." *I love you too much to*

ever let you go. I kiss the top of her head and wrap my arms around her. "Just sleep."

Forty-Three

LULU

"I don't think Luke told you to kill me," Scarlett says, glaring at Mateo from the floor where she's flat on her back, chest heaving from exertion.

"I didn't kill you." Mateo offers her a hand and pulls her to her feet. "You didn't stop me from pushing you down."

"This is only our third lesson," she reminds him.

"And you're going to learn this. If someone gets you flat on your back like that, they can do whatever they want to you. Kill you. Rape you. *Anything.*" Mateo narrows his eyes at me, and I know I'm up next, and *dammit.*

He's brutal.

Mateo is also sexy as all get-out. With all that dark hair and dark eyes, the tattoos, the sheer size of him.

He's massive.

And so strong. There's no way I would ever win in a fight with this man.

Thank God I'm finally over my period, and I don't feel so damn fragile, but still. I'm a total wimp compared to this man.

"Come on, Lu," Mateo says, reaching for my left arm and tugging me onto the mat.

We're in a private room down in the gym, with lots of mats and mirrors and plenty of space to move around.

I feel so clumsy doing this. Scarlett is graceful and lean, and she may not know what she's doing, but she looks good while she's doing it.

Me?

I look like a giant marshmallow getting slung around.

"This is *so* not sexy," I grumble as I join him on the mat.

Mateo's dark eyes go hard and narrow on me. "We're not here to be fucking *sexy*. We're here to work."

"Don't get pissy with me," I counter and watch his jaw flex. "I'm just saying I feel self-conscious. Because I'm fat, and I don't move quickly, and I look ridiculous."

"For the last time," Scarlett says, her eyes on the ceiling, "you're *not* fat! You're curvy. And we both feel like we look ridiculous because we suck at this. Now, stop getting all up in your head and kick his ass."

Mateo smirks but continues to watch me.

"Fine." I blow out a breath. "What do I do?"

He doesn't answer. He advances on me way faster than a man his size should and wrenches my left arm behind my back, and I immediately cry out as the pain sears through me.

Mateo's hands release me, and I cradle my left arm to me.

"Fuck," I whisper as I try to rub the pain out of the joint.

"What the hell was that?" Mateo demands.

"I've had my shoulder dislocated more times than I can count." I shake my head and try to shake it off. "But any asshole who's trying to kill me won't feel bad for me and go for the right one instead, so don't hold back."

"Fuck that," Mateo says, scowling. "Who fucking did that to you?"

"My piece-of-shit father," I bite out and watch Scarlett's face go white. "He liked to hurt me, if you must know. Bruise me. Break me. But his favorite was wrenching this shoulder out of joint as often as he could. So yeah, that hurts, but I'll get over it. Now, try to kick my ass because just thinking about that piece of shit pisses me off, and now I want to fight back."

But he doesn't move toward me. He's watching me, his arms crossed over his chest.

"You hate him."

"With every cell in my body," I confirm and mirror his stance by crossing my arms. "I hope his death is long and painful. And soon. And I hope I get to watch."

He tilts his head to the side. "So you're really not trying to fuck Rome over by spying on him for your father?"

I blink at him, positive I heard him wrong.

"What the fuck did you just say?"

But he doesn't say it again, and the blood in my veins turns to fire.

"Fuck you," I say, moving toward him. "You think I would hurt Rome for a man who not only liked to hurt me but also enjoyed making me watch him torture the people he killed? Watched him hack them up and make them scream and beg and spit and piss themselves? The man who killed my mother viciously in front of my own eyes? You can go to hell because Rome is the first man in this world to show me even an ounce of kindness, tenderness, and gentleness. To make me feel safe."

My hand flies up to hit Mateo across the face, but he blocks me and holds my wrist in his hand, watching me carefully.

"Okay," he says while I continue to pant through my rage. I hear Scarlett sniffle behind me. "I'm going to come at you from behind, and I want you to get out of my hold."

I'm startled by the change of subject, but when I really look at Mateo, I see a change in his face. He doesn't look mad at me like he always has. He's not happy. In fact, he's still pissed, but it's not at me. This is the look of a man who hates my father with the same level of contempt as me. Who believes me.

Who will defend me.

So I turn my back on him, and when he advances on me, wrapping his arm around my neck, I fight to get free, but it's no use. I can't get him to budge, and his bulging bicep is choking me out.

"You're too strong," I tell him, sounding defeated to my own ears.

"You can always get free," he says, talking to us both now. "Remember to go for the eyes, the throat, the balls, and the knees."

He spends time showing us what to do. Over and over again, he shows us moves to help us get out of his hold.

Scarlett masters the crush to the knees.

And I finally manage to poke him in the eye.

I preen when he barks out and releases me, holding his hand over said eye.

"You're not supposed to actually blind me," he growls, but I smile.

"That's for saying that I would do something to hurt Rome. It bruised my feelings."

Scarlett giggles, and Mateo blinks at me, scowling.

"If I do find out that you're a snitch, you'll wish you were dead."

I roll my eyes. "Okay, bad guy."

"I *am* a bad guy," he replies. "And Rome is my brother. Hurt him, and we'll kill you. Painfully."

"I get it. My dad's a mobster, remember? Now, when are you going to give us shooting lessons?" Even though I know how to use a gun, it's not a bad idea to sharpen those skills.

"That's Carson's job. He'll take you this afternoon."

"So basically, the Kings of Vegas are teaching us self-defense," Scarlett says with a frown. "I didn't have that on my bingo card, but I'm not mad about it. Also, how is this my life?"

"You're Luke's," Mateo says with a shrug. "And she's Rome's. You're stuck with us."

Scarlett looks at me, and I grin at her. "Not a bad problem to have."

Forty-Four

ROME

"Goddammit," I grumble, watching security footage of one of my warehouses east of the city. Someone raided it last night, took my product, and set the whole thing on fire, killing six of my men and getting away with about five million dollars of my weapons.

I've watched it at least a dozen times, trying to see if I can make out the men who did it, their vehicles, *anything*, but they avoided the cameras as if they had inside information on where every camera is in the area.

And that pisses me off most of all.

"You look way too moody. And still, super hot."

I glance up at the sound of that sexy voice and find Eloise standing in the doorway of my office in the penthouse. She's leaning on the doorjamb, her arms crossed, in a pair of jeans that hug her delicious curves and a red tank top that gives me a view of her cleavage that makes me want to get her naked and sink inside her.

I haven't fucked her since the morning she started her period a few days ago. She was miserable, but she seems to be feeling better now.

"Come sit on my cock and cheer me up, firefly."

She smirks and pushes off the door, walking to me. "I wish I had time, but I'm headed down to Scarlett's. We're going out to lunch, but don't freak out, we're not leaving the property. We're just headed over to that cute diner on Carson's side of the resort. I hear they have good food."

"You're still taking guards with you." I take her hand and tug her into my lap, bury my face in her neck, and breathe her in. "You smell fucking amazing. How was training with Mateo?"

Eloise chuckles and kisses me on the temple. She pushes her fingers into my hair and snuggles me close.

"Fucking hard," she says. "He's trying to kill me."

"I think that's the point. You said you wanted to learn self-defense. Mateo is the best." He's a Krav Maga master, and he's agreed to teach Eloise and Scarlett how to fight for their lives if needed.

"He's the best, yes, and he's trying to kill us. But it's kind of fun, too. Scarlett and I went our separate ways to shower off all the sweat, and now we're heading out to eat. We're starving."

"Be careful," I say against her neck as I slide my hands under her shirt and let them drift over her soft-as-fuck skin. "If anything happens to you, no one in this world will survive my wrath."

"Careful is my middle name." She kisses me again, and it's like a balm to my soul. "It's just lunch, Rome.

Then I'm coming back here to bake some cookies before Carson takes us to target practice."

"Chocolate chip."

She leans back so she can look me in the eyes and brushes her fingers down my cheek. "Is that a request?"

"Yes." I lightly push a dark strand of hair back from her face and hook it behind her ear. "How is Scarlett feeling?"

"Much better. It's been almost two weeks, and she seems to be healing well. Physically, anyway. I don't know if she'll want to go back to work in the playroom. I know that's none of my business, but—"

"It's your business," I assure her and kiss her softly. "I'll talk with her later, now that she's feeling stronger. I'll have Luke send two guards with you to lunch."

"You're so paranoid."

You have no idea, firefly.

"One of my warehouses was hit last night," I tell her, and her eyes darken in concern. "I don't know who's behind it. So until further notice, yeah, I'm paranoid as fuck, and you'll do what I say."

"Yes, Rome." She kisses my lips, and my cock twitches.

"I'll be putting your tracking device in later today, too."

Her eyes narrow on mine. "Who's doing yours? I can't do it. I hate needles."

"Already done." I take her hand, kiss her fingers, and place them on the back of my neck. "Feel right there."

She gently moves her fingertips over my skin, and when she discovers it, she bites her lower lip. "It's tiny."

"Give me your phone."

She shifts to pull the device out of her pocket and passes it to me. It only takes a moment to download the app and sync it with the tiny capsule, the size of a grain of rice, in my neck.

"Here it is." I turn the screen to her and show her how to check it. "That blue dot is me. When yours is active, it'll be yellow."

"Why yellow?" she murmurs, watching the screen.

"Because fireflies are yellow."

She smiles softly, then wraps her arms around my neck and hugs me hard. "Thank you. We'll do it before I make the cookies."

"Deal." I wrap my hand around her throat and pull her in for a deep kiss. She opens for me, letting me in to glide my tongue over hers, and all too quickly, she's gone, climbing out of my arms. "Get back here."

"I have to go," she says with a smile. "Scarlett's waiting. I'll text you to let you know I'm okay if you want."

She bites that lower lip, and her words hit me right in the chest.

My girl wants to make sure I'm okay.

"That would be appreciated," I tell her with a small smile. "Thank you, firefly."

"No problem." She winks, and then she's off. I watch that round ass sway as she walks away.

Christ. I'll never stop wanting her.

I call Luke, and when he answers, I hear giggling in the background and pinch the bridge of my nose.

"Hey, boss."

"Eloise is on her way to meet Scarlett. I want two men with them everywhere they go."

"Already on it," he says. "But I assigned four."

"Good."

I hang up, and less than five minutes later, my phone chimes, telling me there's someone at the front door. I check the video feed and see it's Julian, so I unlock the door from my desk. A few moments later, he walks through my office door.

"I'm the first one here," he says with surprise as he takes a seat across from me, and I blow out a breath.

Fuck, I'm tired.

He eyes me. "What's wrong? Aside from the warehouse hit last night?"

"We need to talk." I lean on my desk and drag my hand down my face. "About Elliott."

Julian's eyes narrow slightly. "So talk."

"Shit." I shove back in my seat. I don't want to have this conversation.

"Just tell me what he did now."

"He's six months behind in his membership fees with the club," I reply. Julian doesn't foot the bill for Elliott's ... hobbies.

"I'll pay it," he says, and I shake my head.

"I don't need or want you to pay it," I tell my best friend. I don't ask for membership dues from any of my three brothers. "I told you before that I would waive the fee for him."

"No. He has the means to pay himself. If he wants the privilege of the club, he'll pay for it. Christ, he's almost twenty-five years old."

Julian married very young, at the age of just eighteen, and his wife had Elliott right away. Then she died in a hit-and-run car accident. Julian raised his son alone with the help of housekeepers, all while building his own business. He's done a hell of a job, but Elliott is an entitled jerk.

We all know it.

And Julian cleans up after him often.

"I just wanted you to be aware because he's still using the club. And typically, we wouldn't be this ... lenient."

"I get it," Julian replies just as my phone pings again, letting me know the others are here. I push the button, and within seconds, Carson comes walking through the door with Mateo right behind him.

Mateo smirks at me.

"Your girl almost poked my fucking eye out earlier."

The grin spreads over my face. *Good girl.*

"You probably deserved it."

He shrugs one shoulder and leans on the windowsill, crossing his arms over his chest.

"I get to take them to the range in the basement later," Carson says. "It won't be a hardship to show two beautiful women how to hold a weapon."

"Don't make me kill you."

Carson laughs, and then I get right to the point.

"A few things," I say as the men settle around me. "First, I was hit last night, as you know."

"Inside job," Carson says. "I've watched the feed a few times. They knew to avoid the cameras."

"Mendoza's been sniffing around," Mateo offers. "He's pissed as fuck at you."

"He should be. It could be him. If he's in Vegas, he doesn't leave alive. He's been warned."

"What about Rizzo?" Julian asks. "He called me pissed off because we haven't found his precious daughter."

Mateo smirks. "Same here."

Carson's eyes meet mine.

"Did he call you as well?" I ask Carson.

"No. He doesn't have my fucking number."

"Well, he called me," I reply. "And he's pissed. He sounds desperate, and I don't know why. He's not worried about her."

"He's a fucking asshole," Julian supplies. "And I hear your bartender slipped away the other day for a while. Was she meeting with his men?"

I glare at him, and for a moment, I seriously consider pulling my weapon on him. Which is something I never thought I'd ever say. This man is my *brother* in every way that counts.

But I've had just about enough of this bullshit.

"Say shit like that again, and you and I are done."

"It's a fair question," Julian says.

"No."

Julian opens his mouth, but I slap my fist on the desk.

"No."

Forty-Five

LULU

"Hey, babe," Scarlett says as she opens the door of the apartment she now shares with Luke. The day after the incident in the playroom, Luke had all of her things packed up and moved in here, and she's been here ever since. It was actually really romantic, and I know that it made Scarlett feel good. "Come on in. I just have to put my hair up."

She turns to walk to the island in the kitchen and grabs a hair tie off the counter.

"How are you feeling today? Especially after that workout."

She glances at me and shrugs a shoulder. "Itchy. I'm healing, and the skin is a little itchy. But I'm not sore anymore. I'm mostly pissed off that that asshole had the goddamn nerve to hurt me like that. Luke told me that he and Rome took care of him, and I never thought I'd say this, but *good.*"

"I agree with you," I reply and pull her in for a hug.

"Oh, crap, I forgot my phone up at the penthouse. I'll just run up and grab it real quick. Do you want to meet in the lobby?"

"Sure. I have to use the bathroom again anyway. See you in ten?"

"Perf. Sorry about that."

"Don't even worry about it."

I hurry out the door, smile at my guards, and head to the elevator. Two follow me, and two stay behind for Scarlett.

"Forgot my phone," I tell them, and they just nod.

These two aren't particularly chatty, but that's okay. I don't have much to tell them.

I unlock the penthouse door with my palm and push inside. It sounds like Mateo, Julian, Carson, and Rome are in his office, but I don't want to interrupt.

Where did I leave my phone?

I know I had it when I said goodbye to Rome, but where did I go then? *Bedroom?*

As I head upstairs, I consider the tracker. I'm not sure what I feel about having a tracker inside me, but I can trust Rome on that one. Like I trust him with everything in my life, it seems. The fact that he was instantly happy to have one put in his neck, though? That level of ... trust and loyalty still surprises me.

It's no wonder I love that man.

Is it too early to tell him I love him? Not that I've ever been in love before, but surely a few weeks is far too soon, right? Maybe soon, if it feels like the right time.

Finding it on the end of the bed where I left it, I turn

to leave again, and consider waving at Rome, letting him know I popped in.

But as I veer toward his office, I hear someone say a name that sends shivers down my spine.

"I've heard rumors that Rizzo is working with Adam Damien."

I stop cold in the doorway. My feet won't move.

Christ.

I shake my head as Rome's gaze flicks up to mine, and he narrows his blue eyes.

"I won't go back."

"Come here, Eloise."

"No." I shake my head and take a step back in retreat. "I'll leave ... and you'll never find me."

Forty-Six

ROME

Just hearing her say those words makes my blood boil and bile rise in the back of my throat.

She's shaking her head, her throat working as she tries to swallow, and I'm up and across the room, pulling her into my arms before she can say anything else.

"I just wanted my phone," she says against my chest. "I f-f-forgot it. I didn't mean to—"

"Breathe, firefly." I pick her up and carry her into the office, not at all concerned with her hearing the conversation. "I told you that you could come in here whenever you wanted. You didn't do anything wrong."

"Please don't send me back."

"That's never going to happen."

Julian stands, and I set her down in the chair he vacated and glance at my brothers, all of whom look concerned. Her whole body is trembling, and the fear in her eyes reminds me of when we first found her.

What in the hell is going on?

"I won't marry him," she says, biting her lip.

"Who?" I ask, brushing the tears from her cheeks.

"Adam Damien."

I quickly share a look with the others.

"Is that who your father arranged for you to marry?" Julian asks, keeping his voice calm.

Carson looks like he wants to put his fist through the wall and likely kill someone.

"Yes. That was the name." She takes a deep, shaky breath. "I don't know who that is, but that's the name. And I won't do it. So if you're planning to send me back so I'm out of the way and my father can form some sick alliance with that guy, I'll just pack my things and go."

"Stop." I can't hear another word about her leaving me. I tug her out of the chair, sit in it, and pull her onto my lap, not giving two shits that the other three are sharing looks of surprise. "You're mine, and you're not going anywhere. I'm sorry that what you overheard scared you, but it had nothing at all to do with you, firefly."

"But I don't want to cause problems for you." She bites her lip and looks up at me. "If keeping me here is dangerous, if it puts you in danger, I need to go. I can't ... you can't be in danger because of me."

"We've got this covered, pretty bartender," Carson says with a lazy smile. "Don't worry about us."

"I know you don't all like me, and that's okay, but—"

"Who doesn't like you?" I ask with a scowl.

"Maybe that's the wrong word. *Trust.* You don't all trust me. But I do like and trust all of you, and I can't stay if your lives are at risk. I'll figure something out."

I growl and grip her chin, turning her gaze to me. "No. You're not going anywhere. You're not an inconvenience. And if any of them doesn't trust you, that's their problem."

She shakes her head.

"I trust you," Mateo says, surprising me. And by the way Eloise whips around to look at him, I'd say it surprises her, too. "After today, after what you said, I trust you. We're not sending you anywhere."

Julian watches her for a second, then lets out a breath. "I trust them," he says, gesturing to us. "So unless you give me a reason not to, I'll take you at your word."

"We have some business to see to regarding your father and Damien both," I tell her, pushing my fingers through her hair. "But it has absolutely nothing to do with sending you away. You're *mine.* Never forget that."

She blows out a breath, and even though I can see she's calmer, I hate that even that bastard's name sent her spiraling. *But not only for herself. For us.* She was terrified of him—of her father—and rightly so. But her concern for us? Mind-blowing.

"I'm sorry. I'm okay. I'll ... just go have lunch with Scarlett. I might have a drink, too."

"No," Carson says, shaking his head, his expression restrained. Hard. "You're shooting this afternoon, and you'll be sober for it."

"Well, damn." Eloise laughs. "Actually, that works. I'll take my frustrations out on a target."

She kisses my cheek and then stands, but I tug her back and kiss her hard.

"Say the words *I'll leave* again, and I'll spank your ass until it glows red. Do you hear me?"

"I hear you," she whispers. "I'm sorry."

She leaves the room, and when we hear the front door close, Carson rubs his hands together.

"So let's plan how we're going to kill those fuckers. I'm sick of watching her freak out. Let's end this."

Forty-Seven

LULU

Today has been a *lot.*

Between training with Mateo, overhearing my father and my supposed betrothed's name in Rome's office, my freak-out that was *incredibly* embarrassing, having the tracker put into the inside of my arm, and training with Carson this afternoon, I'm spent.

Spent.

God, I'm tired.

"You did good," Carson says as we clean our weapons. "You both have excellent aim."

"She's better than me," Scarlett says, nudging me with her shoulder. "This isn't your first time."

"No." I notice that Carson's eyes narrow on me. "I took lessons behind my father's back."

But then I remember that my dad admitted to knowing about my classes, something I would have *sworn* he didn't know, and now I'm not so sure if he was in the dark about my target practice.

Probably not, now that I think about it.

"Why?" Carson asks.

I've had to talk about my asshole of a sperm donor a lot today. I don't like it.

"Because he was a bastard," I reply simply and glance at Scarlett. Having to explain why I took so long to return to her was not fun. I was much calmer than when I was in Rome's office, but she could still tell I was rattled. From her sniffles when we were learning self-defense to finding out more about my past, needless to say, she was distraught. She hasn't told me her full story yet, but I'm learning there are a lot of buried scars at Rapture. But now to explain why I learned to shoot. "I suspected that I might need to know how one day. But it's been a long time since I've practiced."

"You'll be practicing every day until further notice," Carson says.

"I think it's kind of badass," Scarlett says with a smile. "And Luke thinks it's sexy."

"It *is* sexy," I agree. "You look damn hot when you're shooting that gun."

Carson's eyes gleam with humor. "It's not about that."

"I know, I know." I roll my eyes at him. "It's about self-defense. But it's okay if looking hot while we do it is a bonus. Are you seeing anyone, Carson? Are you married? Kids?"

He simply shakes his head slowly. "Fuck no."

"Huh."

Scarlett smiles.

"What's that supposed to mean?" Carson asks.

"Nothing." I shake my head and set the weapon back in its carrying case. "I'm just surprised, that's all. You're handsome. You're funny. I figure someone would snatch you up."

"I'm also an assassin, and most of the time, I'm an asshole."

I blink at him, not at all surprised about the assassin admission.

Carson is intense. And he looks … *scary.*

"No one's perfect."

His lips twitch at that, and then we're making our way to the elevators, where the guards who have been shadowing us all day are waiting.

"You're not going up with us?" I ask Carson when he doesn't get on the elevator.

"I have work." He crosses his arms over his chest, watching us.

"Have a good night," I call out to him.

"Be careful," Scarlett adds, and Carson's eyes fill with humor again before the doors close.

After dropping Scarlett off on her floor, my two guards ride with me up to the penthouse. I thank them, then walk inside and let out a deep breath. I'm off work tonight, and I'm glad. I need to disassociate for a while. To just put on a mindless TV show or listen to music and simply *be.* Rome will probably be at work all evening, so I'm just going to zone out.

I don't want to think.

I don't want to be in charge or worry about anything.

But before I can walk upstairs to shower and get cozy, Rome comes strolling out of the den, his hands in his pockets.

He's still in his slacks, but he shed his jacket at some point, and his black dress shirtsleeves are rolled up his forearms, showing me some of his tattoos. His blue eyes brighten when he sees me, and a sly smile works its way over his lips.

"You're home." He walks, his body lithe and lean and so fucking beautiful, straight to me, and his hands come up to my face. He kisses me gently at first, then he deepens the kiss, stealing my breath.

If I wanted my mind to empty, he just did a good job of it.

"How was target practice?" he asks against my lips.

"I'm sorry, what? You just kissed all of my brain cells away."

He grins and does it again, drifting those magical lips over mine, and my knees feel weak. My hands fist in his shirt, holding on for dear life as he sinks into me.

When he finally comes up for air, he brushes my hair behind my ear.

"How are you, firefly?"

"Tired. Overstimulated. And now, I'm turned on."

He kisses my forehead. "Are you hungry?"

"Now that you mention it, yes. We have some left-over lasagna. Would you like some?"

"That's too heavy for what I have in store for you tonight." He hasn't stopped touching me. His fingertips drift down my neck and over my collarbone.

"How about some soup and sandwiches? There's still the beef with vegetables I made the other day and grilled cheese sandwiches."

"Perfect." He tips my chin up. "Here's what I want you to do. Are you listening?"

Of course, I'm listening, but I'm also enjoying the feel of his hard, warm body against me.

"Yes."

"Go upstairs and take a shower. I want you to put your hair up in a bun off your back. Dress in something comfortable and come down to eat. I'll get dinner ready."

I frown up at him. "Aren't you going to work?"

"No." He leans down to kiss the top of my head. "I need time with you tonight. Just you and me, baby. I have plans for you. So go do what I say."

I blink up at him. He's more intense than usual tonight. He's still kind and gentle, but his voice leaves no room for argument, and there's an edge in his eyes I haven't seen before.

It's both unsettling and intriguing.

"Okay."

Before I turn away, I step closer and hug him around the middle, my cheek pressed to his chest. His arms fold around me and tighten, holding me close, and he takes a moment to rock me back and forth.

"Breathe, baby."

I smile and take a deep breath, inhaling his spicy scent and soaking in his warm embrace.

"I didn't know how badly I needed this," I murmur against him.

"A hug?" he asks.

"Yeah."

His arms tighten even more, and he buries his lips in my hair. "You're so fucking amazing, Eloise."

I glance up at him and smile at the affection glowing in his blue eyes.

"I think you're amazing. Okay, I'm hitting the shower."

"Good. Take your time. There's no rush."

My legs are weary from all of the working out with Mateo as I climb the stairs. A hot shower sounds like heaven right now.

And when I get to our bathroom, my heart stutters. He bought me my favorite shower steamers that smell like lilac. I have no idea if he went out to find them on his own or if he sent someone for them, but either way, it makes my heart thud a little harder in my chest.

I've fallen in love with this man so quickly. And when he does things like this, how can I resist him?

The inside of my left bicep is sore from where he injected the tracking device earlier today. There's a little bruise the size of my fingerprint, but when I rub over it, I can't even feel it there.

I asked him why he put mine in my arm and his in his neck, and he told me it would hurt worse in the neck, and he refused to let me feel more pain than necessary.

I take my time, washing my body and letting the hot water beat down on muscles that I haven't felt in a long time, if ever, that are whimpering for mercy. I wash my hair and shave all of the things. When I'm finished, I slather lotion all over my body, brush out my hair, and then dry it most of the way before twisting it up into a tight bun on the top of my head.

After pulling on a pair of sleep shorts and a loose tank, I pad downstairs and find my man in the kitchen, warming soup in a pot on the stove.

There are two grilled cheese sandwiches on plates, ready to go.

"I had no idea you were so handy in the kitchen."

He turns and grins at me, and then his eyes take a slow stroll down my body, from the bun on my head to the tips of my toes and back up again.

"I have a few talents you don't know about," he says. "The soup is ready. Have a seat, firefly."

"I can help—"

"Sit."

Again, his tone is hard. Commanding.

Dominant.

Sexy.

I cross to a stool at the island and have a seat. Rome ladles up some soup in a bowl and passes it to me along with one of the sandwiches.

I've just taken a bite, watching as Rome dishes up for himself, when he turns to stand opposite me and casually asks, "Do you have a safe word?"

Forty-Eight

ROME

Those gorgeous green eyes widen as her spoon pauses halfway to her mouth, and she watches me.

"What?"

"You heard me." I take a bite and chew thoughtfully, my blood simmering. "I won't ask again."

I'm in a mood tonight. I want to dominate her. I want to control her.

I need to take care of her.

This piece of myself doesn't often come out to play, but when it does, there's no satiating it any other way.

I need her.

"No," she says simply.

"You need to choose one."

She takes a bite of her sandwich and watches me. "Why?"

I set my spoon down and brace my hands on the counter. "Because I told you to, Eloise."

She swallows hard and clears her throat. "Are you okay?"

"Yes."

"You're kind of intense tonight. Do I need to be scared?"

"I'll never hurt you. I'd kill myself first. The safe word is for your protection and for my information. I'm going to push some boundaries tonight, and I need to know that you always feel at ease with me."

"I do."

I smile softly at her. "Good. I don't want that to change. Your safe word is for both of us."

She chews another bite, taking that in. "I'm not sure what to choose."

"How about this, then? We'll use colors. I'll check in with you to see what color you're at. You'll say green or yellow. Green means you're good to go. No problems. Yellow tells me you don't need to stop, but you're nearing your limits. And at any time, if you say red, we stop. No questions asked."

"Red means I can't do any more?"

"That's right, baby. And you will *not* be shy about using it. That's imperative."

She nods and finishes her sandwich, then pushes her mostly eaten bowl of soup away from her. "That seems easiest. I like it."

She stands to take care of the dishes, but I shake my head.

"Leave it. I'll get to it later. How do you feel right now?"

Eloise licks her lips, watching me. "Curious."

"You should be." I circle the island and take her hand in mine, threading our fingers together and kissing the back of her hand as I guide her to the den. When we step inside, she comes to a stop, and I turn to watch her. To let her come to terms with what's in here in her own time.

"Rome."

"I'm right here, firefly."

She steps to me, as if she's seeking comfort, and I wrap my arm around her, tugging her to my side.

"Talk to me," I murmur before kissing her temple.

"The ropes," she whispers, making me grin. She looks up at me, and her pupils have dilated with lust just at the sight of my ropes laid out on the table. "Please tell me we get to play with those."

"We are going to play, but there are some rules. You'll do what I say, when I say, without hesitation. I will check in on your colors often to make sure you're comfortable."

My firefly nods enthusiastically. "Deal."

"If you need a break, you tell me."

She continues to nod.

"You will not come until I give you permission."

At that, she falters, and I take her chin in my fingers, making her look me in the eyes. "I'm going to edge the fuck out of you tonight. I'm going to tie you up and touch you, kiss you, *fuck you*, but you will not come until I say so."

She swallows hard. "Yes, Rome."

"That's my girl." I kiss her forehead and step away from her. "Take your clothes off."

As she pulls her tank over her head, I reach for the first bunch of purple rope and bring it to her. Once she's fully naked, I hold the rope out to her and nod.

"Touch it."

She smiles as her fingers brush over the rope. "It's soft."

"Yes."

She eyes the other colors on the table, which are different sizes and lengths. "Are they all soft?"

"They are."

Her eyes drift to the other toys I have laid out beside the ropes, and they widen. "Rome?"

"Ask me anything."

"Is that a ... *butt plug*?"

I glance at the toy with the red-jeweled end and grin. "It is, yes. We're going to work up to that."

She takes a shaky breath, then nods once as if steeling herself for what's to come.

But she has no fucking idea.

And I can't wait for her to discover everything happening in here tonight.

"Have you done this in here before?"

"No." I take her chin in my fingers again. "I've never had a woman in my penthouse before you, remember?"

She nods, and I have to admit, I like the look of jealousy in her green gaze at the thought of me doing this with anyone else.

But I need her to relax and feel at ease, so I kiss her lips and brush my nose against hers.

"You're all that matters, Eloise. Only you. You're with me now, and you're my future. That's all you need to think about."

That shaky breath comes out on a long exhale, and she leans into me. "I know. You're right."

"Good. Let's get started. Do you remember your colors?"

She nods. "I'm at green."

"Well done." I kiss her cheek and nod to the rug in the middle of the room. "Stand here. You'll eventually be on your knees, but we'll start here."

She walks to where I indicated and stands with her arms relaxed at her sides, staring straight ahead.

Christ, she was made for this. So trusting. So fucking beautiful.

And so mine.

I roll the full-length mirror into the room and position it about ten feet in front of her. Room enough for me to work but close enough for her to see everything.

She sucks in a breath and watches herself standing here, completely nude, waiting for me to start.

But first, I walk up behind her and press my front to her back, drift my hand down from her collarbone to her hip, enjoying her softness.

"Look at how fucking beautiful you are, firefly. Every curve, every hill and valley is absolute perfection."

Her gaze catches mine in the mirror, and her lips curve up in a soft smile.

"I like seeing us together like this," she admits softly. Her raspy voice makes my cock twitch, so I decide to forgo the ball gag.

I want to hear every fucking sound she makes.

"Me, too," I murmur before dropping a kiss to her neck. "You can relax. Breathe. Listen to me. That's all you have to do."

Her eyes drift shut for just a moment, and when she opens them again, they're glassy.

"That's exactly what I need tonight."

"Good."

Forty-Nine

LULU

oly. Fucking. Christ.

He looks like a devil, standing behind me in the low light of the room, watching me in the mirror. He's so *big*, so tall and broad, and watching his tattooed hands move over my pale skin sends a shiver through me, making my core ache and my thighs clench.

With a knowing smirk, he leans down and presses his lips to the top of my shoulder, and then he's gone, gathering a long length of rope.

He starts at my front, blocking the view of the mirror from me. He loops the soft purple rope around my neck and shoulders, in almost a harness, and knots it just between my breasts, then presses a kiss on my sternum above the knot.

"May I touch you?" I ask him in a rough whisper.

"No." His icy gaze holds mine. "You may not."

I roll my lips in and press them in a line. That almost pushes me into yellow territory.

I love touching him.

I love that I'm one of the only people in his life who's allowed to.

But I'll be patient and trust his process. His body is strung tight tonight. He's not the calm and collected man I'm used to.

I'd like to know what set this off in him, but I keep my mouth shut, my arms at my sides, and enjoy watching him move. His forearms flex as he ties the knots. His dark eyebrows pull together, making a line form between them, and I want to reach up and soothe it with my thumb, but I stay strong, taking him in.

When he's finished looping this soft rope around me, he steps aside, revealing me in the mirror, and I see my jaw drop.

Wow.

He's looped it so perfectly around my breasts, my chest, and shoulders, it looks like a beautiful work of art. The room suddenly fills with soft piano music, and I glance at Rome as he rubs his hand over his lips, taking me in as he walks to stand behind me, looking at me in the mirror.

"Color?"

"So fucking bright green."

His lips tip up in a half smile before he lifts his hand and brushes his fingertips over my nipple, making it pebble.

"Unbelievable," he murmurs, pressing his lips on the ball of my shoulder. "Incredible." He drifts over to my spine, just below my neck, and skims his teeth over my flesh. "Goddamn delicious."

I sigh at his touch, loving the way he feels.

Suddenly, he spanks my ass, startling me. It's hard enough to make my skin heat but not hard enough to make me cry out.

He tips up an eyebrow in the mirror.

"Green."

He moves back to the table and chooses another rope, this one red and thicker than the last one. He unravels it before stepping behind me and looping it around my waist. He weaves it through the bottom of the purple strands and then down around my hips, his knuckles teasing and tormenting me with every pass of the rope.

He has to run it under my crotch, to the side of my pussy, and back up again, but he pauses and brushes his fingers through my slit, making me groan.

"So wet already," he murmurs and kisses my back. "So warm."

I whimper, and he keeps tying the knots. They're so beautiful. I don't even want to think about all of the practice he had to do to make it this perfect.

Don't go there.

This man is twenty years older than you. He's had a lot of life experience. Shut your brain off, Eloise.

"Firefly."

My gaze whips up to his in the mirror.

"Why are you frowning?"

I blink rapidly and school my face. "Sorry, I was in my head."

His eyes narrow, and he tips his head to the side. Then his hand is between my legs again, but not in my slit. He's cupping my thigh, near the crease where my leg meets torso, and I bite my lip.

"Color," he demands, his voice harder than before, his eyes colder than earlier.

"Green," I whisper, but his eyes narrow. "Very green."

His hand moves up, and suddenly, he plunges his two middle fingers inside me, and I cry out, arching into him.

"Christ, you're fucking gorgeous," he mutters, watching us in the mirror. "I want you to stay here with me, baby. At this moment."

I swallow hard as my walls contract around his thick fingers, *so* wanting to come. Needing it.

"Not yet," he whispers against my ear. "How close are you?"

"So close. Rome, please."

He pulls his hand away and shoves the fingers that were just inside me into my mouth.

"Clean me up so I don't get the ropes dirty."

My tongue swirls around his fingers, licking him clean. I won't mention that the ropes will be dirty from my wet pussy anyway, and the smirk on his handsome face tells me he's thinking the same thing.

And he doesn't care.

When I've licked myself off him, his hand drifts down my neck, down my torso over the ropes. I hope he's going to return to my core, to massage that ache out of me, but he simply grins and then lets go.

Damn him!

He chuckles and grabs another length of rope, this one orange, and he weaves it through the purple and starts to loop it down my right leg.

Holy shit, that's pretty.

Rome squats next to me and kisses my hip, my thigh, as his fingers deftly work that beautiful orange down my leg. I've always been self-conscious about my thighs because they're ... *shapely*, and I have cellulite.

But Rome is worshipping that leg right now, and I feel my breath speeding up, just a little, and my eyes have blown wide in the mirror.

My mind is emptying.

I almost feel like I'm floating.

Rome's fingers skim up my leg, around to my ass, which also has ropes zigzagged around it. He slaps me again, but I don't startle this time.

I bite my lip.

My face flushes.

This is the hottest thing that's ever happened to me.

"Color."

"Green."

Is that *my* voice? So raspy. It sounds like I'm in a trance, and suddenly, Rome is right in front of me, his hands cradling my face as he stares down into my eyes with such intensity, it almost brings tears.

"I'm right here," he reminds me.

"Green," I repeat.

He kisses me softly, then moves to my ear.

"You're slipping into subspace, baby. That's right where I want you. But I need you to stay with me for a while yet. I need you to keep responding to me."

"Okay."

I've never seen anything or anyone more incredible than my firefly at this moment. Her pupils are so dilated that I can barely see the green of her irises. Her lips, swollen from my kisses, are parted, and she's breathing in long, slow breaths.

Her skin is flushed.

Her pussy is so wet and ready for me, and we're not even close to making her come yet.

I'll need to put her on her knees in a minute, but first, I grab the butt plug and watch her eyes flare as I put it against her lips.

"Get this wet."

She opens her mouth obediently and licks the small plug. I know she's not used to this, so I'll ease her into it slowly.

But this little red jewel is going to look so fucking beautiful on her.

I glide my hand down her back, over the knots that

are exactly four inches apart all the way down her spine, and then urge her to bend over, which she does beautifully.

I drag the plug through her wetness, circle it over her clit, and she arches her back, moaning.

"You like this?"

She whimpers but doesn't answer me, so I slap her ass once more, loving the way it glows pink for me.

"Answer me with words, Eloise."

"Yes, I like it."

"Good girl." I kiss her ass cheek, over that pink glow, and push the plug inside her pussy, getting it good and drenched, before I drag it up to that tight little puckered muscle and gently, patiently, work it inside her.

My girl gasps again and then moans deep in her throat when the plug is seated inside her, and I push two fingers inside her cunt, loving the way she clenches around me, her walls already quaking with an impending orgasm.

"Oh, you like that."

"Rome."

"You could come just from this plug and my fingers." With my free hand, I press on the red jewel. I can feel it move against my fingers, and she cries out. "Just wait until it's my cock where these fingers are, and how fucking full you'll feel. Or better yet, when my dick is in this perfect ass."

"Oh God."

She starts to quake, to shiver and push against me. I pull my hand free of her, then stand and back away.

"Rome!"

"Not until I fucking say so," I remind her and slap her ass again. "And I can do this all goddamn night, Eloise."

"Fuck."

"What's your color?"

"So fucking green and I want you to make me come."

I grin and push a finger through the rope in the center of her back and bring her back upright, then kiss her cheek.

"No."

"Rome—"

"What is your color, Eloise?"

"I said it's green."

"Then stop complaining."

She narrows her eyes, but I couldn't care less.

I grab a green rope and resume tying knots down her left leg, mirroring the work I did on the right, sure to keep her knees clear so it's comfortable when she kneels.

I can't wait to get her on her knees.

As I press kisses on her inner thigh, her muscles quiver beneath my lips.

Suddenly, her hands are in my hair, and it feels amazing, but she knows the rules.

No touching.

I pull back out of her reach.

"I *need* to touch you," she whispers.

"No."

But her eyes plead with me, filled with that need and longing, so I take her hands in mine and kiss them, then press them to my chest and let her soak me in for a minute.

"Why?" I ask her.

"Because you let me, and it's when I feel the closest to you."

"I've been touching you this whole time," I remind her.

"I know. But it's not the same."

If I'm not careful, she'll bring me to my knees.

"Better?" I ask after a moment and tip her chin up so I can see her eyes.

"Thank you," she whispers. I know she's not simply talking about allowing her hands on my chest.

"There isn't anything I wouldn't do for you, firefly." I kiss her gently and then remove her hands from me. "That's enough now. I have to focus, and I can't do that as well when your hands are on me. I'm going to restrain them."

Her eyes widen, and she licks her lips. "But not behind me?"

I want to kill him just for this look, this goddamn fear, in her eyes.

"Never," I assure her. "In front of you."

She nods, and I grab more red rope and get to work, making knots down her arms and wrists, even between her fingers. Then I cross her arms in front of her, over her belly, so I still have unrestricted access to her tits, and tie them there.

I mastered the art of Shibari in my early thirties, and I've worked my ropes over many women over the years, but no experience was quite like this one. Eloise is in a different league altogether.

Her incredibly soft skin is flushed, and each time my knuckles brush against her, her breath hitches so beautifully, it makes my cock twitch in my pants.

She's back in subspace. Those pupils so wide, her breathing even. I help her down to her knees and walk away from her altogether.

I know I said it earlier.

Unbelievable.

My woman, the love of my life, the only girl I'll ever want again, is kneeling in our home, covered in my ropes. Her feet are crossed at the toes under her perfect ass, and I can see the red jewel just above them. The ropes look like lace, looped over her body and knotted strategically to look like jewelry.

She's a vision.

And she's mine.

Hearing her say that she'd leave today brought out something dark and primal in me. If I could keep her just like this, so she couldn't try to run away, I would.

Without qualms.

Because she'll *never* leave me.

I push off the table, where I've been leaning, watching her, and kneel behind her. She's so far under that she doesn't even raise her gaze in the mirror to look at me.

"Eloise?"

"Green."

I smile and ghost my lips over the ball of her left shoulder, the one that's hurt.

"You're doing so well, baby."

I want to take her to the brink once more before I set my hard, pulsing cock free and fuck her.

I want to make her as crazy for me as I am for her.

"Look at how gorgeous you are in my ropes." She bites her lower lip, and I reach around to tug it free with my thumb, then cradle her throat in my hand, not squeezing, just holding. "Have I told you how perfect your breasts are?"

"No."

"Well, I should be killed for that alone. I fucking *love* every inch of this incredible body."

Now her eyes jump to mine, and she frowns as if she's confused.

"Why?"

I blink at her.

"I don't understand," she continues with a whisper. "You could have *anyone.* Look at you."

Her eyes dance over my reflection.

"You're so handsome. Dangerous. Strong. Powerful." Her voice takes on an edge that I fucking hate. "And I'm ... *this.*"

"You're fucking perfect," I growl next to her ear.

"I'm—"

"Eloise, you're beautiful—"

"Yellow."

I rear back as if she struck me and stare at her reflection. "You need to talk to me, firefly."

"The ropes are beautiful," she says. "And I hope we do this often because I might be addicted to it now."

"That's not what I meant."

"We can talk about it later."

"We'll talk about it now." I wrap my arms around her from behind and hold her against me, watching her gaze in the mirror. "Tell me why you don't think you're good enough."

"Loveland didn't even want to hire me. My dad reminded me on the regular that I'm too fat, too plain, too ... everything."

I shake my head, but she keeps talking.

"And I know that beauty is in the eye of the beholder, but I guess I just don't get it. I don't see it."

"Okay." I kiss her neck, still watching her. "I'll show you. The minute I saw you walk into my club, I knew you were mine. I felt it down to my bones, and I was looking at you through a video camera."

She bites her lip but doesn't interrupt me.

"Your lips are so goddamn fuckable, and I love the sass that comes out of them." My thumb drifts over said lips, and she smiles softly. "Those green eyes of yours will get you anything you want."

"Good to know."

I smirk and continue. "I can't keep my hands out of your hair. Off your body. I've never wanted to touch anyone the way I want to touch you. Your breasts are full, and your pink nipples are every fucking wet dream I've ever had. I love lying my head on your stomach while we watch TV. Your softness is such a contrast to your inner strength. Your legs wrap around me perfectly. And your pussy."

I groan and rest my mouth on her shoulder as I push my hard cock against her lower back, unable to stop myself from grinding against her.

"Christ, there's nothing about you that I don't want. That I don't crave. I *lose myself* in you, Eloise, and I don't ever lose myself in anything."

Tears fill her eyes as she leans into me.

"Thank you."

"If you *ever* question how fucking beautiful you are, you just tell me, and I'll remind you that there's no one in this world I want more than you."

She swallows thickly as my hand glides down the front of her, over the ropes, and between her legs, where she's still sopping wet for me.

"I'm going to fuck you hard, Eloise. And then I'm going to carry you upstairs and make love to you in our bed."

She nods and bites that lower lip, and I pull her onto her feet. Her hands are bound, so I can't put her on her hands and knees on the floor.

Well, I *could.*

But I don't want to make her uncomfortable. That's for another time.

I walk her over to the table and bend her over it.

"Cheek on the wood," I instruct her, and she complies. "Legs spread. Wider."

Fuck, she's a work of goddamn art. That she can't see that agonizes me.

"Color, Eloise."

"Green. Absolutely green."

We're back in the zone from earlier, and it sends a new shot of adrenaline through me as I smack her ass with a loud *slap*.

"Rome!"

Fifty-One

LULU

My ass hums and heats, and I sigh in relief. I was sure I'd just ruined the whole night with my insecurities rearing their ugly head. But Rome was patient and loving, and turned us back around, putting us on the right track again.

Thank God.

I hear the sound of his belt clanging open, then his pants zipper being pushed down, and the rustle of his clothes coming off. My core clenches, and I wish I could see him.

Nothing in this world is as gorgeous as a naked Rome.

His hand moves between my legs to my slit.

"So goddamn wet," he murmurs as he drags the head of his cock—and that glorious piercing—through my wetness now. "This pussy was made just for me, firefly." He pushes inside me, all the way to the hilt, making me groan loudly. "Do you feel this? How goddamn perfect we are together?"

"Yes."

"It's *never* been like this before. Not once before you. Anything I experienced before was an empty fucking husk of what I have with you. Nothing before you matters because it was fucking *nothing*. Do you hear me?"

"Rome."

"Do. You. Fucking. Hear. Me?"

"Yes. I hear you. God, I hear you." The tears are coming now. There's no way I can stop them. His words, his beautiful body slamming into me in long, measured strokes, the delicious feel of his ropes wrapped around me, and all of the reassurance he just gave me are at once overwhelming and the best things to ever happen to me in my life.

"You're all I need in this world," he says, slamming into me. God, I feel so *full* with his big cock, and the butt plug still inside me, and his arms around me, his words. "Don't you come yet."

"Rome."

"Not yet. What's your color?"

I have to think about it, then whisper, "Yellow. I'm so close. I'm right *there*."

He stops, buried deep within me, and I cry out.

"I know, baby." He kisses my neck, my shoulder. "You're almost there. You're doing so well. Look."

I open my eyes and notice that he somehow turned

the mirror to face us when he brought me over to this table, and my eyes go wide at the scene before me.

The view is our profile, so we can see both of us. I'm bent over this table, helpless. And Rome is naked, buried inside me, his pelvis against my ass and hands on my hips, watching me. His abs ripple as he moves, and I can't take my eyes off the V that forms down his hip to his muscular thigh.

"You take me so fucking well," he growls, pulling out so I can see his glistening cock. "Look at that, firefly."

He starts to move again, one hand on my shoulder, the other on the small of my back, and I watch him fuck me, the way my body shakes with every thrust, the way sweat gleams on his skin as he thrusts into me.

And then I feel the orgasm build once more.

"Please."

His blue eyes flare at that.

"That's right, beg for it. Beg for me to let you come all over this cock. To make a mess of me."

"Rome, please."

"Ask for it, Eloise."

"Please let me come on your beautiful cock!"

He roars and pulls me onto him so hard, I see dark spots on the edge of my vision.

"Come. Fall apart for me, sweetheart."

Oh God, yes.

I cry out as I spasm around him, against him. Our eyes are still pinned to the mirror, watching.

And it's the sexiest thing I've ever seen in my life.

As the orgasm continues to move through me, Rome pulls the butt plug out, causing a new wave of shivers, and he smiles.

"You're doing so well, firefly."

I whimper. He pulls out, turns me around, and boosts me onto the table, holding the ropes between my breasts to keep me upright since I can't brace myself on my hands. I wrap my legs around him as he sinks back inside me.

"I need to look in your beautiful eyes." He pauses, grinding his pubic bone against my already overstimulated clit, making me moan. "Don't you *ever*, and I mean *ever* say that you'll leave me again."

I frown and then realize he's talking about earlier today in his office.

That's what this is all about.

"I won't." I shake my head, and he pulls out, then slams into me harder.

"You're *mine*. Today and every day."

"Yours," I confirm and wish I could touch him. "Rome, I need—"

I swallow hard. He said I couldn't touch him.

"Tell me."

"It's okay."

"*Tell me.*"

"I need to touch you. I'm sorry, I know—"

He covers my mouth with his and kisses me hard. I feel cold, hard metal against my skin, and I freeze.

But then I realize he's cutting the ropes off my arms,

freeing them so I can wrap them around his neck and bury my fingers in his hair.

"Mine," he says again.

"Yours."

He's moving like a crazed man, his blue eyes feral as he pumps in and out of me until I can't resist another orgasm that moves through me.

"Yes, baby," he groans and rests his open mouth against my neck as he follows me over the edge. "Fuuuuuuck."

His hips jerk, and I feel the heat of his release bathing the inside of me.

He bites me over my pulse point, then his hands are under my ass and he's lifting me once more, still inside me, carrying me out of the den and up the stairs.

"I need you in our bed," he murmurs against my mouth. "What's your color?"

"Pink," I say with a little smile, and he frowns down at me as he lays me carefully in the middle of the mattress and hovers over me, his elbows on either side of my head, his pelvis nestled against mine, and his cock still buried so deep, I would swear I can feel him in my throat.

"That's not one of the options," he says, brushing his nose over mine gently. The intense, almost angry man from earlier is gone, and now he's gentler.

More tender.

And I love both sides of him.

I don't care that he runs an organized crime syndicate, or that he kills people, or any of the shitty things he does.

Because he's *so good* to me.

"Why pink, firefly?"

"Because I love you." I kiss his chin when he goes absolutely still. "And if I said red, you'd pull away."

He doesn't move.

He doesn't *breathe.*

"Rome?"

His eyes haven't moved from mine. His hands are in my hair. Every ink-covered muscle is tight.

"Say it again." It's the faintest whisper, barely uttered through his lips.

I drag my hands up his sides, over his chest, to his face.

"I'm so completely in love with you that I physically ache with it."

His eyes close, and he lowers his forehead to mine. His hips pull back, and then he's moving inside me again, but in sweet, slow strokes that make my throat close with emotion.

"I love you so much, firefly." He brushes his lips over mine. "So fucking much."

He holds me gently as he makes love to me. His kisses are reverent as if he's drinking in every bit of this moment so he can look at it later.

How could I not love him?

"You are everything," he breathes.

God. I cling to him as the orgasm moves through me. I've never experienced anything like tonight. The ropes, the mirror, his intensity. He's so hard and ruthless with everyone else, but shows me his softer side. His tender side.

And he loves me.

I'm home. I've found my home here with him, and I'll fight to keep it.

I'm never letting him go.

Fifty-Two

LULU

"I'm not paying more than a thousand dollars for a pair of shoes." I shake my head, and Scarlett laughs at me. "I'm serious."

"Rome gave you his black card," she reminds me as she tries on a pair of Dior sneakers. They're *so cute.* And I love them.

I want them.

But I don't like the idea of spending this much of Rome's money.

"Our men have more money than God," Scarlett adds with a grin. "They said we should go out and spoil ourselves today, and that's what we're doing. I'm excited for the spa after dinner. I so need another massage."

"Is your back healed enough for a massage?" I ask her, and she nods.

"Yep. Just scars now. The massage should help that, too. Now, you're getting those shoes. *And* the bag. You're helping me celebrate, remember?"

I bite my lip, looking longingly at both.

I want them.

Scarlett is officially the new playroom manager at Rapture. Rome offered her the job yesterday, and she jumped at it. She doesn't want to have sex with anyone but Luke, and this way, she gets to stay at the club that she loves so much. I'm so excited for her.

But I still don't love the idea of dropping this much of Rome's money.

Suddenly, Scarlett has her phone in her hand, tapping on the screen. She has it on speaker, holding it between us, when Luke answers on the second ring.

"Hey, baby. What's up? Everything okay?"

"Everything's great, and we're having *so much* fun. Is Mr. Alexander with you?"

"He's right here," Luke says. I can hear the frown in his voice.

"It's okay," I say, not wanting to bring Rome into this. "Hang up."

"Do *not* hang up on me," Rome says through the speaker, and that hard tone makes my core clench as heat moves through me. "What's wrong, firefly?"

"Nothing's wrong."

"She's afraid to spend too much money on shoes and bags," Scarlett interjects. "And I told her to buy them, but you're the boss, so—"

"Buy whatever you want, Eloise. Buy the whole fucking store, I don't care. There's no limit on the card. I told you to have fun."

"See?" Scarlett looks smug as fuck. "Told you."

"I have my own money to spend—"

"Scarlett, take me off speaker and pass the phone to my woman."

Scarlett lifts an eyebrow and does as she's told, and I press the phone to my ear.

"Hi."

"Baby, spend the money."

God, I go all gooey when he talks to me like this. Like I'm the most precious thing in his world.

"It feels weird."

"Are you spending ten million dollars on a house or something? Not that you can't. I'd just like to be in on real estate decisions, if possible."

I scoff at that, and I can almost picture the smile on his face. "No, of course not. It's probably less than ten thousand altogether."

"Spend fifty."

"Fifty dollars? I can do that."

"Fifty thousand, and not a penny less."

I frown at Scarlett, who's still listening in unabashedly.

"I can't spend *fifty thousand dollars*."

"Yes, she can," Scarlett says into the phone. "I'll help. We've got this, and we'll make you proud, Mr. Alexander."

"I'm not kidding, firefly. Fifty grand, or you don't get to come for a week."

"Rome—"

"I love you."

And with that, he hangs up, and I'm left staring at

my best friend, my mouth wide open.

"I like that man," Scarlett says as she tosses her phone into her handbag. "I think you should try those heels on, too. The blue ones. And then you're going to try on some ready-to-wear."

"There's no way I can fit in any of the clothing they sell here."

"Psh, yes, you can. And you will."

My phone dings with an incoming text, and I take a breath when I see that it's my man.

Rome: Spend the money. No less than $50k. I mean it.

Me: You're so bossy.

Rome: And you love it.

Me: …

Rome: Eloise…

Me: …

Rome: ELOISE.

Me: I love you. And your bossiness. I'll spend a bunch of your money, sugar daddy.

Rome: I will spank you.

Me: Promises, promises. *kiss emoji* *heart emoji*

"You have such a goofy grin on your face," Scarlett says with a giggle. "You're so in love."

"Yeah. I am." I shrug a shoulder and nod at the saleswoman hovering nearby. "I'll take these for sure."

"And we want to look at your ready-to-wear," Scarlett says.

"Right this way."

Fifty-Three

ROME

I pocket my phone and look up to see Luke watching me with raised eyebrows.

"What?"

"I don't even know who you are anymore."

I roll my eyes, and we continue down the hallway to the cell. "You're being dramatic."

"Nope. I'm not. I've literally *never* seen you get mushy over a woman. I've also never seen you spend so much money on one."

"It's just money."

"Still."

"Tell me you didn't give Scarlett your black card this morning."

Luke shuffles on his feet and pushes his hand through his hair.

"That's what I thought. Eloise is *mine*. Forever. Anyone who tries to even hurt her *feelings* dies. Painfully. Got it?"

"Got it." He nods, and we push inside the cell where two men are strung up, their hands tied over their heads and hanging from hooks. They're gagged, and they're exhausted.

They should be. They ran for miles, trying to escape my men.

It didn't work.

"So Rizzo sent you into my territory even though he was warned not to." I shake my head and pick up a baton, shaking it so it extends to its full length, and then hit man number one in the knee, shattering the kneecap.

He screams.

I grin.

And the door to the cell opens as Julian and Mateo walk inside.

"Where's Carson?" I ask them.

"He's out of town on a job," Mateo says with the shake of his head. "Won't be back for a couple of days."

"Too bad." I rear back and hit Number Two in the hip. "He would have enjoyed this."

"Next time," Julian says with a chuckle. "Rizzo continues to be a stupid cuntface, I see."

"I like that," Mateo says with a nod. "Cuntface. I'm gonna use that one."

"Happy to help," Julian says, and they bump fists.

"How have your accommodations been here, boys?" I ask them and nod for Luke to take the gags out. Number One immediately pukes, making us all scowl. "Jesus."

"Fuck you," Number Two says. "We're not the only ones here."

"Shut it," Number One says, but I shake my head.

"No, by all means, keep talking. Who else is here?"

But Number Two closes his mouth.

Mateo likes to use fire when torturing, so he grabs the blowtorch, turns it on, and goes to town on Number One's back.

"That's what you'll get if you don't talk," I say conversationally. "Who else is in our city?"

"Everyone," Number Two says with a shaky voice. "The whole army."

"Rizzo?" Julian asks.

"Shut. Up," Number One groans through the pain.

"They're going to kill us anyway," Number Two says.

"He's smart," Julian says, nodding. "I like him. He's also a pussy and a piece of shit, but I like him. Is Rizzo here?"

"Yeah." Number Two licks his lips. "Found the girl."

The hair on the back of my neck stands on end.

"Had an inside contact," he continues, and I gnash my teeth.

One of my own is a traitor.

"Gonna snatch her up."

I look at Mateo, whose black eyes narrow menacingly.

I don't know what was said between the man and my firefly the other day, but I can see the shift in how he feels about her.

And right now, he's fucking pissed.

We all are. The room around us pulses with fury, and we're about to take it out on these two.

"I'm calling the men now," Luke says, reading my mind.

"Get them home," I growl and turn back to Number Two. "When are they making the grab?"

"Time is it?" he asks.

"Just after one," Julian replies.

"Should already be done."

I whirl around to find Luke, and when my eyes land on his, I know.

Fuck.

I'm about to burn my city to the motherfucking ground.

Fifty-Four

LULU

"Okay, this is the best day ever," I say as Scarlett and I leave Dior, headed for Chanel. "I only feel a little guilty for spending more than ten grand in there."

"You still have a long way to go to hit your goal. You want lots of orgasms this week, and I don't think your man was bluffing. But don't worry. We'll get there."

I smirk at my bestie and see a spot to get some gelato. "Want some?"

"Yes, but I also have to pee. Will you get me a scoop of the coffee, and I'll be right back?"

"Of course."

Scarlett walks away with her two guards right behind her toward the restroom, and I get in line to buy us each a sweet treat.

Shopping requires calories. I haven't mastered the art of making gelato myself. Maybe that's something I should work on. I *am* Italian, after all. I should know how to make it.

I glance back and only see one of my guards, but then I don't think much of it. I'm sure *they* have to use the bathroom sometimes.

I pull my phone out, skim through the text messages that Rome and I exchanged, and feel the giddy grin spread over my face again.

Things have been ridiculously good since the night we said the L word just a couple of days ago.

Like, the happily ever after of a rom-com movie good.

He loves me. He's going to protect me from all of the shit my father might try, and I'm totally safe with Rome. My job is the bomb. I have friends, and I'm learning so much from Mateo and Carson. Even Julian got in on the training action and offered to teach us how to hack electronics. I don't know why we might ever need that information, but I'm a sponge.

I'll learn whatever the Kings of Vegas want to teach us.

"I thought that was you."

I turn at the voice, then feel shock roll through me, and every hair on my body stands on end.

"The new line at Dior is to *die* for," Loveland continues, gesturing to the bag in my hands with a smile on her perfect face. She's in jeans, a sweatshirt, and sneakers, which throws me off further. I've never seen her so dressed down, not looking like a runway model. "Did you find some good things?"

"Uh, yeah. Sorry, this is a surprise."

"I know, I had to come say hello when I saw you over here. How are things at Rapture?"

I tilt my head to the side. I know Loveland was fired, but I have no idea why. Is it a betrayal against Rome to chat with her? Should I text him and let him know I'm talking to her?

That's silly. She's just an acquaintance who happens to be shopping at the same time as me.

Except she's not even carrying a handbag.

Something isn't right here.

"Things are pretty much the same as ever," I reply, staying neutral. This is so uncomfortable. I wish Scarlett would come back from the bathroom. "It's been busy."

"That's good," she says with a knowing nod. "Rita treating you right in the lounge?"

What is her angle? Loveland has never taken the time to have a conversation with me.

"Rita's always great."

Not in the mood for gelato anymore, I slip out of line and look around for my guards. I still only see one, and he's not even looking in our direction.

Where is the other one?

And where is Scarlett? How long does it take that woman to pee?

"You know," Loveland says, not seeming to be at all interested in moving on, "I could use your thoughts on the cutest Fendi bag I saw over here."

"Oh, I really can't. I'm with a friend, and—"

Her hand reaches out for my arm, and before I can

move away from her, I feel the bite in my skin. I blink in confusion and realize that she just fucking *drugged me.*

"Your friend isn't going to help you," she says with a bright smile as she links her arm in mine and starts walking toward an exit as if we're old friends shopping together. It's getting harder and harder for my feet to move, and by the time we make it out of the doors to the valet parking, I'm stumbling. "Just a few more feet."

Suddenly, I'm picked up from behind and tossed in the back of a waiting SUV. I want to fight, to roll out before the back closes on me, but my muscles won't work.

And then everything goes dark.

Fifty-Five

ROME

"I can't reach any of the guards," Luke says, his face full of fury and worry. "And Scarlett won't answer the phone."

I'm pacing the penthouse, staring at the yellow dot on my phone.

"She's moving," I announce as ice-cold fear settles in my stomach. "Away from the shopping center. Let's go."

"Wait," Julian says, holding up a hand, and I snarl at him. "I know, we all want to go get her, but we need an army, Rome. If all of Rizzo's men are here with him, we need our men, too."

"I'm calling every-fucking-body," Luke says. "And I'm sending a team to that fucking shopping center. Where's my girl?"

"They could have them both," Mateo reminds us, but suddenly, *my* phone rings, and I see that it's Smith, one of the guards with the girls today.

"Talk," I bark into the phone.

"Lulu's gone," he says, wheezing into the phone. "Scarlett's locked in the bathroom. Can't get her out."

"We have people on the way," I reply.

"Too late," he says, and I know what the voice of a dying man sounds like. "Matthews was in on it."

"What about Parker and James?" Luke asks.

"No, just Matthews. Fuck. Sorry, boss. Tried."

He doesn't say anything else, and I know he's gone.

"Get this army together." My voice is hard. "Now!"

IT TAKES TOO LONG.

We have Scarlett back and safe in her apartment more than an hour later, but she's a mess. Sobbing and wailing, and inconsolable. I sent Rita to be with her because I need Luke with me.

I can't keep my own fucking panic down.

He has my firefly.

And I know he won't hesitate to hurt her.

"We should have killed him when we had the goddamn chance," I growl, speaking over something Mateo was just saying.

"He dies today," Julian says, his jaw tight. "None of them walk away from this. We destroy his entire empire."

"It'll be a pleasure," Mateo agrees. "She's not stupid, and she's not weak, Rome. She's been trained well, and I can tell you that she's skilled. She keeps a cool head, and she's almost as good at target practice as you are."

I lift an eyebrow. "This isn't target practice."

"No, but she won't go down without a fight," he replies, and the words *go down* have me swallowing hard. "We have three hundred and fifty men ready to go."

I check the screen for the fiftieth time in the past hour. "They've stopped moving. This must be a warehouse or an abandoned building."

"Looking it up now," Julian says, tapping the keys of his laptop. It feels like it takes him forever, that every single second is an hour that she's gone, and it's making me lose my fucking mind. "It's a ... *house.*"

"Say that again."

He shakes his head, still typing.

"It's a goddamn, motherfucking house. And it was purchased a month ago by Rizzo."

"A big one," Mateo says, looking over Julian's shoulder. "How did we miss this?"

That's what I want to fucking know.

"We need to get eyes in the air," Julian says, "so we know what kind of security we're walking into."

"I'm going now."

"No," Mateo says, and I snarl at him. "Julian's right. We have to do this right because they won't hesitate to take her out, and you know it."

"Christ." I push my hand through my hair and continue to pace. "I can't think."

"We'll do the thinking," Julian says and nods to Luke. "Get eyes in the sky. Drones are best. We need to know what his surveillance is like, and how many people he has on the grounds."

"On it," Luke says, making more calls. "I'm going out with them. I can report to you myself. Don't worry, boss, we'll get her back in one piece."

Fuck.

We'd better.

Thirty minutes later, we have some answers.

Rizzo's *army* is closer to thirty men. Half outside the house, and it seems the rest must be inside, coming in and out.

"Let's go," I say, pulling on a Kevlar vest as I leave the penthouse and head for the parking garage. I'm already armed with my knives, my guns, and enough rage to tear these motherfuckers apart with my bare hands.

Hold on, firefly. I'm coming for you.

It's time to end this.

Fifty-Six

LULU

Everything hurts, and I'm pretty sure someone just punched me in the face.

"She's awake."

I know that voice.

And then it all comes back to me. Shopping. Loveland. Getting drugged and thrown into the back of a car.

I wheeze when someone kicks me in the ribs. I manage to open one eye and see Loveland grinning down at me.

"Wake up, you fucking slut. Jesus, we didn't give you that much."

"Enough."

I'm punched again, and then my father screams, "ENOUGH!"

"I'm just getting started with her," Loveland says with a sneer as I push myself up into a sitting position.

"You won't touch her again," my father says, his eyes full of hate and rage as he glares at me.

I look around, hoping for a way out, but I'm still groggy. My arms and legs are heavy, and I'm in a ... living room.

I'm in a house?

I see men with big guns walking past the windows and a sliding glass door that opens out to a pool.

I'm surrounded.

And I'm alone.

"The only reason you even have her here is because of me." Loveland rears back to slap me again, but I raise a hand and block her. "You little piece of shit."

She manages to hit me anyway, and I see stars. I'm so damn dizzy. I want to throw up.

Jesus, being drugged *sucks.*

I hear the cocking of a gun and then watch in horror as my father shoots Loveland in the chest, the stomach, and right between the eyes.

"Fucking cunt," he mutters as she falls right on top of me.

Oh God.

I try to push her off, but I'm still weak, so it takes several tries before I get the body to roll away. I'm covered in her blood, in her flesh, and the urge to throw up has intensified by about a million.

"I'm so disappointed in you, Eloise."

Oh God. That tone. Fuck.

"I can't marry him."

He tsks and shakes his head and drags his hand down his face. "That's not for you to decide. You'll do what I fucking tell you. Being Roman Alexander's fuck toy is *not* what I have in store for you and will not help to advance this family."

Family? This man has no idea what family is.

With my legs starting to feel stronger, I push up to my feet, but the room spins, and I almost fall again.

"She wasn't supposed to fucking drug you." He shakes his head, glaring at the woman at my feet who continues to bleed out all over the floor.

God. Will that be me next?

Please. Please, Rome, find me. I'm so fucking scared.

He's going to kill me.

"Damien will be here shortly to collect you."

I shake my head, but he storms over to me, and I can't move fast enough to evade his big hand wrapping around my arm and pulling my left shoulder out of the socket.

Fuck.

I scream out in pain. It's so sharp, so fucking *hot*. It sends electricity through me, and not in a good way.

Dad's face is an inch from mine.

"You'll fucking do as you're told, you ungrateful little bitch!"

Smack!

I'm seeing stars again when his phone rings, and he smiles.

"There he is now. Rizzo."

"I'm out," the man says. My dad's face pales, and his body goes rigid with pure fury. "She's been fucked by Alexander. Ever plan to divulge that little piece of information, you asshole? You knew the score, and you didn't fucking deliver. The deal's off."

"Listen, there are surgeries—"

"I said the deal's off."

The phone goes dead, and my father lets it fall to the floor as he turns to me. "You little piece-of-shit bitch. I should have killed you with your mother."

My shoulder is screaming, and I'm nauseous from the pain.

He's going to kill me.

Where's Rome? I want to see him, just one more time before I die. I want to tell him how much I love him. How grateful I am for everything he did for me.

Suddenly, we hear gunfire coming from outside. It sounds like a freaking *war*. So many explosions and smoke in the air. My father grabs me, wrenching my already dislocated arm and pulling me against him as if I'm a human shield.

What a weak piece of shit.

"If I go down," he sneers into my ear, "we both do, bitch."

Fifty-Seven

ROME

As my army takes care of the men outside, Mateo, Julian, and I charge through the front door and kill everyone in our wake, fanning out through the house. It takes all of six seconds to find Rizzo and my firefly in the living room off the kitchen, but I stop cold as I take in the scene.

Loveland is dead at Eloise's feet.

What the fuck? Loveland was in on this?

Rizzo holds his daughter in front of him, his weapon pressed to her neck.

And I can tell that her shoulder isn't right.

This son of a bitch.

"If you let me live," Rizzo says, licking his lips nervously like the piece of shit that he is, "I'll let you marry my daughter. We can join forces, form an alliance."

I tilt my head to the side. "Or?"

"Or I kill her right now."

Eloise's eyes are on mine. She's fucking terrified.

She's trembling, and she's in agony. There's so much blood on her that there's no way she's not injured. Shot. Stabbed.

Jesus, baby.

"You know, it's interesting," I tell him, not taking my eyes off my firefly. I came in this side of the room alone. I can already see Mateo approaching Rizzo soundlessly from behind, and Julian is to my right, just out of sight. "I plan to marry your daughter with or without your blessing. Your approval doesn't mean dick to me."

Her lip quivers. She swallows hard. Her gaze drifts away from mine as if she's disassociating from the pain she's in.

But I need her with me.

"Firefly." Her gaze whips back to mine. "On me."

"We can work this out," Rizzo says with a sharp, nervous laugh. "Damien no longer wants her since you've fucked her and taken her virginity."

Now my girl scowls, and it almost makes me laugh.

Almost.

"I wasn't a virgin when I ran away," she says, and Rizzo's face reddens.

"You're a fucking whore," he growls in her ear, and while he's distracted, Eloise flies into action. She stomps his instep and reaches up with her good hand to poke him in the eye and doesn't miss.

Rizzo howls in pain.

"Down," I shout as I raise my gun and shoot her father right between the eyes.

He falls over Loveland, and I sprint to Eloise, who's trying to crawl away from him.

"Come here, baby."

"It hurts so fucking bad," she says, crying out when I tug her into my arms.

"I'm taking you to the hospital. Where are you bleeding?"

Christ, there's so much blood.

"Did he shoot you?"

Julian, Mateo, and Luke rush in, and Luke immediately helps me look her over. She's crying too hard to answer me.

"She's not hit," Luke says, shaking his head.

"Landed on me," she says between sobs and looks down at Loveland.

"It's her blood?" I ask her and feel relief flood me when she nods.

"Thank God. I'm going to carry you, baby."

"No." She shakes her head. "I have to walk. You'll jostle me too much."

"We have a car right outside," Julian says. "All of Rizzo's men are dead. We need to clear out before the cops get here."

"Wait." Eloise tugs on my shirt, and I lean down, pressing my cheek to hers.

"What is it, firefly?"

"I love you. I didn't think I'd get to tell you again because he was going to k-k-kill me, and oh God—"

"I love you, too. I'm right here. You're safe, my love."

I have so many questions, but the answers will have to wait because I need to get my girl looked at.

"No hospital," Luke says as we rush out to the car. "I have Dr. Asgood waiting at the infirmary with a full staff."

I nod and help Eloise into the car. She winces and cries out as I try to get the seat belt on her, and every moment of her agony is a wound to my soul.

"I wish I could take this away for you," I murmur as I lean in to press my lips to her head. "I wish it was me, firefly."

"I'm alive, and I'm with you. I'll be fine."

Luke turns a corner and hits a pothole, and Eloise gasps and then loses consciousness.

"Fuck, I'm sorry," he says.

"Do it again, and you're a dead man. I don't give a fuck if you're family."

Again, every minute drags on and on, and Eloise doesn't regain consciousness.

Did he hit her in the head? She has bruises spreading on her face, and that makes me want to go back and burn it all down. I hate that the fucker had a quick death when he deserved to suffer for days on end. For what he did to my girl today—I'll never unsee her being used as a motherfucking human shield—and all the years of abuse she suffered. I have her in my arms, but I don't know what she suffered for those few hours when I couldn't get to her.

I'll never forget seeing her with him breathing down

her neck, believing he could strike a deal with me—as if I would treat her as a pawn on a chessboard.

And Loveland? She was part of hurting my firefly?

I need to know what, exactly, happened, and if any more of my people are fucking traitors.

Because they'll all die.

"You have Matthews in the cell?" I demand as I bury my lips in Lulu's hair.

"Yep."

"How alive is he?"

"Plenty alive," Luke confirms and watches me in the rearview. "How long is he going to stay that way?"

"Days." I grin at him. "It's going to be a long, slow death for that piece of shit. I need answers, and he's going to give them to me."

"Christ, you're scary," Luke mutters.

"That's my whole job, remember?"

When we make it to the parking garage beneath my building, I carry Eloise up to the infirmary, and we're immediately surrounded by Dr. Asgood and her people.

"Lay her on the gurney," Dr. Asgood directs, her voice tight and strong. She's good under pressure, which is one of the reasons I hired her to begin with.

It's often a matter of life and death in this room.

"Where's the blood coming from?" she demands, and I shake my head.

"It's from someone else. We checked her over, and she's not bleeding."

"Get the scissors," she barks. "I want these clothes

off. Her left shoulder is dislocated. Everyone out while I take an X-ray."

Everyone files out while she drags a big machine over and manages to get it settled over Eloise to take images.

"You too," she says to me.

"I'm not fucking going anywhere."

"The radiation—"

"I'm. Not. Going."

She sighs, leaves the room, and there's a beeping noise before Dr. Asgood and everyone else return to continue working on my girl.

"Dislocated," she says again. "No fracture. She's been hit in the face, the ribs, her legs. Lots of bruising. I would guess that her ribs are bruised as well. She took one hell of a beating. Poor girl."

Jesus Christ.

"Why is she unconscious?"

"Pain. Fear. The body will do whatever it needs to do to protect itself. You know that."

"If she doesn't live, neither do you," I snarl at the woman, who narrows her eyes at me.

"She's going to be fine. Now get out of my way so I can finish examining her."

"I'm staying right here."

Dr. Asgood shakes her head and wisely keeps her mouth shut as she continues to look Eloise over.

"No head wounds," she murmurs. "No facial fractures. Her jaw will be sore, though."

For fuck's sake.

"Wake up, firefly," I whisper and kiss her hand. "Wake up for me."

"You might want to leave the room while we reset this shoulder."

"Absolutely fucking *not*."

"It's not—"

"Do it," I bark at her.

"She might come to while we do this," she warns me. "And she might come up swinging."

I fucking hope so.

Fifty-Eight

LULU

I wake up disoriented with pain singing through every vein and muscle in my body. God, why does everything hurt so bad? Was I hit by a freaking bus?

"There she is." A woman is crooning at me. I don't know if anyone has ever *crooned* at me before. "Welcome back, Lulu. Do you remember me?"

"Dr. Asgood?" I frown up at her, and then it all comes back to me.

Again.

Tears form in my eyes, and suddenly, Rome's there, my hand in his and pressed to his mouth as the tears flow down my cheeks.

"We got your shoulder reset," the doctor says as she frowns. "That shoulder's been through a lot."

"Yeah." Rome wipes my tears away. I can't look away from him. His blue eyes look ... *scared.*

"You may need surgery at some point. At the very

least, you'll need physical therapy in about a month once you've had time to heal."

I nod, and my head spins. "That drug still isn't gone."

"What drug?" Rome growls.

"They drugged me. Loveland did. That's how she got me to leave the shopping center with her. Oh God. Scarlett! Where's Scarlett? Did they hurt her?"

"She's safe and with Luke," Rome assures me, brushing his hand through my hair. "She'll want to see you as soon as you're ready, but she's fine."

I relax in relief and sniff. "I don't usually cry this much."

"You've had a lot of trauma along with the drugs," Dr. Asgood reminds me. "Tears seem pretty normal to me. Are you dizzy?"

"Yeah, a little."

"Headache?"

"Not really. I'm thirsty."

"We'll get you some water. I'm happy to report that none of the blood on the clothes we cut off you is yours."

"No, it isn't." Cheryl passes me a bottle of water, and I nod in thanks before drinking some of it down. It soothes my dry throat. "I'm so sorry."

I turn to Rome, and he cradles me against his chest, kissing the top of my head.

"Hey, no, baby. You don't have anything to be sorry for."

"She came up to me, startled me, and I didn't trust her."

"Loveland?"

I nod and press into him harder. "I *knew* something was off. One of my guards was gone, and the other one wouldn't look at me."

"Matthews," he says, and I jerk back to stare up at him. His voice is hard and angry.

"Yes."

"He's being dealt with."

That makes me shiver, and I cuddle back into him.

"She pricked me when I wouldn't go with her, and I fucking *knew* she'd drugged me. Took me out of that shopping center, and someone threw me in the back of a car."

He growls against my hair but gently rubs his hands up and down my back.

"I don't know how she came to work for my father, or why, or *anything*. But she was so mad at me. She kept hitting me, over and over again, even after my father yelled at her to stop. But she wouldn't, so he shot her. And she fell on me and bled all over me. God."

I can't stop sobbing. God, I'm such a mess.

"Hey, you're safe. You're safe, firefly. We'll get answers," he assures me. "Right now, I don't want you to worry about any of that. I want you to rest and recover."

"That's exactly what you need," Dr. Asgood agrees. "I don't need to keep you for observation, but I'm only a call away if you need anything. Thanks to that drug, it might be hard to eat for the rest of the day but try to at least get some broth in you. You need calories. Just eat what your stomach will tolerate."

"Okay." I turn my face to offer her a small smile but don't let go of Rome. "Thank you."

"Of course. Let's not do this again."

With a wink, Asgood leaves, and Rome lifts me into his arms. My left arm is in a sling, and I must be on some good pain medication because it doesn't even bother me right now.

It just feels good to be in Rome's arms. To feel his warmth against me.

I might never let go of him ever again. He'll have to carry me behind the bar so I can do my job.

I smirk at that, and he looks down at me in surprise as we ride up the elevator.

"What's funny?"

"I don't want you to ever put me down. You'll have to carry me like this when I go to work."

His lips twitch, and he leans in to gently kiss my lips. "Deal. I have no problem with that. I may never let you out of my sight again."

When we get to the penthouse, he carries me upstairs and through the bedroom to the bathroom. I'm still in the little gown that someone put on me because my clothes were cut off, so when he sets me on the counter, I yelp from the cold marble hitting my bare ass.

"Shit, are you okay?" he asks, clearly panicking, but I laugh.

"It's just cold." I shake my head, then regret that when the room spins. "Whoa. It's okay."

"I just have to start the shower. Can you sit here without me for a second?"

I smile up at him. He's *so* focused on me. His whole body is tight, his face hard, and his jaw tense.

My poor man. He's fighting fear and anger, yet he's still so calm and sweet to me.

"Yes. I can sit here."

But he doesn't turn away. He rests his forehead to mine and exhales, then kisses me so softly it makes my heart melt.

"I'm so sorry, Eloise."

"Nothing is your fault."

"Everything is my fault, but I'm going to do everything in my power for the rest of my life to make it up to you."

His voice is so rough with emotion, I need to comfort him. So I rest my hand against his cheek and nuzzle his nose.

"I'm *fine*, Rome. I'm fine."

He kisses me once more, then makes sure I'm steady on the vanity before he turns to start the water in the shower. He sheds his clothes as the water heats.

"I will say, seeing you march right into that room in your Kevlar vest, gun drawn, so fucking fierce, that in hindsight, it was sexy as hell. I finally got to see you in gangster mode, and it did not disappoint."

"There was absolutely *nothing* sexy about what went on today."

"No, in the moment, I was so scared, I'm shocked I didn't shit myself. But now that everything's okay, and I look back on it, you were hot. If you were after me, I'd be terrified. Good job."

He smirks and shoves his boxers down his legs, then returns to me and cages me in, his hands leaning on the countertop at my hips.

"Did you just give me a glowing review on my *nefarious* job, firefly?"

"I did. Do you want me to leave you a Yelp or Google review?"

"Fuck, firefly. How can you joke right now after what you went through?"

"Rome, if I don't, I'll start crying again. My father tried to kill me today. I don't know if I've even digested that yet. It's going to take a while. So for now, I'm just going to focus on how hot my man is and the fact that you saved me. I love you."

"Fuck, I love you too."

He pulls the ugly gown off me, helps me out of the sling, and lifts me to take me to the shower, stepping under the hot spray. He's careful with my left shoulder, and when his eyes skim down my torso, they harden, and his jaw clenches again.

I follow his gaze and wince.

Shit, I'm covered in bruises.

"I'll be okay." My voice is soft now as the realization of everything that went down today washes over me again. My eyes fill with tears. "My emotions are all over the place."

"Of course, they are. For the first time since my mom died, mine are too." He shakes his head and squeezes my body wash into my loofah, then starts cleaning me up. "I hate that you saw any of that. That Loveland had her hands on you."

"Why was she so mad at *me*? Because you hired me when she didn't want to? That seems stupid. You own the business."

"Her name was Sarah Lowman," he says, and my eyes find his. He pauses in cleaning me for a heartbeat before resuming. "Way back in the day, she and I were, well ..."

And there goes my heart again. But not in a good way this time.

Ugh. I don't want to think about *my* Rome with her.

"You loved her." I feel sick to my stomach.

But Rome drops the loofah and immediately tugs me into his arms, holding me close.

"I thought I did a long, long time ago. But now that I have you, and I know what it feels like to be so fucking in love that the thought of not having you with me paralyzes me and makes me want to rage all at the same time, I'd say that she was just someone who used to be important to me."

He kisses my forehead. My cheek. My lips.

"Seriously, don't be jealous of her."

"Okay, keep talking." I offer him a small smile, and he picks up the loofah and continues washing me.

"She'd been employed here from the day I opened. Shortly after, I found her fucking someone else. I shot him in the head, and I never touched her again."

I blink up at him in surprise. "But you let her stay."

"She was good at her job. And I found that I didn't really care what she did. You need to understand, you bring out feelings and emotions in me that I thought were long dead. You have since the second I saw you."

He brushes his thumb over my lower lip and then gets to work gently washing my hair. He takes the hand-held showerhead off the wall to do it since it's not comfortable for me to lean my head back too far.

"Loveland found that being a Domme was what she wanted. She adopted the name Loveland, and that's who she was after that. She managed the playroom, and until recently, I didn't have any complaints with her."

"Until me."

He doesn't look me in the eyes, but he does sigh.

"She was jealous, plain and simple. I don't do relationships. I don't fuck around with staff or members. That's not to say I was a monk, but Rapture wasn't my playground. It was a safe place for people who wanted to explore sex and a great way to launder a fuck ton of money."

I grin at him, and now he grins back at me.

"But then I saw you, and I was *so fucking mad* at how she spoke to you that first night. I made her chase you down and bring you back."

How have we never talked about this before?

"And whenever she had something shitty to say, I put her in her place. She started dropping the ball as well, and I don't tolerate that. I fired her, kicked her out of her apartment, and washed my hands of her."

"But she was bitter, felt scorned, and pissy. I wonder how she knew to go to work for *my father?* How did she connect those dots?"

"That's something I don't know." He finishes with my hair and grabs me two towels. After wrapping my wet hair in one, he pats me dry with the other before quickly brushing it over himself. Then he helps me dress in some comfortable clothes, putting my sling back on. It's amazing how much that helps with the pressure on the joint.

But I'm so freaking *tired.*

"We'll get the rest of those answers." He helps me with the sling, then pulls me into him, gently holding me in the best hug ever. "Now, how will you be the most comfortable, baby? In the bed? On the couch?"

"Nothing's going to be great for a little while," I admit, wincing as I think about how crappy finding a comfortable position will be. "Maybe the couch?"

"Can I please carry you?"

I smile and kiss his chest. "Of course, you can."

He lifts me carefully and takes me downstairs straight to the couch, where he sits with me like we did that day when I was so sick with my period.

"Come here, my love."

He cradles me against him and peppers kisses on my head, my face.

"How is this?"

Perfect.

Especially because I wasn't sure if I'd ever get this again.

"Good." Perhaps an understatement, but I'm just too exhausted for anything else. "You know, with him dead, it's over."

"It's over." His hand drifts up and down my right arm, soothing me. "You're a wealthy woman, Eloise."

I frown up at him, surprised. "What do you mean?"

"You'll inherit everything your father had. It's substantial."

"I don't want it." I shrug a shoulder and lean into him. "Donate it."

He chuckles and kisses me again. "If you want, I'll arrange for a trust for you until you have some time to sort your feelings out. You'll just have to sign some paperwork."

"Okay." I really don't want anything from my father. I don't need it. But maybe I can put his money to good use somewhere. "I'm so tired."

"You should be. Jesus, what a day."

"Rome?"

"Yes, firefly."

I yawn and then rub my nose against his firm chest. "Are you really going to marry me, or were you trying to piss my father off?"

He doesn't answer for a long moment, so I glance up at him again.

He's grinning from ear to ear.

"Oh, I'm marrying you, Eloise. The first chance I get. Hopefully tomorrow."

I blink at him. "*Tomorrow*?"

"That's right. You have to get some rest today."

"You didn't even ask me."

I bite my lip and try not to smile. I don't need him to ask me.

I'll marry him right now if he wants to, pain medicine or not.

"Eloise." His deep voice does things to me.

"Yes?"

"Look at me."

"Now I'm nervous."

With a chuckle, he tips my chin up, and he's still smiling down at me.

"Will you please marry me, Eloise? I can't live this life without you by my side. I need you every day. I'll never get enough of you. You're the light that finally broke through the darkness of my black heart. You shine so bright, you made me feel human again. That's why I call you my firefly. Because you flew right into my life and lit it up. Stay with me forever. Be my wife."

Well, damn.

I nod. "Yes. I'll marry you."

"Tomorrow?"

I yawn once more, and he cradles me close.

I'm marrying Rome Alexander.

While that is utterly surreal, and we've only known each other such a short time, it feels right.

Nothing has ever felt so right.

Despite all the dark in his world, that existed in my world before I met him, somehow our paths crossed and we found our own *rapture.* I doubt life will ever be easy. He is a King of Vegas, after all, but I know that this man will do everything in his power to make sure I'm happy. So, yes, I'll marry him.

"Tomorrow. First, I just need a little nap."

Epilogue

ROME

Six Months Later

"Christ, you're beautiful." I nuzzle her temple, and her pussy squeezes me *so fucking hard* I almost come right here and now. "Don't you dare come, firefly."

"Rome," she chokes, lifting her hips.

"You like being watched?" We're in a voyeur privacy room, and it's my girl's twenty-fourth birthday.

This is what she asked for.

Of course, there are modifications.

The people watching through the window can only see what I want them to see. But they can see her face, and the way her gorgeous green eyes shine up at me, her mouth in an O, her cheeks flushed.

"Please," she says.

"What do you need, wife?"

She swallows hard, the way she always does when I call her that. It's been six months, and I'll never tire of calling her *my wife*.

I made good on my promise and made Eloise my wife a week after we disposed of her father. She was in too much pain the day after.

"Fuck, I need to come."

"You will. But not yet." I turn her leg out and push it up a bit, gaining more access to her perfect pussy, and lean in harder, making her gasp. "You're fucking soaking this mattress, baby. Do you like knowing that those people out there are watching and listening to me fuck you right now?"

"Oh God."

"Answer me."

I would *never* have done this before her. No chance.

And I don't love it now.

But it seems there isn't anything that I wouldn't do for her.

"Yes." She bites her lip and drags her hand over my side. "Yes, I like it. I need to come."

"Okay, baby." I start to fuck her, hard and fast, and then I lean down to bite her neck hard enough to leave marks. "Come for me. Let them hear you. Let them hear how much you love my fucking cock."

She starts to come apart, screaming beautifully, sending me over the precipice with her.

I pull out and come all over her, marking her in front of all of those assholes.

Mine.

Fucking mine.

And when she's done, I whisper, "Roll over and give the window your back, wife."

She does as she's told, and I walk to the window to pull the shade.

"Show's over," I growl before shutting them out.

"Thank you," she says when I climb over the mattress to pull her against me. "I know it's not your thing."

"I never said *red*," I remind her and kiss her long and slow. "But I'll only ever do this if you request it for your birthday. Because you're *mine*, and I don't share."

"You know, I don't love that another woman probably just saw you naked," she says, as if it has just occurred to her. "Yeah, no. This will be a one-time deal. But it's fun to try new things."

I smirk and hug her close.

Suddenly, she pulls away, her eyes round, and she makes a run for the attached bathroom, retching into the toilet.

I hold her hair back and rub her back in soothing circles.

I wondered when this would start.

"Shit, I hope I don't have the flu."

I can't help but chuckle at that, and she turns to me with a scowl.

"Why would that be funny?"

"You don't have the flu." I help her get cleaned up, then take her back to bed.

Since the incident months ago with her period and

finding the blood in our bed, I've kept track of her cycle. I don't ever need to be caught unaware like that again.

She's two weeks late.

"Ugh, I don't want you to get sick."

"Firefly, you don't have a virus. You're pregnant."

She stills, then she sits up, staring down at me in shock as I brace my head on my hand and grin up at her.

"No, I'm not."

"Yes. You are."

"How do *you* know?"

"I keep track of your periods."

"Wow, that's not unhinged or anything."

"We established that I'm unhinged a long time ago." I jerk her to me and kiss her fiercely. "You've had symptoms. When were you going to suspect it?"

She sighs. "I don't know. I thought maybe I was broken since I wasn't getting pregnant before."

"You're not broken, my love."

"Holy shit. I need to take tests."

"I have some waiting upstairs."

She blinks at me. "You think of everything. It's a little … unnerving."

Eloise lays her head on my chest and wraps herself around me, the way she's done from the beginning as if she's afraid I might get away.

I'm never going anywhere.

And I fucking *love it* when she drags her hands over my abs. I love her hands on me. I can't get enough of it.

"Hopefully, I'm not a shitty mom."

I frown down at her. "No chance of that happening."

"Do we want to keep living here, or do we want to buy a house?"

I roll over her and cup her face, staring down at her.

"What do *you* want, wife?"

She sighs and lifts up to kiss me. "Maybe a house with a yard. I don't know if I want to raise children over a sex club. But we should keep the penthouse, of course."

"Done. We'll start house hunting tomorrow."

She can have whatever she wants.

"Any other requests?"

She grins.

She rarely asks for anything. In fact, just like that fateful day when she went shopping with Scarlett, I've had to convince her to spend our money. It's one of the reasons I love her so much.

That and the way she looks at me, as if I'm her whole fucking world.

"I have everything I ever wanted, Rome."

Fuck yes.

My heart squeezes, and I kiss her hard. "And you always will, firefly."

IF YOU'D LIKE to read a bonus scene featuring Rome and Eloise, you can download it here:

https://BookHip.com/PGLSJDD

· · ·

THE KINGS of Vegas continue in Blood King, featuring Julian and Natasha! You can preorder your copy here:

https://amzn.to/47Zl9m1

TURN the page for a preview of BLOOD KING:

JULIAN

This asshole thinks he's intimidating me.

I'm sitting in Sergei Ivanov's office, across from the man himself, who's puffing away on a disgusting cigar. He's so fucking cheap, he doesn't even have the decency to smuggle Cubans in.

Sergei's refusal to part with money is the reason I'm sitting here in the first place.

"Your son is late," he says with a heavy Russian accent, as if it might be lost on me that Elliott isn't in the room.

"He'll be here," I reply. I don't bother to check my phone or my watch and show any kind of weakness in front of the head of the Bratva.

Elliott will be here.

"I'm a busy man, Mr. Stavros. If you're wasting my time—"

"I'm not wasting anyone's time, and you're not the

only man in this room who has other business to attend to. Let's get started."

Sergei's eyes narrow, and then he grunts, and the man standing to his right sets a black folder on the desk.

"I took the liberty of having my attorney write a contract."

I lift an eyebrow. "A *marriage* contract?"

"That's right."

I won't be signing anything this idiot sets in front of me, but I offer him a congenial smile.

"And what are the terms in this contract?"

"Well, there's all kinds of legal speak here, but basically, your son marries my daughter, and my debt to you is forgiven."

Oh, his debt will never be forgiven.

"What else?"

"I think it's pretty standard. If Elliott cheats on her, he'll have to pay her ten million dollars—"

"You mean *you*."

Sergei's eyes narrow. "That's right."

"And if she cheats?"

"She won't."

My lips twitch. "You seem so sure of yourself."

"My daughter has been raised to be the perfect organized crime wife. She knows what's expected of her. She'll remain faithful, she'll take her punishments, and she'll never ask for a divorce."

She'll take her punishments.

I'd like to pull the gun from the small of my back and fill his head with lead. Better than that, I'd prefer to pull my knife out and flay the skin from his pathetic, fat body.

Instead, I hold his gaze with mine.

"No."

His face turns red, but I don't give him time to argue.

"I'm not signing that or anything else you put in front of me. We've agreed to an alliance between our organizations with the marriage of my son to your daughter. That's the agreement. I won't pay you a fucking dime if one of them fucks up. You have my word that Natasha will be cared for, and while the money you owe me—all one hundred million of it—will be forgiven, it's not forgotten, Sergei. And any future money you owe me will *not* be forgiven."

His jaw is so tight, I can hear his molars grinding together.

"Papa?"

We all glance to the doorway, and I'm pretty sure one of these fuckers just shot me in the head and I'm dead because I'm looking at a literal angel.

This woman is fucking *gorgeous* in a white dress that flows just past her knees and shows off ample cleavage. Long blond hair flows in waves past her shoulders, her eyes are striking blue, the color of Kashmiri sapphires, and her glossy pink lips press in a line with uncertainty.

He's willing to sell this beautiful woman's soul away for a measly one hundred million?

I should kill him where he sits for even considering it.

"You wanted to see me?" Her voice is soft, and her eyes shift between her father and me with unease.

"Yes, come in, malyshka." Sergei hardly looks at her as he waves her in. "Sit."

"I don't want to intrude—"

"SIT!" he yells and slams his fist on his desk, and Natasha hurries to the chair near the one I'm in and takes a seat. Her back is perfectly straight, hands are folded in her lap, one ankle crossed behind the other, and she looks down at the floor obediently.

I'd really like to gut this asshole.

"This is Julian Stavros," Sergei tells his daughter, gesturing to me. "I've arranged for a marriage."

She gasps, her spine snaps even straighter, and those beautiful eyes turn to me. She blinks, looks me up and down, and her cheeks darken.

Interesting.

"I'm marrying him?" she asks timidly just as the door opens once more.

"Sorry I'm late."

I sigh and don't bother to look behind me as Elliott strolls into the room. I can smell the whiskey on him from here, and God only knows what casino he left to get here.

"Elliott," Sergei says with a nod. "This is Natasha. Your bride."

I haven't taken my eyes off her. She swallows hard, a slight frown appearing between her brows.

She wants to object.

She takes her punishments.

"My what now?" Elliott asks, and I finally look up at my son. "Since when am I getting married?"

"If you'd answered any one of my calls over the past three days, this wouldn't be news to you." My voice is calm, because I'll never give Sergei the satisfaction of seeing any emotion from me, but I'm going to have it out with my kid later.

Elliott blinks at me, then looks over at Natasha, and when his gaze rakes over her gorgeous body, his lips spread in a smile. I want to push him out of the way and claim her for myself.

Which is fucking ridiculous.

"I'm so sorry for my manners," Elliott says as he holds a hand out for hers. "I'm Elliott."

"Natasha," she answers, eyeing his hand. She doesn't want to touch him, it's written all over her perfect face, but she holds her breath and slides her hand into his. "Hello."

"Excellent," Sergei says. "Let's have some vodka."

"No, thank you," I reply before my son can drink the man out of house and home. "The wedding will be in six weeks. We'll be in touch."

I stand and stare my son in the eyes.

"Let's go," I say, gesturing with my chin, and he smiles one more time at Natasha before he walks out of the room ahead of me.

When we're outside, he turns to talk to me, but I beat him to it.

"Not here. There are ears. Get in the car."

"But I drove my own car."

"Get in the fucking back seat, Elliott." My patience is wearing thin with my son.

He looks like he wants to argue, but finally sighs and slides into the back of the Range Rover, and I follow him. We have three other vehicles, and ten men with us, and we pull down the driveway and out onto the road.

"What the fuck, Dad?"

"We need an alliance with the Russians."

He's staring at me, his eyes suddenly sober. "I've been seeing Kitty for three months."

"And now you're not."

He shakes his head, and I lay it out for him. "You'll marry her, and you'll honor that marriage, El."

"Or?"

"Or I'm done. No more bailing you out. No more helping you. I'll cut you off and act like I've never met you in my life."

His jaw drops. "You wouldn't do that."

"Wouldn't I?"

I lift an eyebrow, and he knows this is his last chance with me. He knows what's at stake.

He sits back in the seat and stares out the window.

"I guess it's a good thing I like blonds."

<h1 style="text-align:center">About the Author</h1>

Natalie Kane is the dark romance pseudonym for Kristen Proby. After publishing more than 85 titles, the majority of which are contemporary romance, Kristen wanted to dive deeper into the morally gray side of things and is enjoying her foray into mafia romance. This is where the swoon of Kristen Proby meets the obsession of dark romance. Kristen Proby after dark, if you will.

Kristen Proby is the New York Times, USA Today, WSJ, and Amazon top 3 bestselling author of more than 85 titles. When not under deadline, Kristen enjoys spending time with her husband and their fur babies, riding her bike, reading in her library, trying her hand at painting, and, of course, enjoying her beautiful home in the mountains of Montana.

I hope you enjoyed reading this story as much as I enjoyed writing it! For upcoming book news, be sure to join my newsletter! I promise I will only send you news-filled mail, and none of the spam. You can sign up here.
https://nataliekane.myflodesk.com/newsletter